Hidden Crimes

ALSO BY MICHAEL HAMBLING

THE SOPHIE ALLEN BOOKS

Book 1: Dark Crimes
Book 2: Deadly Crimes
Book 3: Secret Crimes
Book 4: Buried Crimes
Book 5: Twisted Crimes
Book 6: Evil Crimes
Book 7: Shadow Crimes
Book 8: Silent Crimes
Book 9: Ruthless Crimes
Book 10: Brutal Crimes
Book 11: Hidden Crimes
Book 12: Vicious Crimes

Michael Hambling

HIDDEN CRIMES

Detective Sophie Allen Book 11

JOFFE BOOKS

Revised edition 2024
Joffe Books, London
www.joffebooks.com

First published in Great Britain in 2022

Cover art by Nick Castle

ISBN: 978-1-83526-898-8

FOREWORD

This is a work of fiction, and none of the characters and situations described in this novel bear any resemblance to real persons or events. Many of the locations do exist. Win Green Hill, in Wiltshire, is owned by the National Trust. Cranborne Chase is a designated Area of Outstanding Natural Beauty. It spans parts of south-west Wiltshire and north-east Dorset.

For convenience, a short glossary appears at the end of this book. It also lists the main ranks within the UK Police Force. You'll also find a short introduction to some of the local food and drink.

CHARACTER LIST

Wessex Regional Serious Crime Unit (WeSCU):
Detective Chief Superintendent Sophie Allen
Detective Inspector Barry Marsh (Dorset)
Detective Sergeant Rae Gregson (Dorset)
Detective Sergeant Stevie Harrison (Wiltshire)
Detective Constable Tommy Carter (Dorset)

Wiltshire Police:
Sergeant Mark Riley
Constable Colleen Jackson

Other Wiltshire Personnel:
Sally Lezinsky (Wiltshire County Forensic Chief)

Gloucestershire Police:
Detective Sergeant Peter Spence

West Midlands Police:
ACC Archie Campbell

To Margaret, the most important person in my life.

PROLOGUE

Betrayal. There it was. The dictionary definition. The word Bridget Kirkbride was looking for, explained in black and white. The word that described how she felt. Totally and completely betrayed. Overwhelmed with a sense of utter confusion. Sick with it all. She was in tears as she slid the dictionary back into its slot on the bookshelf in the sitting room. What a dreadful, dreadful mistake she'd made. All that trust, all that hope, for all those years. She felt humiliated. Manipulated. And if she felt like this, how much worse must Grant feel?

She wiped her eyes and blew her nose. She wasn't ready to let anyone know of her awareness, not yet. She'd need a few days to get her thoughts in order and decide who to contact, who to trust. To think about the possible consequences of this appalling discovery.

She glanced at her reflection in the mirror. Was that image staring back really her? Pale and drawn? Tired, damp eyes? She looked like some kind of ghoul.

She suddenly stiffened. What was that noise? A slight tap. Rustling. Then all quiet again. Was someone on the front porch? She shrank back against the wall and tried to peer through the hall window. No sign of anyone there, but with the morning mist as thick as this it was difficult to be sure.

Bridget pulled her coat from its hook, then crept into the kitchen. If only her mobile phone hadn't somehow disappeared yesterday. And her landline was still down because of the storm at the weekend. The houses in her lane still hadn't been reconnected, although the rest of the village was okay now. She took several long looks out of the kitchen window as she buttoned her coat up and put on her hat, gloves and boots. She needed to be quick. Had she somehow let something slip the previous day? Enough to arouse suspicions? And here she was, alone in the house. The thought of heading down the lane to the village filled her with dread. Too risky. She'd try to get across the fields to Sarah's place. She'd be safer there.

She slid silently out of the door, closing it quietly behind her. No one about. Good. She'd made the right decision.

CHAPTER 1: HILL WALK

Monday morning

Miriam Boateng finished tying the laces on her walking boots and looked up at the sky. Blast. Where was this mist coming from? The half-hour drive here from Salisbury had been in bright, early-morning sunshine. The forecast predicted a morning of blue sky and clear air. What was going wrong? She turned round, waiting for her husband, his fingers like sausages, trying to finish fastening his boots.

'Come on, slowcoach,' she laughed. 'With this mist coming down, we need to get a move on. You're a local. What's caused it?'

Tom Fitzpatrick straightened up. 'It's the time of year. Bright days in March can sometimes do this, up on a hill. It's probably still sunny down in the valleys.'

The duo had parked their car in the small enclosure close to Win Green Hill, the highest point on Cranborne Chase and a well-known beauty spot. They were planning to walk to the hilltop then head eastwards for a spell, before branching off from the straight ridgetop path so they could circle back to their start point. But what should they do now?

Tom looked up at the sky. 'Let's just get on with it. It'll probably clear within a few minutes.'

They zipped up their jackets and set off, hopeful that the haze would thin and break. It didn't. They quickly reached the small cairn on the summit, expecting that they would be able to spot some nearby features of countryside. They couldn't. Everything was hidden in the murk. Nevertheless, they decided to plough on with their chosen route, heading east for a mile or two. Occasionally, as the mist momentarily thinned, they could make out the vague yellow orb of the sun in the sky to their right, but as the path dropped lower, the mist seemed to thicken. Was that right? Should hilltop mist thicken as you get lower? Miriam was unsure. But she wasn't one to give up on a plan, particularly not one that she'd been thinking about for several days. Work-related stress had to be managed, and this was one of her tactics. When the pressure of her work as a consultant in the spinal injuries unit at Salisbury District Hospital got too much, she headed for the hills. It had been weeks since she and Tom had managed an outing. She didn't want to abandon this one just because of a bit of low cloud on a chilly morning in Wiltshire, particularly after a duty weekend trying to catch up on the operations backlog. And they certainly weren't in any danger. The old drove track led east from Shaftesbury towards the Salisbury area and skirted the summit of the hill, but it wasn't exactly the Scottish Highlands. People didn't die because they fell into a peat bog or off a cliff. There were no such things as bogs or cliffs on these chalk escarpments. Moreover, the main track was extremely easy to follow. You simply couldn't get lost.

Miriam and Tom walked on, slowly losing altitude, heading for the point where they would swing south on a side path that descended towards the nearby village. There they would pick up a footpath that led them back up to Win Green and their car. Miriam looked around her. The mist was thickening. Would they spot the junction? Should they consider abandoning their plan? The side path would be much narrower, snaking its way through wooded areas, becoming fainter as it led them across fields. Up here it wasn't a problem, but if the mist was thickening in the narrow valley, they had a chance of veering off the path, getting lost and missing their lunch booking. That just wouldn't do. They'd booked a table for one o'clock in the area's best country pub, recommended by so many of their friends, and were due to meet up with one couple who they hadn't seen for more than a year.

She suddenly jerked back as a dim figure loomed out of the mist ahead of them, hurrying in a direction at right angles to the path they were on. It was gone almost as soon as it had appeared.

'Did you see that?' she asked Tom.

'What?' came the reply. 'Sorry. I was trying to check the map.'

'I saw someone crossing the path in front of us.'

Tom shook his head and replaced the map into its waterproof sleeve.

Miriam walked on. Where were they? This was getting more than a little disconcerting. She could only see a few yards ahead of her — they would never be able to spot the side path. Maybe they should turn back. This was no longer an enjoyable stroll on a quiet March morning, admiring the views from the high ridge. The air was getting noticeably chilly, and she was starting to worry. She turned to speak to Tom, but he wasn't there. She stopped, waited. Had he passed her? Was he ahead of her rather than behind?

She looked around in a panic. Another figure loomed ahead, eerie in the mist.

'Tom?' she called.

The figure was hurrying across the path rather than along it, just like the one a minute or two ago. But this person was carrying something. A walking stick? A thick pole of some type? That meant it wasn't Tom. He wasn't carrying walking poles today, having forgotten to load them into the car this morning. She turned around again.

'Tom?' she shouted again, this time louder. 'Tom! Where are you?'

There was no answer. She turned through 360 degrees but saw nothing that would help her get her bearings. A distant scream brought her heart into her mouth, and she was about to scream herself when Tom appeared at her side.

'Sorry. Blasted laces came undone.'

'Did you hear that? It sounded like someone screaming.'

'I heard something. Not sure what it was though. Maybe a buzzard.'

A faint wail drifted through the air. Was it a crow screeching at something? Was it a human voice?

Another scream, much fainter this time.

Miriam grabbed Tom's arm. 'Let's head back to the car. I'm scared.'

* * *

While at the pub, Miriam phoned the police about the strange noises she'd heard on the hillside that morning. She and Tom returned to the scene an hour or so later to meet a couple of local officers and have a look around, now that the mist had cleared. The whole area looked benign. Beautiful, in fact. They could see for miles in the clear air.

'Look, Dr Boateng. We've been along the path. We've had a good look round and there's nothing out of the ordinary as far as we can see. It could just have been a bird of prey. Their calls can sound like a scream. We can't assume that every loud noise out here in the sticks means someone is up to no good. We'll report it and it'll get logged. That's all we can do at the moment.' Sergeant Mark Riley followed his colleague back into their car and they drove away.

'They're probably right,' Tom said. 'There could be all kinds of explanations.'

Miriam scowled at him. 'That's hard coming from you. You know me better than anyone. Them? I'm not really surprised. I could see it on their faces as soon as they got out of their car. Mad black woman. Probably into voodoo and stuff.'

'Why didn't you tell them you're a consultant surgeon?'

'What, and upset their preconceptions? It shouldn't matter to them who I am. I may well have witnessed a serious crime, and I reported it in the correct manner. Why should my own role in society matter the slightest?'

Tom sighed. 'Because it does make a difference, even though it shouldn't. If anything ever came to court you'd make a stunningly effective witness, you know that. They ought to know that too. They ought to know that your testimony would count more than most.'

She frowned. 'Maybe they do. He was watching me closely. Not sure about her though. Seemed a bit of an airhead.' She turned towards their car. 'Let's go home. It's not been the day I'd hoped for. I think I need a cup of tea.'

* * *

'What a pain in the arse.' PC Colleen Jackson was navigating around a series of sharp bends as she spoke. 'What does she think she's doing, calling us out here on a wild goose chase? Haven't these people got anything better to do with their time than waste ours? I ask you.'

Her boss, Mark Riley, sat tight-lipped for a few seconds before speaking. 'I don't think she made it up, if that's what you mean. She heard something. She saw people.'

Colleen snorted. 'Yeah, but I bet it was something totally innocent. Someone falling over. A crow cawing. Even someone deliberately playing silly buggers with them. She's probably a fantasist. Most of them are.'

Mark turned in his seat and looked at her. 'She's a doctor. Up at the hospital, in the spinal unit. My mum got treated by her and she's really good. Didn't you notice the way she spoke? Really precise. She could make mincemeat of you in any debate, Colleen Jackson. Anyway, what do you mean by saying *most of them are*? Is this your racist side coming out again? I thought you've been warned about that.'

Colleen curled her lip and said nothing.

Meanwhile, back at the Win Green car park, a slightly grubby grey Ford was slowly heading down the exit track towards the road. A pair of small binoculars lay on the front passenger seat beside a camera. The car turned right along the lane, then, after a mile or so, took a left at the junction with the main A30, heading towards Shaftesbury. The driver was frowning despite the glorious afternoon sunshine.

CHAPTER 2: IN THE WOODS

Wednesday morning

Duffy Edgington was an apprentice farmworker at Boldswood Farm on Cranborne Chase. Long gone were the days when a farm employed someone as a specialist shepherd or cattle-worker. Nowadays you had to be a jack of all trades to work in agriculture. Sheep, cows, horses, tractors, fencing, drainage. You name it, it would be part of the job. She loved it though. She was only recently out of agricultural college, and this was her first placement. And what a wonderful placement it was, situated in such a beautiful upland area of chalk escarpments intersected by wooded valleys. If the farm manager were to offer her a permanent job at the end of her apprenticeship, she'd accept it like a shot.

She'd been known as Duffy since she'd started at primary school as a five-year-old. In fact, she'd chosen the name herself. What normal parents would call their only daughter Daffodil, for goodness' sake? She'd never been anything like a daffodil, either in shape or spirit. Daffodils were tall and slender. She was shorter than average and curvy. Daffodils were coloured yellow or lemon. She hated those colours, preferring more vibrant reds and oranges, often set against black, the colour of her hair. So she'd altered her name at the earliest opportunity and never regretted the change. She no longer admitted to the original, telling anyone who asked that her name was Duffy, and if they didn't like it, well, they'd just have to lump it. She hated daffodils with a vengeance. If anyone brought her a bunch as a springtime gift, she'd compost them as soon as she could get away with it, usually after she'd stamped on them first. Tulips were acceptable, daffodils were certainly not.

Today she was replacing a section of loose fencing wires on the edge of a wooded area and had Sookie, one of the farm dogs, with her for company. The dog sat patiently watching as she began to replace some of the corroded fixings and check that the wires were tight and secure, then he lay down and dozed as the sun began to show itself through the thinning cloud. Duffy mopped her brow with a tissue. The weather had been unpredictable lately, with alternating periods of mist and sunshine. It was partly caused by the folds in the landscape and the variations in wind direction. Spring mists had been appearing as if from nowhere, then vanishing just as mysteriously. It was one of those things that country people were used to, particularly in this area of rolling upland, criss-crossed by wooded valleys. It was late morning by the time she reached the end of the main stretch of fence. The enclosed field butted up against an area of dense woodland, shaded by the lie of the land. It felt chilly in comparison to the sun-soaked area that Duffy had just been working on. The woods were already carpeted by the first green shoots of ferns. By midsummer the whole area would be thigh-deep in their fronds. The track that ran alongside the fence she'd been checking doubled up as a public footpath, running downhill from the ridge track and Win Green Hill. That's why the fence had to be kept secure. Its purpose was to keep livestock in and walkers out.

Duffy took a swig of water and looked around. Her next task was to check the fence that ran along the side of the field, at right angles to the path. But maybe she'd first have a quick look at the rather more ramshackle fence separating the footpath from the woods. This was little more than a boundary marker. In reality there was little need to keep people out of the woods, but in bygone years country landowners had wanted to stake their claim to the land so had put fences up everywhere. It was about time this one came down. It performed no useful function. She wandered along the path for a few dozen yards, followed by the elderly dog, still sniffing about among the leaf litter. She stopped. It looked as though someone had crossed the fence. A faint trail of flattened ferns was just discernible, leading into the middle of the wood. Something glinted on the ground a few yards ahead, so Duffy moved forward to have a closer look. A slim bracelet by the look of it. Why would it be here? She moved on. There was a deep ditch beyond, almost filled by years of accumulated musty plant debris. More flattened undergrowth lay ahead. One small region of it looked somehow disturbed, although Duffy couldn't decide precisely what seemed wrong with it. She got closer. The detritus in the ditch nearby didn't look right either. Dead leaves and twigs didn't naturally end up in such arrangements, and there was one branch with residual green leaves on it. It had somehow been torn from a nearby bush.

The smell hit her as she approached. Clouds of flies lifted from the ditch then resettled. She'd brought a stick with her, so she used it to poke around for a few seconds. There was something under the debris and the dimensions of it began to worry her. It felt as if it was between five and six feet long and a foot or two wide. Maybe just under a foot deep. Surely it couldn't be? She used the stick to push more debris to one side. Sookie's tail, usually wagging furiously when out exploring, dropped and his ears lay back against his skull. He wasn't happy. He gazed at Duffy with sad eyes and gave a low whine.

Clothes. The outline of feet. What looked to be a head.

Duffy backed away, a hand to her mouth, then hurried back to the pickup truck. There was no mobile phone signal down here in this steep combe. She'd need to get back to the farm. She felt sick.

* * *

A police squad car drew to a halt in the farmyard and the passenger door opened. A middle-aged officer stepped out and looked around. He saw the young woman approaching.

'Duffy Edgington? I'm Sergeant Mark Riley. You phoned in to report that you've found a body?'

Duffy was still red-eyed and pale. She nodded but didn't speak.

'Can you take us to the location? Sorry to drag you back there, but it'll be quicker to have you with us rather than trying to follow instructions.'

'Okay. I'll take the pickup. You can follow.' She turned to a dog sitting nearby, watching her. 'C'mon, Sookie.'

She slapped her thigh and pointed to the back of the truck, then climbed into the cab. It only took five minutes for the two vehicles to wind their way along the track and into a shaded area of dense woodland.

'Do you think she's another fantasist?' Colleen Jackson said. 'I mean, what are the chances? It'll be a dead deer or something.'

'She looked a fairly sensible type to me, Colleen. Let's just go and see and save the cynical comments till later. What do you say?'

Colleen scowled but stayed silent. Mark was fast getting fed up with his stand-in squad car partner. The keen new recruit he usually worked with was currently on holiday, and he found it hard to adapt to Colleen's cynical, gnarled personality. She seemed to have a down on everybody and everything, added to which she seldom smiled. Even when she did it was usually at some poor sod's expense. Warped, that's what she was. Mark wondered what had helped to create such a miserable personality. Maybe she'd always been like it. And she was only in her mid-thirties. What was going on in her personal life? He dreaded to think.

He realised that the pickup in front was coming to a halt part way through a wooded area. He stopped the car, climbed out and walked forward to join the young farmworker, then waited for Colleen to catch up. They walked through the woods in silence until they came to a heavily shaded area on the edge of a dip. Duffy pointed, then stood back. Mark took the pole he was carrying and began to push bits of dried debris away, exposing more of the body. It looked to be fully clothed and was lying in a shallow ditch, much of it still covered in dried leaves, dirt and dead bracken. Mark could make out patches of a mottled jacket and what looked to be denim trousers. The few bits of skin on display were badly discoloured and crawling with insects. He spoke into his radio.

'It's a human body. Looks to be female, but I might be wrong there. Can you report it up the chain? We'll stake out a cordon and leave it be until Forensics get here. Who's in charge now?'

He listened carefully for a while, then spoke to Colleen. 'It's this new Wessex unit that'll be in charge. We've to secure the area.' He walked across to Duffy, who had remained several yards away. 'Best if you head back to the farm. They can speak to you there.'

Duffy looked puzzled. 'They?'

'There's a new Wessex unit just been set up. It'll be them who take charge, though one of our own Wiltshire guys is likely to be first on the scene. Stevie Harrison. He's a mate of mine. Good bloke. The others won't be far behind.'

Duffy drove back to the farm, leaving Mark pondering. He remembered the call-out a couple of days previously, when that doctor had reported hearing strange noises in the mist. If it was linked, then two days had been wasted. No doubt he'd get ticked off for not taking her report seriously enough. He scratched his grizzled head and looked across at Colleen.

'C'mon. Let's get started.'

CHAPTER 3: THE TROOPS ARRIVE

Detective Sergeant Stevie Harrison felt proud to have been asked to join the newly formed Wessex Serious Crime Unit. WeSCU, as it had come to be named, had been set up as a trial project, using government funding direct from the Home Office in Whitehall. It had inbuilt flexibility. The team members kept their prior roles in their base counties of Dorset, Wiltshire and Somerset, but would step into their WeSCU roles while investigating crimes that could draw upon their expertise. It was a win-win setup. Sparsely funded rural counties could share knowledge and resources when needed and the team members gained wider experience. He could understand the government's interest in the plan.

Stevie hadn't been the obvious choice for the Wiltshire member of the unit. He knew the position was earmarked for a fellow Steve, DS Steve Gulliver, who'd worked with the original Dorset Violent Crime Unit on a case some years before. But that Steve had simultaneously been offered a DCI role in his home county of Devon, one that he'd have been stupid to turn down. So here he was, Stevie Harrison, in a new role in a shiny new serious crime unit. He knew that he had the Dorset-based DS, Rae Gregson, to thank for the suggestion to apply for the role. She'd started her police career at the same time as Stevie, both of them working as rookie uniformed officers on the same beat in Salisbury. They'd moved into CID work at the same time, and their friendship had endured Rae's gender transition. She'd moved to Dorset several years earlier and had clearly blossomed in her new role. Had Rae put in a good word on his behalf? Stevie had been both surprised and pleased to land the job, and his newly pregnant wife, Sharon, had been over the moon. He was ambitious, and the new setup was exactly the kind of role he'd been looking for since becoming a detective. Added to which, during cases, he'd be operating alongside three experienced cops, all held in high regard. Sophie Allen herself, of course, along with second in command DCI Polly Nelson from Somerset and DI Barry Marsh. Of course, the person from the new unit he knew best was Rae Gregson. Rae was already an insider, being a protégé of the boss, Sophie Allen. Stevie had always got on well with her when she'd been in Wiltshire before her transition. She was professional to the core and worked like stink. But he wasn't averse to hard work himself. It got results. The trans bit? Well, live and let live, that was his motto. That was how they'd maintained their friendship, even after she'd transferred to Dorset. And she had a quietly winning personality, even if she could appear to be a bit too serious at times. That was probably a reaction to her own insecurities. The other member was DC Tommy Carter, from Dorset, another good bloke, although still a bit wet behind the ears. There was talk of another DC joining but nothing had been fixed yet. Stevie's only concern was that the new unit might be a fifty-fifty split between men and women in terms of numbers, but the two at the top were both female, so the power split wasn't even. Did that matter though? All three of the senior officers seemed to be professionals to the hilt, although a bit guarded. Maybe the pressure would be on them to show that the new initiative got results. Not so much him though, as a junior-ranking member. In some ways Stevie was relishing the future. It could give his career a much-needed boost. Other people would be drawn from local forces as and when they were required. And here was the first case for the new unit, in his own backyard.

He'd been visiting the Salisbury nick when the call came through about the body found in the woods out west near the county boundary. A rural crime, then. More common than people thought. So many folks held the mistaken view that serious crimes occurred exclusively in towns and cities. Not so. Idyllic countryside settings had their fair share of violent occurrences, but maybe they didn't reach the press quite as often as their urban counterparts. Taking the population distribution into account though, the stats showed not too much of a difference. Stevie knew this from the number of nasty crimes he'd investigated in seemingly perfect villages with thatched cottages dotted along country lanes.

The local uniformed cop at the scene was Mark Riley, a sergeant with a lot of experience. He'd have done things right. Stevie and Mark knew each other outside work. They were both semi-regulars at one of Salisbury's curry restaurants and often exchanged views on their menu favourites.

Stevie drew to a halt behind Mark's squad car. Any time now and the lane would fill up with cars and vans, so he parked neatly, climbed out and headed into the woods following the taped pathway. The two uniformed officers looked up as they heard him approach and Mark waved.

'We've kept clear,' he said. 'Nothing's been moved since we first arrived and had a peek.'

'Maybe your buddy can go back to the track now I'm here,' Stevie suggested. 'It'll be bedlam in no time, and we need someone to direct traffic and log arriving personnel. The forensic unit will be here in about ten minutes.'

He turned back to the body for a closer look. He could see why Mark Riley had thought the body might be that of a woman — the few wisps of hair that showed through the muck and debris that covered the head, the shape and fit of the jeans on the exposed parts of the legs. And the few bits of shirt he could see had a feminine style of colouring and pattern. He shouldn't make assumptions though. Too many of his colleagues had come a cropper that way.

He turned away from the body and took a careful look around. The ground sloped upwards slightly all around. The ditch the body lay in was aligned east to west, heading off in both directions. Had it been dug for drainage long ago? The whole glade had an ancient, forgotten feel to it. Small saplings grew out of the undergrowth, thrusting their way upwards in an attempt to find strong sunlight. Their attempts would be doomed. Old mature trees lined the area and kept much of the sun out. The only type of tree that seemed to be making some headway in the dim light were some scrappy-looking hollies. He noticed a line of moss-covered stones some yards away, following the line of the ditch. An old stone wall? Most of it had collapsed and a few rocks lay close by. Many others were probably hidden under the deep layer of undergrowth.

Why here? What was that body doing in a place like this? Maybe the victim had been despatched here and the killer had quickly shoved it into the ditch, covered it with debris and then beat a hasty retreat. But, then, why assume murder? Could it have been natural or some kind of bizarre accident? They wouldn't know until after the preliminary forensic examination.

Stevie turned back to Mark. 'Any other paths?'

'Not really. There are a few animal trails crossing through but they're not proper paths. Deer, maybe?'

'What are your thoughts, Mark?'

The sergeant shrugged. 'She's been killed by someone. Look, you need to know that there was a report of some screams being heard around here a couple of days ago. We were called out to do a check. Nothing suspicious at the time. The couple who reported it were up on the ridge but couldn't see anything because of the mist, or so they said. When we arrived, it was afternoon, and the sun was out. And they'd had a pub lunch with a few drinks. We didn't know how much to believe them.'

'How reliable?'

Mark looked unhappy. 'She's a doctor. I think Colleen there, my slightly cynical partner, may have upset her. Colleen is a bit anti, you see.'

Stevie looked at him closely. 'Anti what?'

Mark pursed his lips. 'Anti just about everyone. Asian, Chinese, Italians, gays, left-handers. You name a minority and Colleen will be anti them. All except the Irish. Her mother's from Dublin.'

Stevie was puzzled. 'And this doctor?'

'Black. Her name's Miriam Boateng. She's a consultant up at the District Hospital.'

'Right. And your buddy Colleen let some of her feelings out, did she?'

Mark nodded grimly. 'I warned her she might get herself into trouble one day. Although this doctor hasn't made a complaint yet. At least nothing's reached us if she has.'

'Okay. We'll need to speak to this Dr Boateng. If it's me, I'll try to smooth things over. In the end, though, it'll be the SIO who'll allocate jobs.'

'Who'll that be?'

Stevie shrugged. 'Probably Barry Marsh. He's a DI from Dorset. Good bloke. It's unlikely to be the DCI, Polly Nelson. She's based across in Somerset, but she's currently heading up a team looking into the rape culture in local colleges and schools. My guess is that it'll be us and the Dorset contingent who'll take it on. And we'll probably see a lot of the boss, the DCS. Not today, though. She's in Taunton for the start of this probe that the DCI's running. But we can expect her around tomorrow. This'll be the unit's first big case, so she'll want to make sure it goes well.'

'Another woman?' Mark's voice was neutral, as if he didn't want to let his inner feelings out.

Stevie smiled. 'Modern times, Mark. Changed times, in fact. Gotta get used to it. If you ask me, it's a definite improvement on the way things used to be. More teamwork. More discussion. More openness. Maybe you don't see it on the uniformed side, but compared to when I first joined CID, well . . .' His voice tailed off. 'Some of the guys in charge then were real moody bastards, only interested in their own empire building. Everything hinged on what a case could do for their own careers.'

* * *

Stevie's predictions proved to be correct. Soon after the arrival of the forensic unit, a car arrived and out stepped Barry Marsh and Rae Gregson. Stevie gave them a short factual summary and led them through the trees to the crime scene. A forensic tent had been erected and the specialist technicians had made good progress in clearing debris from the body. Their initial thoughts had been correct. The body was that of a woman, possibly late middle-aged from her appearance.

The senior forensic officer turned to face them.

'Sally Lezinsky,' she said, holding her hand out. 'I guess you're the SIO.'

'Barry Marsh,' he replied, grasping the offered hand. 'This is DS Rae Gregson. You'll already know Stevie.'

She nodded, her white-capped head dipping slightly. 'I guess this is an important case for you all. New unit and all that.'

Barry could see her eyes twinkling behind her glasses. 'It's more of a collaboration than a takeover, Sally. We'll be relying on you and Stevie a lot. Local knowledge.'

'Forensic science doesn't recognise county boundaries. We'll do the same job as always. I've worked with Dave Nash, your guy in Dorset, several times.'

Rae couldn't help butting in. 'George Clooney mark two, you mean. Adored by women across the county.'

'Well, yes, I can see that. I wasn't going to say anything. Anyway, shall we get on? What I can tell you, even this early in the process, is that there's a big head wound on the left side of her skull. Normally I wouldn't want to give details until after we've managed a thorough examination, but the wound is pretty obvious. You'll have to wait a bit longer for anything else though. She didn't have a mobile phone with her, by the way. My initial thoughts are that she might have been here for two or three days, but you'll have to wait for confirmation of that from the pathologist.'

The detectives watched as the rest of the body was uncovered, photographed and finally lifted onto a stretcher. They followed Sally outside. Barry turned to Stevie, the local detective.

'Where can we set up an incident room? Anywhere convenient nearby?'

'We could do it back in Salisbury, but it's nearly twenty miles away. The nearest town is Shaftesbury, but that's no good. It's across the county boundary, in Dorset. There'd be all kinds of complications. I reckon the community hall down in Millhead St Leonard might be the best bet. It's the nearest village, a mile or two down the valley. What do you think?'

Barry was noncommittal. 'Let's go and take a look. Rae, you stay here. We shouldn't be long.'

* * *

Many of the buildings in the village centre looked ancient. Gnarled trees, many of them oaks, made it look rather like the hamlet that time forgot. The bed of a stream, carrying water down from the hills, ran in a ditch beside the road, with small bridges spanning the flowing water to the gateway of each house. It looked a damp sort of place. How did the village cope in times of flood? What would the house insurance costs be? Barry shook his head and followed Stevie to the village hall. They'd been forced to park beside the small village green even though the hall had a good-sized car park. Several vans filled much of the available space and workers were loading exhibition material into the vehicles from the hall. Stevie hurried inside to find the caretaker while Barry had another look around the village centre. This more detailed look didn't alter his earlier thoughts.

'We're in luck,' the local detective explained when he came out of the hall after a few minutes. 'There's been a village history exhibition, but it finished yesterday. The other bookings can be easily switched to the church hall. I've just had a word with the chair of the trustees.'

Barry didn't answer. If truth be told, he wasn't keen on using halls like this. The security implications always worried him. Too many people had keys and felt they had the right to use them, no matter what they were told. A lock change would be needed if they were to end up here.

The two detectives walked inside, dodging a large display of historical illustrations that was being carried out. Once inside, Barry felt much more positive. The interior was a good size, with several small rooms that could be used as offices. It was light and airy, with a good heating system judging by the ambient temperature. It was also well fitted with electrical sockets. It might do, he thought. And it would give the distinct advantage of close proximity to the crime scene.

An overweight man in blue overalls walked across to them, a scowl on his face.

'So, you lot might be commandeering the place for a while? That mucks us up good and proper.'

Barry felt indignant but kept his feelings in check. 'And you are who, exactly?'

The man narrowed his eyes. 'The senior caretaker. Joe Hammond.'

'I'm DI Barry Marsh, currently in charge. Your chair of trustees didn't see it that way when he offered the hall's use to DS Harrison here. He thought it important to show community support to what might prove to be a detailed investigation. It looks ideal for us, but the decision hasn't been finalised yet. And don't worry, we'll be paying for it. We'll keep you informed of our plans. Thank you for sharing your thoughts with us.'

The man pivoted on his heels and stalked away, muttering to himself. Barry waited until he was out of earshot before turning back to Stevie.

‘Might have to keep an eye on Mr Grumpy there.’ He grinned. ‘The place should work, Stevie. Good idea. Can you do the usual and get it kitted out? I’ll contact the boss with the decision, then get back up the road to see how things are developing. If there’s time, try to see this doctor you were telling me about, the one who called in about the noises. We need to know exactly where she was when it happened, then organise a search. There might still be bloodstains somewhere up there on the hill if what she heard was linked to our body.’

CHAPTER 4: WITNESS

Barry suggested that Rae accompany Stevie on his visit to interview Miriam Boateng. Rae wondered about her boss's motive. She guessed that he was still feeling his way in this new setup. Maybe he had some doubts about Stevie and wanted the opinion of someone he trusted.

She followed the tall figure of the Wiltshire detective to his car. Of course, she'd known Stevie earlier in her career during her spell in Salisbury. She already knew he was a good bloke and a thorough worker. Barry could be a bit of a worrier sometimes. Unnecessarily so.

They chatted about things past and present during the twenty-minute drive to Salisbury District Hospital. Dr Boateng was waiting for them in her office.

'Two detectives,' she said once they settled into their chairs. 'You're taking this seriously, then.'

They'd already agreed that Stevie should take the lead, as the local officer. This left Rae free to watch, listen and analyse. 'A body's been found, Dr Boateng. There'll be a press release later this afternoon, so it'll be on the evening news.'

Miriam looked momentarily shocked. 'Who was it?'

'We don't know yet. It might be someone local to the area, but we can't be sure. You can help us by taking us through what you saw and heard two days ago. There's a short report already on file but it's a bit thin. So if you can go through it again, it would be really helpful.'

Miriam recounted the events in a precise and structured way. Rae took notes and watched. She was impressed. It was rare to find a witness who was so organised in her thoughts. But then, Miriam was a senior surgeon, used to organising complex procedures and making detailed decisions.

'How did you feel when you heard the screams?' Stevie asked.

'I was shocked. Make no bones about it. The fog was so dense I could hardly see a thing. And the cry that followed the scream was haunting. It was a wail, long and drawn out. Maybe it had become distorted in the thick mist. Can that happen? The second sound was fainter.'

'The report says that these figures crossed over in front of you from south to north. Is that right?'

Miriam frowned, her facial skin showing its creases. 'Well, that's what I thought. Tom and I had intended to walk west to east along the top of the ridge. That would have meant anyone crossing in front of us was moving north to south or vice versa. But I've been thinking about it since. The path kinks a bit around there and, when we turned back towards where we parked, we had to make several changes to find the main track. I spotted the sun at one point, a faint disc in a break in the mist. It wasn't where I expected it to be. It's possible we'd drifted further south than we meant to. I checked the map again last night. There's a shoulder sticking out, pointing south above the valley. We might have been on it.'

'Meaning the figures could have been crossing that shoulder rather than the ridge top?'

Miriam nodded. 'Exactly. And that would have made it west to east.'

Stevie glanced at Rae for a second. This changed things. 'That's really useful, Dr Boateng. It makes a stronger case for a link to the body we found.'

'Down in the valley?'

'Yes.'

Rae made a comment. 'If it was in the valley the sounds would have been channelled up to you and caused that spooky echo effect. It may have also disguised the direction they came from.'

Miriam nodded. 'I can see that.'

'The report on file looks okay, Dr Boateng. It had the essential detail, except for what you've just told us. I'd judge the two officers took you seriously enough in the circumstances.' Rae wanted to remove any possible unease that the doctor might feel towards Colleen Jackson's attitude. During the drive to the hospital, Stevie had passed on the comments that Mark Riley had made about his junior.

'I guess you're right. The sergeant seemed thorough enough.'

Rae went on. 'The case is being handled by WeSCU, the new serious crime unit for the Wessex region. Stevie here is a Wiltshire cop, but I'm based in Dorset. So there are no boundaries for us.'

'I can see it makes sense,' Miriam answered. 'The county boundary is really close just there. I guess the nearest town is Shaftesbury? And that's in Dorset.'

'As I said, county boundaries aren't a problem.' Stevie handed her a card. 'If you remember anything else, please get in touch right away.'

* * *

Millhead St Leonard's village hall was a hive of activity by the time the two detectives returned from their interview with Miriam. Desks had appeared, extension cables were being placed along walls, laptops were being set up and network connections checked. Rae looked around her and laughed.

'What is it?' Stevie asked.

'No chairs,' she replied. 'Maybe they've forgotten. Will we have to use the hall chairs until the proper office chairs arrive?'

'Is there a problem with that?' Stevie sounded puzzled.

'Oh, yes. Long hours of desk work. We need proper office chairs.'

Barry had joined them in time to overhear the last comment. 'The van had a puncture,' he explained. 'They'll arrive soon. How did you get on with the doctor?'

'Good. She's reliable. No problem with her story, though she does say her sense of direction was a bit suspect that morning. She reckons they might have strayed from the main path onto a shoulder, meaning the figures she saw could have been moving from west to east.' They moved to a map spread out on a side table. 'Look, the people she saw could have come up via the western coombe, then crossed the shoulder, heading back down the eastern valley. And that's where the body was found. It fits.'

'We've got off to a good start for once, then,' Barry replied. 'A reliable witness. Shame it was so misty though. No more recollections from her? No description of these two figures?'

'No. That would be too much to expect, boss. I think it's gonna be another tough one. It's a bit weird, don't you think? The way the body was carefully hidden. Someone really didn't want it found. It could have lain there for months, even years. It's what Stevie here was saying as we drove back. It was sheer good fortune for us that Duffy was doing some fence repairs in that location and had her dog with her. Otherwise . . .' Rae let the sentence hang.

CHAPTER 5: LOCALS

Sophie Allen, newly appointed as a chief superintendent and in overall command of WeSCU, pulled up in the centre of Millhead St Leonard. She was early. In fact, she hadn't expected to be here at all until the next morning, but Polly Nelson had got the Somerset-based team, the one investigating college rape culture, so well organised that Sophie had felt a little redundant. Anyway, getting here before anyone expected her had an added bonus. It gave her an opportunity to do something that she always found worthwhile. The chance to wander around incognito, sounding a place out, trying to judge what kind of a town or village it really was. And this little village was a real beauty. Quaint cottages? Tick. Village green, complete with duck pond? Tick. Thatched roofs? Tick. Historic church? Tick. It was really something to behold, even though it was late afternoon by now and the sun was soon to disappear behind the high ground to the west.

She saw what must be the village hall, over on the other side of the green. Several vans were unloading equipment, watched by a sour-faced man in blue overalls. No, wrong — he had been watching the kit transfer, but he was now watching her. Interesting. He must be the caretaker that Barry had warned her about. This, of course, was the problem with being a detective. Always looking around. Always watching. Always noting people. Like the elderly woman just coming down the side path from the church, a rather vacant look on her face. And the younger woman, toddler by her side, leaving the village shop with a heavily laden bag. Groceries probably. It was all rather fascinating. Maybe she should visit the shop and buy some biscuits or cakes for the team. Show her support right from the start.

Sophie wondered if the shop would be so old-fashioned that it would still have across-the-counter service. Not so. It was set out in a more modern minimarket style. She picked up a basket and headed for the grocery aisle in search of biscuits. Chocolate ones, of course. That's what they liked. And some Eccles Cakes, always a winner. She took the basket to the till, where a woman was watching her keenly.

'Just passing through, are you?' she asked as she scanned the items.

'Sort of. Looks a bit busy out there.'

'Summat's happened. There's talk of a body being found up in the woods. Must be summat like that, with all this going on. Looks like they've taken over the village hall. Vinegar Joe won't be pleased.' The woman grinned.

'What, because of his name or because the hall's being used?'

The woman rolled her eyes and laughed. 'The hall, of course. That's not his real name.'

Sophie kept a straight face. 'I'd never have guessed. Personality problems?'

'God, yes. Miserable old sod. His real name's Joe Hammond but, well, you can guess. He sets everyone off. Never be nice when you can be nasty instead. That's his approach.'

'So, what's the rumour mill saying?'

'Well, we don't know any details yet, though it's reckoned to be a woman. Course, you can guess what everyone's talking about. Trying to think who it might be. You know, who hasn't been seen around for a few days.'

'Who are the favourites? Anyone you know?'

Maybe that was a question too far. The shop assistant suddenly looked at Sophie more carefully and clammed up, frowning. Sophie paid the bill. 'Thanks,' she said.

'Who did you say you were?' the assistant asked.

'Well, I didn't. But since you asked, I'm with the police, the chief superintendent. The boss, you could say.'

The woman scanned her up and down. 'I'd have never known. You don't look it.'

Sophie had been wearing a grey skirt suit earlier in the day but had called in at her Wareham home and changed before driving north-west to the Cranborne Chase area. She was now wearing khaki-coloured soft-cord trousers and her favourite tan-leather bomber jacket. She put a finger to her lips and winked. 'I'm in disguise,' she said. 'Incognito. Keep it to yourself.'

The woman's eyes widened. 'Of course,' she said. 'You can rely on me.'

Sophie left the shop and wondered where to wander next. The church? Along the street past the village school? The choice was taken from her. The moody caretaker was standing by her car, looking at it.

'Is there a problem?' she asked as she approached.

'You're very close to that double yellow.'

'*Close* being the operative word. I'm not actually on it. And you are Mr . . . ?'

He ignored the implicit request. 'We don't like untidy parking here.' He really was a sour-faced individual.

'So do I get some kind of penalty point for that? Do you want to see my licence?'

He didn't reply.

'Or were you just admiring my car and the way I've parked it so carefully?'

'It's usually locals who park along here.'

'Ah, I see. I've nicked someone else's regular spot. I'll tell you what, I'll move it once those vans have finished unloading. There'll be room by the hall then.'

He looked at her suspiciously. 'Are you summat to do with the police, then?'

'Yes, I am *summat* to do with the police, as you put it.'

No point in continuing this particular conversation. She turned away and walked towards the church. Another of her weaknesses. Old church buildings, and this one was a stunner, built in the Early English style. It was a near-perfect example, and the setting — on a low mound to the west of the village green, surrounded by old, gnarled yew trees — was a dream. She made her way around the west side of the old building, looking at some of the moss-covered gravestones. The only sound she could hear was the twittering of birds. It really was a lovely setting. She stopped and looked around her, breathing in the air. Was it her imagination or did the air itself have a tinge of ancient history to it? Probably just mildew from the decaying leaves.

Sophie heard footsteps and looked up as a figure approached from the front of the church. He was middle-aged, greying at the temples, and was wearing a dog collar.

'Can I help you in some way?' he asked. He too was looking at her suspiciously. Was there something in the water around here that made the men so touchy?

She smiled at him. 'Not really. I have a weakness for old churches. I was just having a nose around.'

He nodded solemnly. 'Feel free. If you're staying locally, you'd be welcome to join our services.'

'Thanks, but I won't take you up on that offer. I love the buildings but feel rather less for what goes on inside them.'

He stared at her coldly, then frowned. 'I see.'

This was a rather different response to the one she'd had some years ago from Tony Younger, the Dorchester vicar who, in similar circumstances, had invited her in for a tour followed by bacon sandwiches in the manse. He'd found her response amusing. Maybe Tony was a rarity among modern clergy.

'Are you with the police?'

She nodded.

'Are we allowed to ask what's going on?'

'A body was found this morning in the woods. We're investigating the circumstances. That's all I can say.'

He was looking hard at her. 'You're with the investigating unit, are you?'

Sophie gave him a cool smile. 'That's right. I'm the chief super. Sophie Allen.'

His face crinkled into a rather forced smile, and he held out a hand for her to shake. 'Well, if there has been a suspicious death, it's good that it's being taken seriously. I'm Gordon Wentworth. I'll help in any way I can. I hope all my parishioners will do the same. I know most of the people around here and they're a good lot.'

'Thanks. We'll let you know when we need your help. I'd better be going.' She held up her shopping bag. 'Biscuits for the team. Gets things off on the right foot.'

His expression had already returned to its former solemnity. She turned and made her way back to the green. School had finished for the day and a small crowd of parents and children were standing opposite the village hall watching all the comings and goings. Sophie looked at her watch. Someone from the inner circle would have spotted her car by now and told Barry. She'd better not keep him on tenterhooks any longer. That would be cruel.

CHAPTER 6: MISSING LETTERS

Barry felt an elbow nudge into his ribs.

'The boss is here,' Rae whispered. 'I thought you said she wouldn't make it until tomorrow morning?'

'You know what she's like,' he replied. 'Anyway, I knew she was around. I spotted her car parked across by the green about fifteen minutes ago.'

'You could have warned me,' Rae murmured. 'I might have been picking my nose or something.'

Barry merely snorted, then walked across to greet Sophie. She was looking around at the activity — desks being set up, laptops and printers connected, filing cabinets being moved.

'Looks good, Barry. Everything going to plan?'

'So-so. The hall's in a good location. The body was a couple of miles up the valley. Middle-aged woman. Serious head wound. We've just got the first clue to her identity. Probably Bridget Kirkbride. She lived alone in a small cottage up one of the lanes that leads north-west towards the ridge.'

'Close to where she was discovered?'

Barry pursed his lips. 'Not directly. There's a shoulder of high ground between the valley she lived in and where her body was found. We were just looking at the map. It fits in exactly with a possible witness who heard screams up on the hill two days ago. Rae and Stevie have already interviewed her.'

Sophie turned to Rae. 'Reliable?'

Rae nodded. 'Oh, yes. Very. She's a surgeon in Salisbury. Out walking. No problems there.'

'Well, that makes a welcome change. Forensics?'

Barry answered. 'They're up at her house now, with Stevie. Do you want to go for a look-see?'

It was Sophie's turn to snort. 'Barry, really. You should know me better than to ask a pointless question like that.'

'I was just thinking of your new role. A lot of chief supers don't get involved with the nitty-gritty. That's what I've heard.' He stood back, waiting for the inevitable reaction.

She gave him a withering look. 'Sod that approach. Not that I'm going to throw my weight around and take over. It's your baby, Barry.' She looked at him more suspiciously. 'You were just trying to wind me up, weren't you? Maybe you've been working for me for too long.'

Barry and Rae were already walking towards the door. 'My car?' Barry asked.

'Okay,' Sophie replied. 'I've done a lot of driving today and could do with a break. And I'm not riding in Rae's new little banger unless I'm forced to. I've got a thing about old sports cars. One of my early boyfriends had one when I was still at school. He drove so wildly I was sick in it, so that romance didn't last very long.'

Rae was indignant. 'We don't all drive like that, ma'am. That kind of thing is the fault of the driver, not the car.'

Sophie opted to stay silent but didn't look as though she was convinced.

* * *

Bridget Kirkbride's home was the last dwelling on the narrow, winding lane. Beyond the small cottage, the route deteriorated into a muddy track that led across a field and uphill to a shoulder of high ground. It was difficult to see much detail because of the rapidly fading light.

'How sure are you of her identity?' Sophie asked as they approached the front door. They were all wearing forensic overalls.

'Oh, it is her,' said Barry. 'Stevie called just before you arrived. Several photos in the house match up closely. And no one's seen her for the last couple of days, which is unusual. Everyone knew her, you see. Apparently, she was a mainstay of village life. Fairly quiet but always helpful, that was one description from a neighbour. He said that her death made no sense.'

The house was small and neat. Surprisingly it didn't feel cold inside. Sophie felt the radiator in the hall — still warm, so the central heating must still be on. Stevie Harrison and Tommy Carter came out of the sitting room to meet them, both covered from head to foot in pale-blue forensic suits. Forensic technicians were active throughout the house: taking photographs, dusting for fingerprints and searching for unusual stains. Sally Lezinsky, the local forensic chief, came out of the kitchen and held out a gloved hand to Sophie.

'Heard a lot about you,' she said.

'I hope most of it is good,' came the reply. 'Are we able to take a look around yet?'

Sally pulled her head cover back, exposing a tousled mass of pale ginger curls. 'Phew. That's better. I get too hot in these things. Yes, fine. Keep your suits on while you're in any of the other rooms. We've finished out here, so you can de-hood, like me.'

'Anything showed up?' said Barry.

'Not yet. It's a nice place, but you'll see that for yourselves. Just check with whoever's in each room that it's okay to go in.'

'Of course,' Barry replied. 'It's just to get a feel for the place.'

'By the way, we haven't found a mobile phone, either on her body or here. And the line's not working to her home phone. We've just found out that some of the other houses lost their landline connection in last week's storm, but the others have been reconnected. We're chasing it up with the phone company.'

'So she might have been unable to contact anyone?'

Sally nodded and left.

They moved into the sitting room. It was comfortably furnished in autumn colours, browns and golds, and had a homely feel. A TV sat in one corner and an old-fashioned radio stood on a shelf on the other side of a fireplace that still held a pile of grey ash.

'We guess she boosted the heating in here on cold evenings with a log fire,' Stevie explained. 'These old cottages can be a bit chilly in winter.'

'I live in one,' Sophie replied. 'It's exactly what we do.'

Several photos sat beside the radio. They showed a smiling middle-aged woman and a young man with a similar face shape. A small shelf-level hatchway near the back corner of the room gave convenient access to the kitchen, ideal for a few plates or cups.

They moved to the kitchen, surprisingly modern in its fittings. It was neat and tidy but not obsessively so, a practical neatness rather than something neurotic. There was nothing out of the ordinary, a point agreed by the forensic officer who was just finishing off in the room.

'The same in all the other rooms,' he said. 'Not really anything obviously out of place.'

They climbed the stairs and peeked in the two bedrooms. The main one was clearly lived in, with a jumper and skirt draped across a chair near the foot of the bed. A pair of low-heeled court shoes lay under the chair, the left one laying on its side. A basket-weave laundry container sat in another corner with a few items of clothing in it. Above it, a shelf held a row of books, mainly romance novels and light fiction.

The second bedroom had a more masculine feel, but it lacked any sign of recent occupation. A couple of outdated football annuals lay on a bedside table and a few clothes were hanging in the wardrobe: trousers, an informal jacket and a couple of brightly coloured shirts. The small laundry basket was empty.

'Someone younger?' Sophie asked. 'The man in the photos, maybe?'

'That's what we thought,' Stevie replied. 'The neighbour said her son lived here, but he moved out when he started college in the autumn. It was just the two of them. Oh, and that bracelet that was found at the crime scene? It's probably hers. A neighbour described it to us.'

A forensic officer was still working in the bathroom, so Barry and Sophie stood in the doorway and watched. The small, mirrored cupboard above the sink held only women's items, although a shelf in a lower cupboard had a box with an electric razor inside. There were few other signs of any masculine presence.

Sophie felt that a profound sadness seemed to linger over the small home. Was it really there or was she just being oversensitive, the result of coming to the end of a long and tiring day?

'I've seen enough for now,' she said. 'Feel free to stay if you want to, but I'm heading back down the valley. I'll walk. I could do with some fresh air.'

Rae opted to go with her while the other three detectives chose to remain in the cottage for a while longer.

'What are your thoughts, Rae?' Sophie asked as they walked down the lane in the early-evening twilight.

'There's nothing obvious is there, ma'am? No signs of a break-in, nothing out of place in the house. You'd think it might be a case of mistaken identity, but whoever killed her was right up close, with something heavy to hand. You know that we're having trouble contacting whoever's the next of kin, don't you? There isn't a husband. She was never married.'

'In that case, I suppose it'll be the young guy in the photos. A son?'

Rae grimaced. 'Yes, Grant's the name. But we can't trace him. Not yet, anyway.'

Sophie frowned. 'You know what that usually means, don't you?'

'That he was the killer? Yes, of course. We've only had a chance to speak to a couple of the neighbours so far. They say the two of them were devoted to each other. That the son was a lovely young man. And that he hasn't been seen at college for the past couple of days. We're still trying to trace him. There's only one other close member of the family. The dead woman's sister. She lives in Shaftesbury, apparently. We haven't managed to trace her yet either.'

'It's early days. Maybe you're expecting too much too soon. The body was only found this morning, for goodness' sake.'

'Maybe you need to tell Barry that. He's worrying.'

Sophie turned to face her. 'I already have. Barry's a perpetual worrier, like me. It's what makes him so good. Cops who don't worry about things can miss stuff.' She sniffed the air and looked upwards. 'Red sky. It should be a fine day tomorrow.' She looked back at Rae. 'I had a quick chat with three locals before I joined you in the hall. You might want to tell Barry. The local shopkeeper probably knows a lot of what goes on here. She's a bit of a gossip though. I think her name's Wendy from the sign above the door. Maybe you met the caretaker, one Joe Hammond. He's a real moaner, suspicious of everyone and everything. But I also bumped into the vicar, Gordon Wentworth. Reserved sort of man, but he said he'd help in any way he can. Said he knew most people in the area.'

'You're not coming back in, then?'

'No. I'll just get in the way. I'll pop back tomorrow morning, though. We need to trace her movements leading up to her death. Can you organise that, Rae? Tell Barry.'

* * *

Barry was still in the cottage when his phone rang some thirty minutes later. He listened to the message carefully before turning to Tommy Carter and Stevie Harrison.

'That's the agricultural college where the Kirkbride son, Grant, was meant to be studying. He hasn't been seen since last week. According to the admin people there, they've tried phoning but clearly the landline's been out of action and there's been no response from his mobile.' He paused for a few seconds. 'I think I need a few words with your forensic chief, Stevie. Let's face it, this place has been empty since those screams were heard two days ago, assuming that's when our victim was killed. That's plenty of time for someone to get in, search the place and remove anything incriminating. I want her to double-check all the doors and windows for any signs of an entry, however slight. There's something going on here that doesn't add up.'

'Whoever did it might have had a key,' Tommy suggested. 'Where might this son be? You'd expect him to have a house key, wouldn't you?'

'That's what bothers me,' came the reply. 'I'll get Rae onto it with you, Tommy. Stevie, I want you to check everyone in the surrounding area who might know where he is. Any girlfriends and so on. Get a couple of the local cops to help if you need to.'

CHAPTER 7: DESPAIR

Thursday morning

The village of Millhead St Leonard was shaped like the upper half of a starfish. The base of the village was spread out along an east–west axis, following the line of the river and the main road. Not that the latter was a transport route of any significance. It probably had been important in the early part of the twentieth century, but the completion of a trunk road between Salisbury and Blandford Forum, one that bypassed the villages, had left it of only local significance. Two small streams joined the river in the village centre. One trickled in from the north-west, the other from the north-east. Lanes wound their ways up both valleys, each lined with houses — some old, some built rather more recently. The two lanes were cul-de-sacs, each shrinking to a mere farm track or footpath at the upper end.

Sarah Wilkinson lived near the top of the north-eastern spur with her husband, Neil. Her close friend Bridget Kirkbride lived at the top of the north-western spur, about a mile away across the high ground that separated the two valleys at their northern ends. But maybe she didn't live there now, not as a living, breathing, sentient being. Sarah had heard the news that Bridget's was probably the body that had been found in the woods yesterday. Well, maybe *news* wasn't the right description. An increasingly urgent rumour was a more apt alternative.

Sarah was in a state of emotional turmoil. She'd tried to eat a little breakfast, encouraged by Neil, but after yet another phone message had come in from yet another neighbour, she'd been unable to keep even that small amount of food down. It just didn't make any sense. Bridget was such a lovely person, such a kind-hearted soul. Who would have wanted to harm her? It was just beyond belief. Surely the rumours couldn't be true. These people must be mistaken. It was mischievous to spread such false tales, causing unnecessary anxiety and fear, that was what Neil had said. But Bridget was not answering her phones, neither her mobile nor her landline. She wasn't responding in any way to messages or social media posts. Her neighbours had reported that there had been no signs of life for several days. And last night had brought the final confirmation: rows of police and forensic vehicles parked outside Bridget's cottage. What other explanation could there possibly be? Neil was still insisting that it was probably all some kind of tangled mix-up, but Sarah knew deep down that something awful had happened. She'd finally got angry with him when he'd made yet another attempt to come up with a different explanation.

'Oh, for God's sake, Neil. Get real!' she'd finally shouted at him. He'd stalked out of the room and was now nowhere to be found, not even in the garden. He must have gone out for a walk.

She heard a car draw up outside and looked out of the lounge window. Two people, a man and a woman. They had a businesslike look to them. Police? Sarah felt a sense of terror gripping her heart. Even so, she glanced in the mirror to check her dark hair was moderately tidy, straightened her necklace, tugged the sleeves down on her jumper and went to the door.

There were standards to be maintained, even in the most challenging of circumstances.

'Sarah Wilkinson? I'm DS Rae Gregson. This is DI Barry Marsh. We understand that you are probably Bridget Kirkbride's closest friend. May we come in, please?'

Sarah's hand went to her mouth. 'Oh, no,' she whispered. 'Is it true then? Bridget's really dead?'

'We don't know for sure, Mrs Wilkinson. Which is one of the reasons we're here. May we come in?'

Sarah was wringing her hands. 'Oh, yes. Of course. Sorry.' She showed them into the lounge.

The man took over. 'We have an as-yet unidentified body that we suspect is hers, but we can't contact her next of kin. That would be her son. One of the neighbours mentioned that you were probably her closest friend. Do you have his contact details?'

'Oh, I think so. Somewhere. Let me think. This is all such a shock.'

The woman took over again. 'It's bound to be, Mrs Wilkinson. Can we call you Sarah?'

'Yes. It's not on my mobile because I never called him, but I think it might be in my address book. His phone number, I mean. I'm a bit old-fashioned that way. I'll get it.'

'Shall I put the kettle on, Sarah? I think maybe you could do with a cup of tea.'

Sarah, who was out in the hallway rummaging through a drawer, called back, 'Oh, yes. I'll be with you in a moment.'

She took a small pocket book back to the lounge and showed the man the relevant page, then joined the woman in the kitchen.

'Is it really her?' Sarah asked.

'I don't think there's much doubt,' came the reply. 'Does she often wear a silver bracelet? Like this?'

She extracted a photo and passed it across. Sarah put her hand to her mouth and nodded. It took her several moments before she could speak. Even when she did her voice was weak and quavery. 'Yes, that's hers. Someone said it might be murder. Several people, in fact.'

'We're treating it as a suspicious death.'

'Bridget hasn't been answering her phone. Not since Monday. I know the phone lines came down last week in the storm, but they were repaired quite quickly. And she hasn't answered her mobile. I was getting really worried.'

'So, you are her closest friend?'

'I suppose so. She's a really nice person, so kind to everyone. I just can't believe it. Why would anyone want to harm her? It doesn't make sense.' She started to cry.

The policewoman went on to make the tea and extracted three mugs from a wall cupboard. Sarah put a tray on the table and transferred the teapot and mugs onto it, along with a plate of biscuits. She was about to pick the tray up, but her hands were shaking too much. The detective put a hand on her arm as if to calm her, then lifted the tray.

'Don't worry. I'll do the carrying. Do you know the son well? Grant, isn't it?'

Sarah nodded. 'He's at agricultural college up near Gloucester.'

'Well, let's go through, then you can tell us what you know.'

The senior detective, the ginger-haired man, was still sitting in his chair, but Sarah wondered if he'd been around the room looking at her photos. That's what detectives did, didn't they? On the TV, anyway.

'Did you find the number?' Sarah asked him.

'It's the one we already have. And the address. You don't have any others?'

She shook her head. 'No, sorry.'

She noticed that he looked perplexed, worried even.

'We can't contact him on that number, nor on any others we've found. The college say they haven't seen him since last week. Can you rack your brains? Is there any other way to contact him?'

Sarah thought hard but had to give up. 'No. That mobile number was the one Bridget used.' She put her hand to her mouth again and turned pale.

'What is it?' the junior detective asked.

'Bridget told me on Sunday she was having trouble contacting him. She was really upset. It wasn't like him. They were very close, and he always called her, every week.'

'We understand that Bridget has a sister who lives in Shaftesbury. Do you have her details?'

'She's in a care home. She suffers from early-onset dementia so I'm not sure how helpful she'll be. But the address is in the book. Let me show you.'

Sarah pointed out the relevant address and the junior detective made a note of it.

'There's no one else?' the man asked. What was his name again? DI Barry Marsh. That was it. The other one, the woman, had said her name was Rae Gregson.

Sarah shook her head. 'Bridget was a single parent, never married. That caused a bit of a stir when she first arrived in the village with Grant as a baby. Some of the locals are a bit stuck in the past with views that wouldn't be out of place in Victorian times. But most of them got over it eventually. She worked as the village librarian until the place closed ten years ago. Those awful cuts. She tried her hand at other things. She takes in sewing and runs a little alterations business. That's how she gets by. She always said she wasn't going to get rich, but it paid the bills.'

'How old was Bridget?'

'That's easy. She had her fiftieth birthday party just over a week ago, on the Saturday evening. That was the last time we saw Grant.'

'We?' He looked puzzled.

Sarah shrugged. 'Any of us, I think. Certainly Neil and I. But Bridget told me the same thing just a few days ago. That she hadn't seen Grant since the party, and he didn't seem to be answering his phone. She was getting a bit worried.'

'So tell me about the party. Was it a happy occasion?'

'Oh yes. Bridget was positively glowing. She's an attractive woman, Inspector. She's got a quiet personality but she's a bit of a looker.' Sarah suddenly put a hand to her mouth. 'Oh, God. I mean, she was. I just can't get my head round it.'

'Did she have a partner or boyfriend?'

'Not for some time, no. She was seeing a man. He was some kind of advertising executive, but that ended when he went off with a much younger woman. That was a couple of years ago. I don't think she's had a regular boyfriend since.'

'Any irregular ones?' the younger detective, Rae, asked.

'I couldn't say. If she did, she kept it quiet. Better that way around here. People can be a bit, you know, quick to condemn.' She was frowning again.

'Have you thought of something?' Rae asked.

Sarah nodded. 'I hadn't thought of it before. It's just that they both got a bit tense on the evening of the party. Bridget and Grant. With each other, I mean. It was odd.'

'Can you explain?'

'I overheard him say, *Don't trust him, Mum. He's a snake.* And she kind of snorted in response. She said something like, *Don't be ridiculous.* I've only just remembered. And before you ask, I've no idea who they were talking about.'

'Had anyone just arrived?' Rae was leaning forward in her seat.

'A group of people. I think they'd just come up from the pub. They must have met up in there for a pre-party drink. They were a bit noisy, if I remember. I can't remember who they were. Neil might know. He was with them.'

'Neil?' Barry asked.

Sarah rolled her eyes. 'My husband. Normally we'd go to a party together, but I was across helping Bridget get things ready. I took my dress with me and changed there. Neil was meant to be arriving ready for the start, at seven thirty, but he didn't roll up until well after nine with the pub lot. I wasn't particularly happy about it.'

'And did the tension last long between the two of them?'

Sarah shook her head. 'No, not at all. It couldn't. They're both such nice people and they're so close. But Grant didn't stay long. He said he had to get back to college. I think a taxi came for him soon afterwards and took him into Salisbury for a train.'

'Do you think anyone else overheard this disagreement between them?'

'I don't know. It's possible, I suppose.' She suddenly looked horrified. 'Do you think it caused all this?'

Barry pursed his lips. 'Probably not. But we need to check.' He glanced up as he heard a door open at the rear of the house.

'That'll be my husband,' Sarah said. She called more loudly. 'In here, Neil.'

A man looked around the door from the hallway.

'These are police detectives, dear,' Sarah added.

The man merely nodded. He clearly didn't know whether to come in or go away, so the DI beckoned him into the room. The two detectives stood up in order to shake hands. Courteous, Sarah thought to herself. Maybe they've been trained that way. She stood up and joined her husband, holding onto his arm.

'It *is* Bridget, Neil. The body found yesterday. I feel . . . devastated.'

Neil frowned. 'So why are you here?'

The younger detective, Rae, spoke. 'We understand that Sarah was probably her closest friend and confidante. We needed information about her son, but we've also been talking about her recent birthday party. You were there?'

He nodded. 'Yeah, but a bit later in the evening than Sarah. I don't remember anything odd happening. Why's the party relevant?'

'It may not be. But it's likely it was the last time Bridget saw her son.'

'He left soon after I arrived. I didn't speak to him much.'

'Who else was with you? We understand you came up from the pub.'

Neil frowned again, this time more prominently. The sideways scowl was directed at his wife. 'That's right. I needed to see someone there and bumped into the others while I was having a quick drink.'

'Who was with you when you arrived?'

'Wendy Draper and her husband. They run the village shop. Joe Hammond and his missus. He's the caretaker for the local hall.'

'We were a bit surprised he was there,' Sarah interrupted. 'He's a bit prickly, but you've got to stay on the right side of him if you want to use the hall. Bridget doesn't like him really but couldn't afford to leave him out. She runs a knitting group there. She'd have never heard the last of it if she'd left him off the list.'

'Dougie Dillon was there too. He didn't really have an invitation but thought he'd try to sneak in anyway. Anything for free booze and a nosh, that's Dougie. And the Kellaway girls.'

'They live together,' Sarah explained. 'They're very dramatic. Quite lively. Good to have at a party.'

'And they like a bit of quality plonk,' Neil added.

'And that's it?' This was the detective again.

'I think so.'

'What about the vicar? Didn't he come in with you?' Sarah looked puzzled.

'What, Gordon? He wasn't in the pub. Perish the thought. No, he caught up with us just as we arrived at Bridget's house.'

The male detective spoke, aiming his question at Sarah. 'Was there an invitation list? It's just that you mentioned one and we haven't found anything like that, as far as I'm aware.'

'It was more than a week ago. Maybe she binned it soon afterwards.'

Neil broke in. 'You're barking up the wrong tree, if you ask me. No one at the party would have done anything like that. She was too popular. A lovely woman, in every way.' He suddenly went quiet and looked embarrassed.

Sarah glanced at the detectives. The woman was watching Neil with a look of deep interest. Sarah felt sick again as she watched Neil slide out of the room.

The DI spoke. 'Could you put together a list for us, please, Sarah? We've got the people who came in from the pub, but there were others who arrived earlier, is that right?'

Sarah nodded. She felt too nauseous to speak because of the thought that had just entered her head. Had a semi-drunk Neil been trying it on with Bridget yet again? At the party when he thought no one was watching? Had he been the 'snake' that Grant had warned Bridget against? Oh, God. This was all too much.

CHAPTER 8: THE KELLAWAY GIRLS

It was the mid-morning briefing and Tommy Carter was looking dubious.

'Isn't it a bit of a mistake to focus on people who were at that party? I mean, it was a good week or so before the murder and there could be loads of motives for someone wanting to kill her.'

Barry, in charge of the meeting, frowned. 'We're not focussing on it, Tommy. I agree with what you're saying. But we always start any investigation by talking to the people who knew the victim best, as well as neighbours and acquaintances. We're assuming that most of the people she knew were there, so speaking to all the guests gets us off to a flying start. And when we talk to them, can we all make sure we double-check their memories of who was there? At the moment the only names we have are the latecomers who came up from the pub. There were bound to be a lot of others and we need to talk to them all. Plus, other people she knew who weren't there. It's not our only line of enquiry anyway. The forensic teams are still searching up in the woods and Stevie's local squad are trying to trace her movements in the twenty-four hours prior to her murder. Once we get their reports, we can widen our approach.'

Tommy looked downcast. 'Sorry, boss.'

Rae elbowed him in the ribs. 'Don't take it personally, Tommy. You were right to speak up with your thoughts. None of us are immune from missing something obvious. That's why we meet and talk like this.'

Tommy looked a little more cheerful. 'It's just that I say some stupid things sometimes. Like just then.'

Barry went on with what he'd been saying. 'You and me, Tommy. We'll see the Kellaways and then try to see this Dougie Dillon person, whoever he is. Rae and Stevie, you take the hall caretaker, Joe Hammond, and his wife, and then have a chat with Wendy Draper. She runs the village shop. We're just looking for background at the moment, tracing other people at the party and other friends. Don't give too much away. It's early days yet.'

'What about the vicar? What was his name?' Stevie asked.

'Gordon Wentworth,' Tommy said instantly.

Barry grinned. 'See, you're spot on with the facts, Tommy. We'll add him to our list. I think the super had a few words with him yesterday but just in passing. Shall we get going? Back here at one? We might even see the boss again. She's gone to Gloucester to chase up the missing son.'

* * *

Sarah Wilkinson's description of the Kellaway girls as dramatic proved to be spot on. To Barry they seemed to be more the type of middle-aged women you'd expect to find living in the bohemian enclave of a large city rather than a small, rural village in deepest Wiltshire. Edie was tall, angular and dark-haired. Minnie was shorter, rounder and fair. Both were sporting theatrically dark eye make-up, along with headbands that wouldn't have looked out of place in the Charleston era. They both came to the door on hearing the bell's overdramatic ring and stood listening to Barry's introduction with eyes wide and mouths open.

Edie put her hand to her almost non-existent bosom. 'Oh, my goodness,' she gasped. 'So, it is true! How dreadful.'

Her partner stroked a hand across her brow. 'I feel quite giddy. Please come in. I think something strong is called for. Don't you think so, Edie, darling?'

'Brandy, Minnie. You get it while I escort these people into the drawing room. I think we all need seats. I know I do.'

She led the two detectives inside and through the first doorway. 'I'd better explain, Inspector. Our full name is Kellaway-Brockhurst. I'm Edwina and Minnie is Minette. I'm a Kellaway and she's a Brockhurst. We're married. I think we caused a bit of a stir when we first appeared in the village five years ago. We probably still cause a stir at times, but heigh-ho, we don't give a toss. We do our bit for the local community.'

'We won't take up much of your time, Ms Kellaway-Brockhurst.'

'For God's sake, just call me Edie. It's too much of a mouthful otherwise. Have a seat.'

Barry and Tommy each sat on a soft chair facing the sofa where Edie perched. Minnie appeared, carrying a tray of glasses and a brandy decanter and set it down on a small table beside the couch.

'Not for us, thanks,' Barry said. 'Water would be good, though. It's thirsty work, all this talking.'

This time it was Edie who left the room, leaving Minnie to act as host. 'So how can we help you, Inspector? We'll do anything we can. Bridget was such a dear friend. A real gem and a truly lovely person. We're both utterly shocked.'

Minnie's eyes were like saucers, made more dramatic by the dark kohl shadow and thick mascara. Just like her partner a few minutes earlier, her hand rested on her breast, though Minnie's bosom was rather more pronounced. Edie returned with two glasses of iced water.

'Thanks. Several things, really. We want to build up a picture of Ms Kirkbride and her life here. We need to speak to all of her friends, so we're making a start on the guests at her recent birthday party. I understand that you were both there?'

'Indeed, we were,' Minnie replied. 'It was a lovely do, wasn't it, Edie?'

Edie nodded enthusiastically. 'Oh, yes. Lots of interesting chat. I take it you know the group of us who met up in the pub first? Most of the people already there when we arrived were her neighbours, people who live in West Street. It was a fine evening, so most of us from East Street decided to walk to her house. That's why we were in the pub for a while. We toddled down to the village centre, had a couple of drinks while we assembled, then made our way up West Street. It's only ten minutes. We're all very law-abiding, Inspector. No drunk drivers. We don't like them around here, not after Wendy Draper's mother was killed by one a few years ago. A hit-and-run.'

'How did you get back? Wasn't it a bit of a trek for those living at the top end of East Street?'

'We had a minibus arranged. We all chipped in, so it worked out cheap.'

'Can you remember who was already there? Apart from Ms Kirkbride and her son? Oh, and we know about Sarah Wilkinson.'

'Poor Sarah,' Minnie sighed. 'Married to that man. He tries it on with us all, you know. What a bore it is, having to fend him off once he's had a couple of drinks.'

'He needs to be put in the stocks,' Edie added, a mischievous look on her face. 'All the village women could throw rotten fruit at him. That'll teach him.'

Minnie was frowning in concentration. 'Martha Marshall, Bridget's next-door neighbour, was there. She was by herself, as usual. She's very *churchy*. Spent the evening talking to the vicar. He looked bored out of his skull.'

'Peter and Valerie Bailey. They live opposite her,' Edie added. 'They're nice.'

'Fred Golbie. You know, the retired darts champion. He lives down the road from Bridget. He's by himself too, though he had a woman with him when he first moved in.'

'A real slapper,' Edie added, giggling. 'We were all agog to find out why she'd upped and left but he wouldn't let on, would he, Minnie? But Bridget must have felt sorry for him. She had a soft spot for anyone who was single. We kind of half expected her to start a lonely-hearts club but she never did.'

'Just the knitting group,' Minnie added, rolling her eyes. 'Not exactly the height of excitement. I think that's everyone.'

Barry watched the two women carefully. 'Can you tell us about this Dougie Dillon? He was with you coming up from the pub, we understand. Yet he didn't have an invitation.'

Minnie narrowed her eyes. 'So you know about him. That Sarah Wilkinson. She's a gossip and a half, isn't she? Yes, he was there. He was in the pub, as usual. Once he heard us talking about the party, we couldn't get rid of him. I reckon he had a bit of a thing for Bridget. Don't you agree, Edie?'

Edie widened her eyes. 'Ooh, yes. That would have solved all his problems if he could've hooked Bridget. Money, a nice home, status, invitations to things rather than him constantly having to gatecrash. Not a hope, though.'

Minnie laughed. 'No, not a hope. Can you imagine an urbane, well-dressed, middle-aged man? Neat and tidy? Always saying the right thing at the right time? Knowledgeable about food, drink, current affairs and the arts? Well, think of the exact opposite. That's Dougie.'

'Bridget let him in, though. We said she was kind-hearted. She always took pity on waifs and strays.'

'That's Dougie,' Minnie added. 'A waif and a stray. Swears a lot too.'

'Where would we find him?' Barry asked.

Minnie glanced at her wife before replying. 'At the timber yard just along the valley. He saws wood.'

'All day,' added Edie, drily. 'Every day.' She rolled her eyes again.

'And that's everyone who was at the party?' Rae said.

'Think so,' Minnie replied.

'So, let me ask you something different,' Barry went on. 'Where were you both on Monday morning?'

The two women looked troubled, as if they hadn't expected to be asked this obvious question.

'We were in Shaftesbury, at the shops,' Minnie said. 'Monday can be such a depressing day, can't it? We almost always head into town to have a look around. We visited a little boutique we like then the supermarket. Then we had lunch in the little café at the top of Gold Hill. So picturesque with that stunning view.'

She looked across at Edie and they exchanged a smile. 'Well, if that's everything we've got things to do.'

'What are your lines of work exactly?' Barry asked.

'We edit *Cranborne Life*. It's a free monthly magazine. Well, saying we edit it is a bit of an understatement. We also do the reporting and interviewing, don't we, Edie?'

Her partner nodded enthusiastically, her fair hair bobbing to and fro. 'Absolutely. We also do the page make-up and organise pretty well everything. We bully people into advertising.' She giggled. 'We started it from scratch when we came here. It's going great guns.'

* * *

'How far is this timber yard?' Barry asked as he steered the car out onto the valley road heading east.

Tommy looked carefully at the map he held. 'About two miles, boss. It should be on your right, just before we reach the main road to Salisbury.'

The valley was heavily wooded in parts, with occasional areas of open field in which sheep and cattle grazed.

'It's pretty, isn't it?' Tommy said.

'King John had a hunting lodge around here somewhere,' Barry replied. 'Apparently Cranborne Chase was one of his favourite hunting grounds.'

'Is that the same John of Robin Hood fame?' Tommy asked.

'Probably. I think we've only had one John. Can't be sure though.'

The timber yard and sawmill appeared after the next bend, so Barry slowed and pulled in to the entrance. The office was a wooden shack on the edge of the empty carpark. They could see a middle-aged woman watching them as they walked towards the building. She smiled at them expectantly as they entered.

'I'm afraid we're not here for wood,' Barry said. 'Can we have a couple of minutes with one of your workers, Dougie Dillon? We're from the police. DI Barry Marsh and DC Tommy Carter.'

The woman's smile faded somewhat. She pressed an intercom button and spoke into a microphone. 'Dougie, you're wanted. The cops are here to take you away.' She looked back at the two detectives. 'That should bring him.'

'Scare him, more like,' Barry replied. 'He'll be on edge now.'

'What, Dougie? Don't be daft. He's as hard-bitten as they come. I'm Sue Gazzard, by the way. I own this place.' She rose and stretched out a hand.

Barry grasped it firmly and explained the purpose of their visit. 'We're trying to have a few words with all of Bridget Kirkbride's friends.'

Sue raised her eyebrows. 'Dougie? A friend of Bridget? Ha! Who told you that?'

'Well, he was at her recent birthday party.'

'Yeah, I heard about that. I'd have shut the door on him if he'd turned up uninvited to a party of mine. Too soft-hearted, that's our Bridget.'

'Did you know her well?'

'So it is true, then? Sort of. Not close enough to get invited to her party, but she was a good person. She didn't deserve whatever happened to her, no way.' She looked up as the door opened and a dishevelled-looking man came in.

'You can use my office through there.' She pointed to a door. 'And if I can help in any way, just give me a bell.' She turned to the man. 'Tell the truth now, Dougie. None of your porkies or you'll likely end up in hot water.'

Tommy repeated the introductions once the door to the office was closed behind them and they were seated. Dougie looked nervous, his eyes flickering between the two detectives, the window and the door. It looked as though he desperately wanted to make a run for it. He was dressed in grubby dungarees and heavy work boots. Fine bits of sawdust stuck to his clothes, skin and hair.

'We just wanted to ask you about the party you went to at Bridget Kirkbride's house a week or so ago,' Barry said.

Dougie looked at him suspiciously. 'I just turned up on the off-chance. I weren't invited or anything. I don't really know her. Didn't, I mean. It's tragic.'

'How did you hear about the party?'

'In the pub. Saturday night, weren't it? Always there. I got chatting to Neil Wilkinson. He thought it would be a laugh if I tried to get in. Everyone'll be a bit posh, that's what he said. Could do with someone like you there, Dougie. Stir them all up a bit. So I thought I'd give it a go.'

'And was there any problem with Bridget?'

'Nah. She just giggled a bit and said, "Come on in, then." Anyway, I said I'd fix her broken back gate, so it was worth it for her.'

'Did you see any friction there? Any arguments?'

'Nope. But Sarah gave Neil a hard time. He should've been there at the start, s'what she said. That's Neil for you. He was in a mood for the rest of the evening. Except when Bridget was around. I reckon he's been trying it on with her for months. He's a bit of a chancer, like me.' He laughed.

Barry seemed to be pondering this information, so Tommy broke in. 'This back gate. Where does it lead?'

'A footpath goes up over the hill and down to the top end of East Street. She could get to it right from her back garden.'

'How did you know the gate was broken? Surely it was dark by the time you arrived?'

'She told me.' Dougie seemed to clam up after that. Did he somehow think that he'd said too much?

'Do you own a walking stick, Mr Dillon?'

The man nodded but said nothing.

'Have you used it recently?'

He shook his head. 'Not been out of the village much this month. Too bloody busy at work.'

CHAPTER 9: VINEGAR JOE

Stevie had wanted to visit Wendy Draper in the village shop first but the caretaker, Joe Hammond, was lurking in the car park as he and Rae left the hall. He was clearly the type of person who was around when he wasn't wanted or needed, so was the opposite true? Would he have vanished by the time the detectives wanted to speak to him? Stevie thought it better not to take a chance on it.

'Glad you're around, Mr Hammond,' he said to the somewhat sour-faced individual. 'We need to pick your brains about something. Come in for a few minutes, please.'

Hammond didn't say anything as he marched inside, glancing around him as he entered as if to check on the state of the building.

'A bit overcrowded in here,' he scowled. 'There'll be some scrape marks on the walls by the time you've finished, I bet.'

'In that case, we'll pay for any touch-up needed,' Stevie said. 'We want to ask you about any recent contact you had with Bridget Kirkbride. Take a seat.'

'What? Am I a suspect or summat? That's a bloody outrage, thinking I done it.' Hammond accompanied this remark with a scowl that was obviously created for the occasion.

'Have you heard the expression, *eliminating someone from our enquiries*? That's what we're doing,' Stevie explained, patiently.

The man was only partly mollified. He looked at them suspiciously and merely grunted.

'You were at Ms Kirkbride's party last week. We assumed the guests were her closest friends.' Stevie waited to see the reaction to this statement.

'Yeah, we was there, me and Mary. People rely on us, you see. To keep the hall ticking over, ready for when anyone needs it. It's one of the most important bits of the village. The single most important one, if you ask me.'

Stevie decided not to ask him. What would be the point? Wouldn't some people put the village pub, the shop or the public toilets first? He chose a different angle. 'Is your wife a caretaker as well? I didn't realise that.'

Hammond looked shifty. 'Nah, but she helps me out sometimes.'

Stevie could see the explanation. Hammond was the only official caretaker, but probably expected his wife to muck in when it was inconvenient for him to work. Interesting.

'Can you remember who was at the party?' Stevie asked.

Hammond worked his way through the same set of names they already had, with no surprise additions.

'You and your wife went to the pub first, we understand. Is that right? Who else was there?'

'Wendy Draper from the local shop. The Kellaway pair. That was meant to be all. But Neil Wilkinson was there for some reason, talking to Dougie Dillon. He got a bit of an earful from his wife when we arrived at the party. He should've been there earlier. Bloody moaner, that woman is.'

'Whose idea was it to meet in the pub first?' Rae asked.

Hammond pulled a face. 'I dunno.'

'Did you talk to the son, Grant, while you were there?'

Hammond shook his head. 'Nothin' much in common with 'im,' he replied.

'Anything unusual happen at the party? No strangers there?' was Stevie's next question.

'Nope.'

'How did you get on with Bridget Kirkbride, Mr Hammond?' Rae asked.

The caretaker shook his head again. 'Well enough. The wife knew her better than me though. Even so, not as close as some of the others in the village.'

Stevie took over. 'Do you know of any disputes or feuds in the village? People who don't get on?'

Hammond snorted. 'Course not. We're a close lot round here. We all rub along fine.'

'So you're not aware of any reasons for Ms Kirkbride's death? No enemies?'

The man shook his head again. 'No.'

'Well, thanks Mr Hammond. We may want to speak to you again.'

The two detectives walked across the green to the village shop. A woman, presumably Wendy Draper, looked up expectantly as they entered.

'I saw you talking to Vinegar Joe,' she said. 'The man who never smiles.'

'Not the most popular person in the village, then?' Stevie commented.

'Hah,' she replied. 'Full of his own self-importance, is our Mr Grump.'

'We're just having a quick chat with people who seemed to know Bridget Kirkbride best,' Stevie explained. 'Starting with the people at her recent birthday party. You were there with your husband? Can we have a few minutes of your time?'

'Sure,' Wendy replied. 'Billy, my son, is in the back. I'll get him to take over the shop for a while.'

She walked through a doorway and called to her son, then beckoned the detectives through into a small back office. They found seats around a small desk.

'You arrived in the middle of the evening. Is that right?'

'Yeah. Me and Rog met up with some of the others in the pub.'

'Why was that?' Rae asked.

She shrugged her shoulders. 'I think it was something some of the men arranged. We went along with it. It seemed a good idea once we'd decided to walk to Bridget's. A good stopping-off point, halfway.'

'Was it a good party?'

She shrugged. 'I s'pose so. It didn't set the world on fire, if that's what you mean, but it was something a bit different. Saturday nights can get a bit boring around here. Not much to do.'

'Was there any friction?' Stevie asked.

'What, apart from Dougie Dillon trying to gatecrash?' Wendy replied. 'It worked too. He got in and nearly drank the place dry, him and Neil Wilkinson. Both as drunk as skunks. Though Bridget didn't seem bothered. She was a bit preoccupied.'

'What about the other people already there when the pub group arrived? The people who'd arrived earlier?'

'Oh, you mean Bridget's neighbours? The Baileys? That's Val and Pete. They live right next door to Bridget. A quiet couple. Retired. Then there was Fred Golbie. You know, the retired darts champion.'

The two detectives merely nodded. If truth be told, neither of them were remotely interested in televised darts.

'Did you see Bridget's son, Grant?' Stevie went on.

'Ah, now. There was something. I was in the kitchen with Sarah Wilkinson, and I heard a comment Grant made to Bridget as they walked by. Something about someone being a snake. No idea who he was referring to though. He seemed upset. But he left soon after that.'

'Is there anyone in the village that knew Grant well? A friend maybe?'

Wendy thought for a few moments. 'He was a quiet boy, kept himself to himself. Always pleasant enough though. Our Billy might know.'

She called her son through, but he was uncommunicative and said he hadn't kept up much contact with Grant since the older boy had left school, so the two detectives left. Tommy glanced back as they crossed the road outside the shop. Billy Draper was watching them through the shop window, his brow furrowed in concentration.

* * *

Billy didn't know what to do. He was fifteen and had spent his whole life living in the rooms above the shop. He'd gone to the local primary school, followed by a secondary education at the state school in Shaftesbury. He was hoping to stay for a few more years there, in the sixth form, to study for a technology-based qualification. Agricultural engineering — that was the future in an area like this. He had always been fairly contented with his life. School, football, occasional parties with a few friends. And then odd things had started to happen. Unexpected things. Really nasty things. He'd quietly withdrawn from some of the organisations that had formed a part of his childhood, but no one had really noticed or made any comments, not even his parents. And now this. Could Grant have somehow become a victim? And had his mum found out? Is that why she was dead, and he was missing? Grant would be dead too, of course. It was only a matter of time before his body turned up somewhere.

Billy wasn't just scared. He was terrified. He realised just what a sheltered life he'd led. And now this. It was like looking down from the top of a sheer cliff, staring into the raging sea below. And knowing that one false step could be fatal. He needed to back away gently and keep his head down.

CHAPTER 10: DOUBLE GLOUCESTER

It was a puzzle. Why had Grant Kirkbride decided on Gloucester as his preferred place to study for a degree in agriculture? Admittedly it had a really good reputation, but so did a number of other colleges that were rather nearer to his home. Didn't everyone say how close the relationship was between Grant and Bridget? And how thoughtful the young man was? If that was really the case, why opt for a college that required such a convoluted train journey, one with two or three changes? Dorset, Wiltshire and Hampshire all had well-regarded agricultural colleges that would have had only half of the travelling time of this one.

Sophie was in the office of Peter Benning, the deputy principal, looking at Grant's records.

'As you can see, he returned after the Christmas vacation as expected and seemed to get stuck into his work really well. He showed really good potential. No one has a clue as to why he just vanished from campus last week. One day he was here, attending classes as usual. The next, he'd gone. We waited a few days then tried to contact his mother, but we couldn't get through. That's when we got the local Gloucester police involved, but they've found no trace of him. It's all a bit worrying.'

'Is there any record of why he chose to come here in the first place? On his original application, I mean.' Sophie was more troubled than she was letting on. The young man's disappearance had echoes of a story in her own distant past, one that she tried to keep hidden from view, locked up in a dark recess of her mind.

The deputy principal turned to Grant's original application form. 'Here. He mentions his wish to put some distance between himself and where he lived. He doesn't seem to expand on that.'

Sophie studied the wording carefully, trying to spot what lay behind the words. There could be any number of reasons for the young man's choice.

'What I can say is that he was close to his mother. She came up here for all the events open to parents. Grant won a prize last term and she was obviously proud of him. I'd hazard a guess that if he was trying to get away from someone, it wasn't her.'

'And there's been no clue of any type as to where he might have gone?'

The man shook his head. 'Not that we've identified, nor the local police. They took our concerns seriously and sent someone up here quickly.'

'I'll call on them for a quick visit next,' Sophie replied.

'Is there some special concern?' he asked. 'Considering that you're a chief superintendent?'

'Yes. His mother has been found dead in suspicious circumstances. It'll be in the press tomorrow, I expect.'

'By suspicious circumstances, you mean murder?'

'That's not official yet. But a close family member going missing at the same time usually means one of two things. Either they're responsible or they've also been killed. The question is, which is it in this case?'

Professor Benning looked shocked. 'I'd opt for the latter. He's such a pleasant and responsible young man. But isn't there a third option? He might have gone on the run to escape the killer. Surely that's worth considering?'

'If he'd disappeared after his mother's death, yes. But this was a few days before. It doesn't quite add up, does it? This is all in confidence, by the way.'

'Of course. We'll do anything we can to help, Chief Superintendent. Grant is a popular young man, both with staff and his peers.'

'It would be useful if I could speak to his closest friends. Could that be arranged?'

'Of course. Leave it with me.'

* * *

Sophie was half-watching the young woman student at the back of the small group. The discussion had yielded little of value, merely emphasising what Sophie had learned from Professor Benning, that Grant was a popular and quiet-mannered young man. He was sociable, reliable, a good mixer and a keen runner. All of his friends had said the same kind of thing — apart from the silent student at the back, the young woman. Nikki? Was that how she'd introduced herself? Sophie wondered if she'd have to catch her alone.

The short meeting drew to a close and Sophie thanked the students for their help.

'Will you keep us informed?' one of them asked. 'We're worried about him.'

'Of course.' Sophie looked at Nikki, hanging back as the others filed out of the office.

'Is there something you want to say?' she asked. 'You can trust me.'

'I made a bit of a blunder with Grant,' Nikki replied, her voice almost a whisper. 'We'd become close friends. Well, that's what I thought. Then I got a bit drunk at a party and came onto him when we got back to our rooms. They're in the same corridor.'

Sophie could sense the awkwardness Nikki was feeling. 'What happened?'

'I put my arms around him and pushed him up against the wall. I started kissing him hard. I really fancied him and thought he felt the same.' She gave a small sob. Sophie waited.

'He went as white as a sheet. He looked terrified. It scared me. You know what most boys are like. They lap up that kind of thing. They can't wait for a girl to come on hot to them. He was the opposite. I said sorry and backed off, fast.'

'Did you see him again?'

'Yeah. He was fine the next day when I went looking for him. He told me not to worry, that everything was okay. We even had a real snog, and he was totally cool about it. I'd even wondered if he might be gay, but he wasn't, not by the reaction I got that time. I could feel it.' She blushed. 'We went back to my room. You know. It's hard talking about it. I think it might have been his first time.'

Sophie put a hand on the young woman's arm. 'It's important for me to know, Nikki. Thanks for telling me. Here's my contact details. If anything else occurs to you, promise you'll get in touch immediately.'

'He had cut marks on his arms. They were very faint, but I spotted them. He clammed up when I asked him about them.' Nikki paused. 'Do you think something bad's happened to him?'

'Let's hope not. That's all I can say at the moment.'

* * *

Sophie had always liked Gloucester, even as a child growing up in Bristol, the much larger city some thirty miles south. Her Auntie Olive and Uncle Frank had friends there, and would occasionally take their young niece on a day trip to visit the cathedral and several nearby cafés and pubs. Until a few years ago, Sophie had been completely unaware that her lost grandparents lived in the smaller city and that her father had grown up there.

She left her car in a city centre car park and made her way to the station. From there she walked through the nearby streets, heading for the area where her grandparents still lived. It started to rain so she put her umbrella up, then she rounded a corner, almost cannoning off a man hurrying the other way. She momentarily lowered the brolly to get a clearer view of her surroundings. A jeweller's shop was situated to her right. She stopped dead and began to feel queasy. Surely not? She took several deep breaths and stepped closer to look at the shop sign. Yes, it was a family-run business that had been at that address for more than a century. It was the one. This must be the exact spot where her father had been murdered late at night nearly fifty years ago, killed by a member of the gang who'd broken into the shop, shot because he was unlucky enough to be in the wrong place at the wrong time and could have identified the thug left on watch, the psychopathic Charlie Duff. Misfortune at its most cruel. Had Grant Kirkbride somehow been afflicted by a similar misfortune? Had something equally tragic befallen him? The more she'd learned this morning the more Sophie had felt that there could have been a double tragedy in which both mother and son were victims. And how many family members would find their lives upended as a result? This, of course, was the second part of the double-whammy that a violent crime always left in its wake. The victim, upon whom the media focussed, along with any subsequent court case. But then there were also the surviving family members, left to deal with the fallout for the rest of their lives. In her own case, her grandparents, who'd lost their only child. Her mother, forced to endure the hardships associated with being an unmarried single mother at a time when society was so condemnatory. Sophie herself, growing up without the father figure she'd longed for as a child. Her own daughters, missing their maternal grandfather. An act of brutality that may have lasted less than a minute resonated down the decades, its consequences rippling out to affect future generations. Would the same be true for the

Kirkbrides? A careless act of casual violence that left a scar across time and space?

'Can I help you? You look a bit lost.' An elderly man was looking at her with concern on his face.

'No, thanks. I'm fine. I was just daydreaming.' She smiled at him.

'Oh, that. I do it all the time. But I've got an excuse. I'm old. You're not.'

'Maybe you can tell my wrinkles that.'

'Laughter lines,' he said. 'Not wrinkles.'

Sophie returned to her car and drove to her grandparents' house. Florence had been in hospital for a while, after receiving another round of radiotherapy, but she was home again now. She looked tired and ill though, despite her best efforts to put on a show for her granddaughter.

'It's lovely to see you, Sophie. Will you be staying for lunch?'

'I'd love to, Gran. Then I'll need to be off. I've spent much of the morning at the agricultural college, on a case.'

'Troublesome?' James asked.

'Could be. I get the feeling it might be another of those tricky ones, where nothing is quite what it seems. But at least the visit has given me an opportunity to pop in and see you both. And it's great to see you back home again, Gran, and looking a lot better than two weeks ago, in hospital.'

'I don't remember that visit. Was I asleep?'

'Yes, but don't worry. Jade held your hand the whole time.'

James broke in. 'She started to feel better the next day. Maybe Jade has got the magic touch.'

'How's her romance progressing? George, isn't it?' Florence always showed a keen interest in her two great granddaughters.

'Well, it's still as strong as ever, as far as I can see. That's since the early summer, nine months ago. There must be something in it, mustn't there?'

'She brought him across to see us back before Christmas. What a pleasant young man.' There was a twinkle in Florence's eye.

‘He’s certainly several steps up from her previous beaus. It’s not easy for him though, being a Dorset cop and with me as his girlfriend’s mother. I’ve occasionally wondered about teasing him, but that would be too cruel. He must get ribbed enough from his colleagues without me having a go as well.’ She laughed. ‘Things should be a bit easier for him from now on though. I’m spread across three counties, so he won’t be seeing so much of me.’

‘And a chief superintendent to boot,’ James said. ‘We’re both so proud of you, Sophie. But isn’t it rare for someone of your rank to be so hands-on? Wouldn’t a junior officer normally deal with a student going missing?’

‘It’s like I said on the phone, Gramps. I could have sent someone junior, and they’d have been here all day. Because it was me, I got straight in to see the vice principal and he had all the information I needed at his fingertips. I’ll be back in the incident room mid-afternoon, and with a couple of fresh insights. Anyway, me not being there gives Barry space to flex his muscles. It was a fortuitous day when he joined my first big case in Dorset. You’ve met him — the one with ginger hair. He’s getting married at Easter so he’s a bit on edge. This case is just what he needs to take his mind off what’s in store.’

Florence looked worried. ‘Is his fiancée that bad?’

Sophie laughed again. ‘Not at all. She’s just right for him. He’s just a worrier, that’s all.’

CHAPTER 11: BODY

Sophie had been heading south on the M5 motorway, halfway to Bristol, when a rushed call came through from Gloucester police. The body of a young man had been pulled out of a reed bed on the River Severn, just south of the town. Dark-haired. About five foot ten. Late teens or early twenties. She found the next junction, turned around and headed north again.

The riverside scene was familiar to her, as it would be to anyone in her line of work. A taped off area with a forensic tent. A gaggle of onlookers being kept at bay by tape stretched across the riverside path. Police vehicles lined up along the nearby roadside. She parked her car and walked towards the police checkpoint, presenting her warrant card to one of the officers on duty.

'Detective Chief Superintendent Sophie Allen. WeSCU.'

'Yes, ma'am. I was told to expect you. The DCI is over there.' She pointed to the tent, half hidden by the personnel seeming to swarm around it. One of the officers looked to be Peter Spence, the DC who'd dealt with cold cases some five years earlier, at the time of the discovery of the body of Sophie's long-lost father. Was he in the murder squad now? He'd impressed her with his considered calmness. No surprise if he'd been promoted.

A tall man stepped forward, hand extended. 'DCI David Greenaway. Good to have you here so quickly, ma'am.'

'No need for formalities, David. And thanks for smoothing the path for me. Can I get suited up and have a quick look at the body?'

Once she was safely enclosed in the usual white suit, the small squad entered the tent. The body was still lying on the sling that had been used to bring it ashore. Sophie only needed a quick look.

'That's Grant Kirkbride. I've seen photos of him at his home in Wiltshire and I spent this morning browsing through his records at the agricultural college. Has the cause of death been identified yet?'

'A serious blow to the back of the head. We think he was out running along the riverside path. Once in the water there was no real hope for him.'

Sophie thought back to her conversations with Grant's fellow students that morning. 'His friends at college said that he was a keen runner,' she said. 'Maybe this was one of his favourite routes.'

'It fits, doesn't it? DS Spence knows more. He was looking into the lad's disappearance.'

'Maybe I can have a word?'

'Of course. We'll need to find ways of working together on this.'

Sophie left the tent and had a word with the officer who was lingering outside. 'Peter? Do you remember me?'

He was watching her carefully. 'Of course, ma'am. I hear you're a chief superintendent now. Congratulations.'

'I know I thanked you last time we met, but there's no harm in repeating it now. I was always grateful for the way you dealt with my father's case. My mother could have become a wreck so easily but she didn't, and that's in no small part due to the way you handled it. You're a DS now? Good for you. I'm sure it's deserved. Anyway, onto what we're here for. I'm pretty certain he's Grant Kirkbride. Your boss told me you've been involved in tracing him. I wonder if we should share our thoughts. I've been at the college this morning with his friends and staff.'

'I heard that you were in earlier, speaking to one of the team about his disappearance. So, it's a double murder?'

'Seems that way. It looked to me as if he'd been in the water for some days. If that's the case, he was killed first, before his mother.' She looked the younger detective in the eye. 'Could you be our liaison up here? Would you be happy with that?'

'Of course. I'll check with the DCI but he's probably thinking along the same lines. You're running this new WeSCU team, aren't you? Is it your first case?'

Sophie gave a dry laugh. 'For WeSCU, yes. For me, absolutely not.' She looked at her watch. 'I'd better be off. The rest of the team are ploughing through the witnesses back in the depths of rural Wiltshire. We've got the late briefing in a couple of hours.' She stopped, thinking hard. 'Do you want to be there? It'll help both squads.'

'I'll check with the boss, but it makes sense. Thanks, ma'am.'

* * *

The mood was distinctly downbeat at the late afternoon briefing.

'Nothing obvious,' Barry reported. 'There are some quirky people in the mix, maybe more than we might expect, but nothing cried out to any of us. Dougie Dillon, the gatecrasher at Bridget's party, is an unscrupulous chancer, and we can imagine Neil Wilkinson trying his luck with anything in a skirt once he's had a few, but neither of them struck us as obvious suspects. We can't see any motive for the Kellaway pair to murder anyone, particularly someone as highly thought of as Bridget Kirkbride. No one we spoke to had a bad word to say about her.'

'Same here,' Stevie volunteered. 'By the way, the team looking into her movements have got nowhere. We don't think she went out the day prior to her murder. As far as the villagers are concerned, they're all a bit quirky in some way, but aren't most people? There was nothing that caused either of us to raise our eyebrows.' He glanced across at Tommy.

'Not even the caretaker,' Tommy added. 'He's a bit of a misery guts, as you know, but we couldn't see him killing anyone in cold blood.'

'And it's a different ballgame now, isn't it, ma'am?' Barry added. 'With her son being killed like that — well, it adds a whole new perspective. What's the latest news, by the way?'

'Let me check.' Peter Spence, the Gloucester detective, had remained as a silent observer until this point. He called his boss on his mobile and listened carefully to the latest news.

'Preliminary thoughts are that he's been in the water for nearly a week. That means he was killed several days before his mother.'

Barry frowned. 'What are your thoughts, ma'am?'

Sophie put her hand to her brow. 'It's a tricky one. It's got the feel of some pre-planning about it, and it means we may be looking at the wrong end. So the key might lie in the past of one of the victims. Or even both of them. If Grant was killed first, then he would probably have been the more important. Bridget came afterwards, so maybe she knew something that the killer couldn't afford to come to light. That kind of fits in with what you've just said about the locals. No one with an obvious motive yet. Who else did you speak to?'

Barry summarised for the team. 'All of her neighbours, not just the ones at the party. They're a quiet lot, except maybe for the darts player, Fred Golbie. He sticks out a bit, but he seemed genuine enough. He didn't raise any suspicions.'

'And the vicar? What's his name? Gordon something?'

'Gordon Wentworth. He seems pretty innocuous. He's a very cautious bloke. Hadn't you already spoken to him?'

Sophie nodded. 'Just briefly. He had a bit of a guarded attitude, I thought. But then I'm comparing him to Tony Younger across in Dorchester, so maybe that judgement is a bit unfair. Tony had a very refreshing take on things for a church minister, whereas I can imagine this one being a bit dry and dull. Maybe that's what parishes like this one prefer. Someone who doesn't rock the establishment boat too much. Tony rocked it continuously, as far as I could tell.'

'Are they married yet?' Rae asked. 'You know, him and the glamorous, leather-trousered lady.'

Sophie laughed. 'You're just envious, Rae Gregson. I keep wondering if that look would suit me. I bet you do too. And, in answer to your question, no. She promised me an invitation to the wedding whenever it happened and nothing's arrived yet. I still don't know how he copes with someone as flamboyant as Pauline.'

CHAPTER 12: CHURCH

Friday

Sarah Wilkinson was a worrier. She knew it herself. She always had been, from her teenage years onwards. She was a pessimist, a glass-half-empty kind of person, always thinking that something dreadful was probably lurking around the corner, waiting for her to lower her guard before striking. She tried hard to mask her naturally pessimistic character from others, but she guessed that many friends and neighbours realised her true nature. Neil certainly did. He was always chiding her, telling her to *cheer up, it might never happen.* Well, it had. And with a double dose. First Bridget and now Grant.

She'd hardly slept a wink last night, worrying that Neil was somehow involved, even though she was convinced he was no killer. It was just that the police might not realise that. He was always making a play for Bridget once he'd had a few drinks. Sarah's best friend had regularly rebuffed his advances in good humour, but people would have noticed. And that meant the police would find out sooner or later. It also wouldn't take them long to discover that Neil had regularly taken Grant fishing until a couple of years ago. And then to learn how their relationship had descended into acrimony when young Grant had discovered that Neil had cheated in the annual angling competition a year earlier. She knew none of that could possibly provide a motive for two murders, but what if the police settled on Neil as an easy option? What if Neil blustered and lost his rag, something he was prone to do when under pressure? What if he somehow ended up unintentionally incriminating himself?

It was like living through a bad dream. She needed some fresh air. She slipped into her coat and walked down to the village centre, hoping that it would be too early for other residents of this sleepy village to be out and about. It was a false hope. People stood on corners exchanging news, all eager to get the latest gossip. Sarah tried to avoid the small clusters of villagers but was inevitably drawn into exchanging a few words with several groups. They knew she had been Bridget's closest friend and that Neil had helped Grant during the boy's teenage years. Moreover, they also knew of the 'Great Angling Scandal', as it had come to be known. Sarah also suspected that the whole village knew of Neil's penchant for chatting up attractive women and getting himself into hot water as a consequence. Maybe other wives could have laughed it all off and made a joke of it. Not her. She was a worrier, and everyone knew it.

She'd set out from home on an aimless wander but quickly realised that this was no good. People expected her to stand and chat. Better to pretend that she was somehow busy, then she could force herself away saying, *Sorry! Got to go! Things to do!* But where was she meant to be doing these things? She soon found herself down in the village centre, approaching the hall. It seemed to be a hive of activity, with rows of vehicles in the car park and along the edge of the road outside. Best avoided. She veered off across the green and found herself approaching the church. Gordon Wentworth, the vicar, was just coming out of the manse, looking preoccupied. He gave a gentle wave when he saw her but didn't smile. Did anyone feel like smiling with this double tragedy hanging over the village?

And as the parish priest he'd be expected to act as a listening ear for so many worried people.

'How are you holding up, Mrs Wilkinson?' the vicar enquired.

She shook her head, unable to speak.

'I'm making sure the church is open all day at the moment. If you feel the need for solitude and prayer, it's there for you.'

'Thank you, vicar,' she whispered.

She changed direction and walked to the church. Maybe some solitude and prayer was just what she needed to get her jumbled thoughts into some kind of order.

* * *

Sarah's husband, Neil, was a systems analyst and IT consultant, and ran his own small business from home. He wasn't at home just now, though. He'd gone for a drive around the local roads, hoping to think things through. It didn't really help. Mid-morning saw him returning home, hoping that a coffee was ready for him. No such luck. Sarah was nowhere to be found. He checked the time, wondering if a walk in the fresh air would help. Another thought struck him: if he chose the right route and timed it right, he'd arrive at the pub just as it opened. If he hadn't got his thoughts in order by then, a couple of drinks might help them on their way. Nothing like a bit of alcohol to simplify a complicated problem. He set out along the footpath at the back of the houses, the less direct route down to the village centre. He was less likely to be disturbed by other locals, keen to dig the dirt.

He was realistic enough to recognise the mess he was in. Half the village knew that he'd always lusted after Bridget and that she'd regularly had to rebuff his advances. It was a crime for a woman to have a body as desirable as hers and yet do nothing with it. Well, he didn't think she was doing anything with it. Or at least, very little, as far as he knew. Could she have been a lesbian? That might explain it. After all, he kept himself in pretty good shape, wore clean clothes and scrubbed beneath his finger nails. What other reason could there have been for her regular rejections? Right now, though, his actions might well have landed him in hot water. With the cops. There'd been some penetrating looks beamed his way during their visit to the house yesterday morning. They were probably still weighing him up. And that was before they'd had a chance to find out about the angling competition fiasco with Grant. Now the lad had been found dead they were sure to come calling again. How best to divert them? The story had to be a good one. He knew what Sarah thought — that he should tell the truth. But, in his mind, that would be a bad move. There were rather too many skeletons in his closet to start opening it up for public scrutiny now.

In the end he decided that honesty was the best policy, as long as he kept close control over the extent of that honesty. Tell the police everything about the angling scandal that had led to the rift with young Grant. Put his hands up to accept the blame for that embarrassing incident. Everyone seemed to know about it anyway, so the cops would find everything out sooner or later. If he got it off his chest at least he'd retain some control. If he was contrite enough maybe it would head them off and they'd go looking elsewhere. It could work.

Neil's timing was immaculate. These final thoughts coincided perfectly with his arrival at the pub. Just right for a celebratory drink. Or two.

* * *

Dougie Dillon heard his phone ping and felt it momentarily vibrate in his pocket. An incoming message. He stopped what he was doing and took a quick look. Neil Wilkinson. In the pub, wanting to meet for a chat. What? The man had money, influence and an ever-forgiving wife. Dougie experienced the exact opposite. He was always short of cash, no one ever paid him much heed and his wife had walked out on him years before. Maybe he should end his friendship with Neil, given it had led to a series of mishaps that nearly ruined his own reputation but never appeared to cause Neil any serious difficulties. The man was Teflon-coated. Nothing nasty ever stuck to him for long.

How could he go to the pub right now, or even in the next couple of hours? The boss here at the sawmills — Sexy Sue, as most of the workers referred to her — watched him like a hawk. She was watching him now, through the window of her office. Even if he was allowed to leave, he'd lose pay and suffer some pointed comments from her. She let everyone know who was boss, and Dougie had few illusions about his standing within the workforce. At the very bottom.

No, let Neil stew in his own juices for a while. Maybe that would bring him down to earth a bit.

* * *

Billy Draper stepped down from the school bus and slid away from the green towards the safety of his home. There were just too many cops around, hurrying in and out of the village hall carrying clipboards, getting into vans, climbing out of cars, speaking into phones. It was like a juggernaut on the loose. Did he want to talk to a juggernaut? Not yet, if ever. But if he didn't say something, who else would? Did anyone else even know?

He walked through the shop to the rear, merely nodding to his mother, who was serving a customer. He climbed the stairs to the flat above, went into his room and threw himself onto the bed. Why did life have to be so rubbish?

CHAPTER 13: VICAR

Barry looked up from his desk at the sound of approaching footsteps. It was Tommy, the unit's junior detective.

'Sorry to bother you, boss. The vicar's arrived for a "brief chat", as he puts it. I thought you'd prefer to speak to him.'

Barry sighed loudly. 'Yes, you're right. It had better be me. He'll have influence here. Where have you put him?'

'In the little vestibule. He says he doesn't have long.'

Barry made his way to the small cubby hole they'd laughingly labelled Interview Room 2. The door was open, and he could see the minister squashed into the corner seat. The man rose as Barry entered, his hand outstretched.

'Good of you to come in, Mr Wentworth. You were next on our list.' They both sat down. Tommy squeezed himself onto the last available seat.

'Well, Mrs Wilkinson told me that you were speaking to all of poor Ms Kirkbride's acquaintances, particularly those who were at her recent birthday party. I have a free hour just now, so I thought I'd save you the bother of looking for me. How can I help?'

'How did you come to know Ms Kirkbride so well?'

'She lived in the parish. I try to get to know all of the residents. You never know when they might need some spiritual guidance.'

'But she wasn't a regular churchgoer, was she?'

'Not really, no. Just occasional. But she helped to run the village youth group and I sat on the committee. That's how we got to know each other.'

Barry thought for a few moments. 'Enough to invite you to her birthday party? Most of the other people there were close neighbours or friends.'

'I see why you're concerned, Inspector. Was I another gatecrasher, like Mr Dillon? That's what you're wondering. No, of course not. We were both signatories to the bank account for the youth group. A cheque needed signing and I phoned her to arrange a convenient time. She told me to come along to her party and she'd do the deed there. And then she told me I could stay for a bite to eat. I didn't have any other plans for the evening, and I live alone. I enjoy a bit of socialising as much as the next man, so I jumped at the chance. She was a very warm person, Inspector. A real boon to the local community. That makes it a doubly tragic loss.'

Barry frowned. 'Doubly?'

'Well, her death is a tragedy in itself. But the loss to the village. She'll be missed. What did you think I meant?'

'The fact that her son, Grant, has also been found dead.'

The vicar looked shocked. 'I wasn't aware of that. Are you sure?'

'We don't release news of a death unless we're sure, Vicar.'

'No, of course not. I should have realised that. So it really is a double tragedy. How awful. How did it happen?'

'He was found in the Severn, in Gloucester. Near his college.'

'Oh. A drowning, I expect.' He looked at Barry questioningly, but the detective didn't give a direct response.

'Did you speak to Grant at the party?'

'I don't think so. I hardly knew him. I think someone told me that he left quite early, after arguing with his mother.'

'Who told you that?'

The vicar put a hand to his head. 'Sorry, I just can't remember. It could have been anyone who was there.'

'Did Ms Kirkbride ever talk to you about her son? You were on the committee together, after all.'

He shook his head. 'Not that I can recall. As I said, we weren't that close.'

'Can you remember the other party guests? We need to identify all the people who knew her best.'

'Of course.'

Gordon reeled off a list of names, all people the detectives had already interviewed. Nothing new here, then.

'Can you think of a reason why someone would have killed Ms Kirkbride? You probably have as much insight into the local community as anyone. Has anything ever struck you as odd or unusual?'

The vicar looked puzzled. 'As regards Bridget Kirkbride? No, not at all. It really doesn't make sense. As regards the community as a whole, again I'd have to say, not really. We have our share of low-level villains, as do most parishes like this, and occasional acts of petty vandalism. But nothing that comes anywhere near this. It's been a shock to everyone. I spoke to your chief superintendent a couple of days ago and I've been pondering it all ever since.'

'Yes, she told me.' Barry thanked him and indicated that Tommy should show the vicar out. He then sat for several minutes thinking.

He collared Sophie as soon as she appeared late in the day. 'The vicar said something that made me think,' he said. 'He couldn't identify any possible reason for Ms Kirkbride's murder. What if the son's death was the important one, the one with a real motive, and she was killed because she knew something that might have been a pointer?'

Sophie listened carefully. 'I was beginning to wonder the same thing. Grant's death preceded hers by a couple of days, we think. So it could have been someone from the village. They had time to get back, make some plans to deal with the mother, then carry them out.' She glanced at her watch. 'The local pub will be open. Do you fancy a look-see? Get a feel for the place? You never know, we might pick up on something interesting.'

He laughed. 'And that's your only motive, is it?'

She smiled mischievously but said nothing.

* * *

The Archers Inn, set on the south side of the village green directly across from the village hall, was a typical country pub. It was built from local stone and was thought to be well over two hundred years old. Dormant Virginia Creeper tendrils covered the front wall, and several bench seats lined the pavement. No one was sitting on them in the chilly March air, preferring to be inside. Smoke drifted up into the night sky from the chimneys. Barry sniffed the air. Wood smoke. Log fires, then. They went inside and he noted the momentary pause in conversation as the locals spotted them. At least he assumed they were mostly locals, enjoying an early-evening drink or meal. He realised that his boss's eyes weren't glancing around the room like his. They were fixed on the ale pumps at the bar.

'Interesting,' she said. 'Local brewery. I haven't tasted them. What'll you have, Barry?'

'Okay, I give in. I'll have the same as you.'

'No, you won't. I'll pick two different ones. It'll give me a taste of both.'

A young man began to move across to serve them, but he was gently pushed out of the way by a middle-aged, dark-haired woman displaying a prominent bust within a low-cut top.

'You're the police,' she said. 'I've been watching you all coming and going for the past couple of days. Wondered when you'd get round to coming in here.'

'First things first,' Sophie replied before Barry could speak. She pointed to the two handpumps. 'We'll have a pint of each. So you're Lisa Sutcliffe?'

The woman looked momentarily surprised.

'Your name is above the door, and we do look at licensee records occasionally,' Sophie explained with a gentle smirk. 'I'm Sophie Allen and this is Barry Marsh. And the handsome young man there is your son, I take it? He has your eyes and nose.'

'Well, that's us well and truly sussed,' Lisa replied. 'No escaping your eagle eye, is there? We do good food, by the way. None of your lot have been in to eat yet. I thought we'd be doing some good business from you. Tight-fisted, are they?'

'Hardly. It's been nose to the grindstone since Wednesday. Once I loosen the leash a bit you'll probably be seeing some of them coming in.'

Lisa laughed and looked at Barry. 'She's a hard woman, is she? Too bloody right. We want good value out of our taxes, not a lot of shirkers.' She pushed the two glasses across the counter. 'Getting anywhere, then?'

'Of course,' Sophie replied, taking a slow sip from her glass. 'That's good. Tell me, was Bridget in here regularly?'

'Not really. More of an irregular. She came in for an occasional lunchtime meal, mostly on a Thursday or Friday. But only when she was with someone.'

'Go on.'

'Maybe Sarah Wilkinson. Or the Kellaways. Or someone from the youth club committee. That was sometimes after one of their meetings. That would be of an evening, just for a drink. She was generous, you know. She paid for more than she got back. She wasn't a big drinker. Just the occasional gin and tonic. She had a good figure and I guess she wanted to keep it that way. Same with food. Always small portions of the fattening stuff like chips or pasta.' She stopped suddenly and looked serious. 'You know what? It doesn't bloody make sense. Of all the people around here, she'd be the last I'd ever think would get killed like that. The world's gone bonkers. It's bad enough with all the mad stuff going on around the world. And now Bridget Kirkbride's been found dead in the woods. It's changed my view of things, I can tell you.'

Lisa moved away to serve another customer. Sophie and Barry took their drinks across to a small corner table.

'That's what everyone says,' Barry said. 'Exactly that. She was the last person anyone here would expect to become a murder victim. They're all bemused.'

Sophie looked at him. 'Apparently. Someone knows the truth, Barry. Someone around here knows a secret and they're not ready to share it yet. You think the same, don't you?'

He nodded, frowning. Sophie swapped the beers over and took a sip of the second one. 'Even better,' she said.

* * *

It was late evening. The two senior detectives were sitting in the near-empty incident room, looking at the initial report from the autopsy of Grant Kirkbride, emailed down from Gloucester. It very much looked as though Grant's body had been in the river since the prior weekend, probably the Saturday. There were few signs of injury other than the head wound, but this was more serious than had at first appeared.

'I wonder if it means it wouldn't have been treated as particularly suspicious on its own,' Barry said. 'It's the fact that his mum was murdered a couple of days later that draws it out.'

'That's what Peter says in the email. The probable interpretation would have been that he slipped on the muddy ground, hit his head on the low wall that edges the river, then slid in unconscious and drowned. It's only when you add the context of Bridget's death that you're likely to start questioning things.'

'It could all be coincidence. We have to consider it, Sophie.'

'I know. Cover all possibilities, as always. But let's face it, how likely is it? I had a good look round when I was there yesterday. It's an ideal spot for someone to lurk about, waiting. Bushes to hide behind. It was dark and wet. And Grant always went running at the same time, along the same stretch of the river and in the same direction. If I'd wanted to kill him, that's exactly the way I'd have done it. He'd already passed the most treacherous spots, the sections that were muddier and more slippery. He'd got through them safely, but they're all out in the open, less attractive to someone waiting in ambush.'

'So you think he's the key? He was the prime target?'

Sophie nodded slowly. 'It's likely, don't you think? But I think the answer's down here, not in Gloucester. Though I did get an interesting insight from one of his friends, Nikki. She told me that she gave him a surprise snog and he nearly collapsed in terror. She thought he might be gay, but things had switched around the next day, and he was more relaxed. She assured me he wasn't gay.'

Barry looked puzzled. 'What do you think that all means?'

Sophie shook her head. 'Could be nothing, but we can't afford to ignore it. She reckoned he was a virgin. Well, before she got her hands on him. Seems odd for someone who was twenty and as good looking as him. I wonder if he had some kind of hang-up.'

'Is that a criminological term?'

'Bloody hell, Barry. Don't get all technical on me!' She looked back at the report in front of her. 'There's the other interesting snippet. Nikki said she'd caught sight of some scars on his forearms and the pathologist has confirmed it, though they're old ones. He used to cut himself. Usually a sign of severe mental stress.'

'So what's next?' Barry said.

'Repeat what you've been doing for the last couple of days. But this time the subject's Grant, not Bridget.'

'I thought you might say that. We're primed and ready to go.'

'Sleep first,' Sophie said, standing up and yawning.

* * *

Paul Sutcliffe had been watching as the two cops left after they'd finished their drinks. Maybe they were decent sorts. They'd brought their empty glasses to the bar, depositing them on the counter before heading towards the exit. His mum had sometimes told him that was a sign of people who were thoughtful and considerate.

He sighed as he locked the pub's front door and switched off the lights. How could he possibly broach the subject with anyone, let alone two coppers? It would cause such deep rifts among people. But would anyone believe him? He had no evidence. It was all guesses, and that was the problem. Nothing was as it seemed. And he knew one other thing for sure. He could never stay in the village afterwards, not once he'd opened up about it.

The key thing was, did anyone else share his suspicions? What about that much younger lad, Billy Draper? He'd looked completely haunted when Paul had spotted him a couple of times recently. Did he know something? Maybe it was time for him to try and find out a bit more, then decide what to do. The trouble was, might he end up dead himself if he went too far?

CHAPTER 14: YOUTH CLUB

Saturday

Barry was chairing the early-morning meeting in the incident room. He looked around at the people facing him, some looking decidedly tired after the non-stop efforts of the past few days.

'We've decided to shift the focus to Grant. That doesn't mean that we ignore Bridget's death completely, and some of you will still be involved in that part of the investigation. We can set aside Grant's recent life as a student in Gloucester. The local team are investigating that, and Pete Spence is in regular contact with us about progress. We're interested in his life up to then. We start with the schools he went to. The village primary school and then his time at secondary in Shaftesbury. We want to know what he was like, his interests, who his friends were. You know the kind of stuff. Stevie, you take that. He was a member of the local youth group here in the village. Rae, you find out who was running it and interview everyone involved. Again, find out what people thought of him. Was he popular? Was he reliable? Who were his friends?'

Stevie and Rae noted what they were being asked to do.

'Tommy, you take his background in the village. Find out if he had part-time jobs or volunteered in any way. Did he have any enemies, for whatever reason? See if there's any dirt on him. I'm going to pursue his interest in angling. That means seeing the club organisers and following up a possible link to Neil Wilkinson, who used to take him fishing, as far as I know. Steer clear of Wilkinson if his name crops up locally but let me know. Please leave him to me or the chief super. Everyone clear? Finish your coffees and let's get going.'

'Does that mean that this Wilkinson man is our prime suspect?' Tommy asked.

'No, I'm not saying that. At the moment he's just a person of interest but his behaviour is a bit suspicious.'

* * *

The village school was small, with fewer than three dozen children. One member of staff remembered Grant from when he'd been a pupil more than a decade earlier, and had agreed to a meeting at the weekend, on one of her days off, after a football match.

'He was a really nice boy,' Helen O'Rourke told Stevie. 'Never a problem. He was quiet and reliable. Worked hard too. In a way, I was surprised he didn't do better in his exams at secondary school. I know Bridget was a bit disappointed. She'd expected him to get to university. I think quite a few people did.'

'You don't think you'd all just misjudged him?'

Helen glared at him. 'No. I don't misjudge my pupils, officer. Certainly not ones like Grant. He had really good potential. Intelligent and with a good memory. His lack of achievement later on just doesn't make sense. His mum was stumped by it. He changed somehow, when he was in his early teens. She must have wondered what it was, but I don't think she ever found out. She never told me anyway.'

Stevie made a mental note to find out a bit more about the local drug scene out here in the villages. They were often cultural deserts for young people, and more than a few teenagers had probably drifted into drink and drugs to escape the crushing boredom. Helen's description closely matched one of the observed behavioural changes of teen drug use.

'Did you see Ms Kirkbride often?'

She shook her head. 'No. It was just a case of our paths occasionally crossing. Which wasn't very often, to be honest. I live in Broad Chalke, officer, a few miles away. I'm only here in Millhead for work. I'm not really up to date with village gossip. I liked her though. She was very talented, you know. She worked freelance as a children's book illustrator.'

'We knew she was an artist of some kind.'

'Very highly regarded. She illustrated some top sellers.'

'And Grant didn't want to follow a similar line?'

'Obviously not.' She glanced at her watch. 'Is there anything else? If not, it's time for me to switch to normal family duties.'

'Not at the moment, though we may be back in touch. Thanks.'

Stevie made his way back to his car. The fifteen-minute drive to Shaftesbury, where he was due to meet the deputy head of Grant's secondary school, would give him time to put his thoughts in order. Helen's comments had been interesting.

Several teachers at the high school remembered the teenage Grant well, with the current deputy particularly knowledgeable. He had been Grant's head of year. His observations differed little from those Helen had described. A talented, pleasant boy who had somehow failed to live up to expectations. But there had been no obvious signs of drug use. Grant had become withdrawn in his middle teenage years, but no one knew why. The boy had clammed up when asked about it.

Stevie left feeling that he'd made little progress, other than discovering that something had darkened the life of Grant during his mid-teens. Maybe something that wasn't even relevant to the investigation. He'd have to record it though.

* * *

Rae wasn't finding it any easier to gather hard facts about Grant's time as a member of the village youth club. She'd hoped to find some formal records, lists of members, maybe even historical attendance lists, but no such luck. Apparently there had been a committee of sorts but it had obviously been very informal in its approach. Shoddy, in fact. The present committee chair, interviewed at her home, was extremely condemnatory.

'I don't know what they were thinking of,' Annabel Linklater said. 'There's nothing at all worth looking at. It was all far too casual, as far as I can see. I took over three years ago, soon after we moved to the village, and I'm a bit horrified, to be honest. They didn't seem to take on board that they had a duty of care towards the youngsters, let alone the legal aspects. Shoddy, that's what it looks like to me.'

'Who was running things?'

'That's the problem. I can't tell. Someone had walked out and left the village a few months before I arrived. Someone else had died. I've never been able to tell who had any legal responsibility. There's no paperwork. I've never been able to find anything.'

'So you can't tell me anything about the years that Grant Kirkbride was a member?'

'I can't even confirm in any formal way that he was a member. You're going to have to rely on people's memories. And good luck with that!' She snorted.

'Have you been able to identify anyone who helped out? Anyone at all?'

'I think that Neil Wilkinson helped sometimes, though it was more to do with taking some of the lads fishing. He's sometimes mentioned it. Wendy Draper told me that she sometimes volunteered and so did poor Bridget. She sometimes brought Sarah Wilkinson with her. The vicar used to pop his head in occasionally, although he had no direct responsibility, apparently. The group met in the village hall, where you're based, not the church hall.'

'Any ideas of what the youngsters did? Activities?'

'Well, we inherited a ping-pong table and a couple of small snooker tables. All the balls were missing though. Someone mentioned that there might have been a football group, though I don't know where they played. There isn't a proper pitch in the village. Look, so you know how bad it all must have been, there wasn't even a bank account. Everything was cash in hand. When I said I found nothing when I took over, I meant it literally. Absolute zilch. I was horrified, I can tell you.'

Rae left feeling despondent. Neil Wilkinson was off limits, according to the boss, though she'd better call Barry about the man's connection to the youth group. Wendy Draper was the shopkeeper who'd been interviewed by Stevie and Tommy a day or two ago. She decided to try to find Tommy and take him along for this chat. She liked pairing up with Tommy. He was refreshingly open and could sometimes spot a novel opening to pursue.

Tommy was still in the incident room, looking worried. Nothing new there.

'It's hard, boss. How do I make a start in the job the DI gave me? I need something to get me started on Grant's background, and I can't find anything online. I was hoping to find something on social media but I reckon this lower end of the village is in a mobile phone blackspot. Either that or Grant wasn't into it, for some reason. And that's unusual, isn't it? For someone his age, I mean.'

'Absolutely. It is odd. Anyway, I need you for a while. I need to visit Wendy Draper in the shop and you saw her on Thursday, with Stevie. It might smooth things if you came with me. I'll explain on the way over.'

* * *

'My husband worked in investment banking,' Wendy told them after she'd finished serving the solitary customer. 'But he hated the cut-throat atmosphere. We had just enough savings to get started here. My aunt lived in Shaftesbury and she told me about this shop being on the market. It was exactly the right thing for us to move here. Not quite so sure about Billy, though. It's a bit quiet for youngsters. There's not much to do.'

'That's what we've come to see you about, Mrs Draper,' Tommy explained. 'The youth club. Grant Kirkbride was a member, we believe, but it's tricky finding any details. The current organiser couldn't help the DS here very much.'

Rae broke in. 'I've just seen Annabel Linklater, as Tommy said. But she's relatively recent, isn't she? You might be able to help us with the years before, when Grant sometimes went along.'

Wendy folded her arms and frowned. 'Grant was a quiet boy. Always polite and helpful when he was there. We thought he might stay on and become one of the leaders, but he suddenly stopped coming.'

'When would that have been?' Rae asked.

Wendy shrugged. 'Now you're asking. Probably when he was about fourteen, coming on fifteen. Don't ask me why. I was only one of the occasional helpers, just going along maybe one evening a month when Billy started. He was about twelve at the time.'

'How often did the group meet?' Tommy asked.

'Every Friday evening. But it was a bit chaotic sometimes. Old misery guts, the caretaker, didn't like kids, you see. He reckoned they got the place messy. He'd sometimes forget to unlock the place for the group and kids would be hanging around outside until someone could find him and get the key. He did it on purpose, we were sure of it. He's come to heel now though. I know Annabel can be a bit bossy and likes everything just so, but she kicked up so much stink the first time Joe Hammond tried the disappearing trick that he's toed the line ever since. He still hates the kids though. Acts as if he hates everybody, does Joe.'

'So there was never any clue as to why Grant stopped coming?' Rae said.

Wendy shook her head, causing her dark curls to flop backwards and forwards across her cheeks. She pushed her hair back. 'Time I got my hair tidied up,' she said. 'No. No one knew why, and Grant didn't say. Bridget never knew either, 'cos I asked her. Billy's a good couple of years younger than Grant but he knew him slightly. I don't think he knows anything, but you can ask him. He's upstairs. I'll call him.'

She disappeared through the doorway into the back, and they heard her voice, then the sound of footsteps going upstairs. She was back with them a couple of minutes later. 'He must have gone out for something. Sorry. He was there just a few minutes ago. Maybe you can call back later.'

'Wasn't there a youngster in the back of the shop just before we went in, Tommy? I thought I saw someone through the window.'

'Sorry, boss. I didn't notice.'

'Is there a back entrance? Let's go round and have a look.'

* * *

Billy had been hiding in his bedroom, lying down in the narrow gap between his bed and the wall, unable to be seen from the doorway. Things were getting worse. How much more of this could he stand? He waited until he could no longer hear voices, then crept down the stairs and out the rear door. He looked up. The two detectives were standing there, watching him.

'Hello, Billy,' the woman said. 'Can we have a chat?'

CHAPTER 15: DARK AND BROODING

Neil Wilkinson looked uneasy. He fidgeted constantly in his seat, even though it looked perfectly comfortable. He kept running his fingers through his thinning hair then rubbing his brow. What was bothering the man? All Barry had done was ask about his angling trips with the young Grant.

'Yeah, I took Grant fishing most weeks. An evening or a Saturday morning. He was a junior member of the local club and I was on the committee. I organised things for the youngsters.'

Again, Barry noticed the guarded response. The man was picking his words just a little too carefully.

'Are you still a club member, Mr Wilkinson?'

Neil shook his head. He looked as if he wanted the earth to open up and swallow him.

'Why not?'

'There was a sort of misunderstanding, so I left. They expected everything to be done by the book and I'm not that sort of person.'

'Is that when you took up shooting?'

Wilkinson looked shocked. 'What do you mean?'

'You're a member of the local gun club, aren't you?'

'Oh, I see. It was about then. I did some bits and pieces of shooting before then, but when I stopped fishing it took over.'

'Did that affect your friendship with Grant? I mean, if you left the club and stopped taking him fishing.'

Wilkinson shrugged. 'I suppose. Though he was growing up fast. I thought he maybe had other interests by then.'

'So you stopped taking an interest in him?'

'It wasn't like that. You make it sound as if I abandoned him. I wasn't a father figure or anything. I just took him fishing every so often.'

'So was there a father figure in Grant's life? If it wasn't you, was there anyone else?'

Again the shrug. 'Never really thought about it.'

'Was that when you became friendly with Dougie Dillon, when you left the angling club?'

Neil seemed more relaxed now. 'Yeah, now you come to mention it. Hadn't really thought about it before. Dougie was already a member of the gun club. It was him that said I ought to join. I was at a bit of a loose end, so I did.'

'What kind of things did you talk about with Grant when you went fishing?'

'What?' Neil sounded genuinely bemused.

'Conversation. Didn't you chat?'

Neil shook his head. 'Not much. We always moved apart on the bank. I kind of left him to his own devices until it was time to pack up.'

'Did he ever mention a girlfriend? Or any other relationship?'

'No. He was a quiet lad, didn't say much, especially as he got older.'

Barry thought for a moment. 'Did you ever wonder why he chatted less? Do you think he was under some kind of stress?'

Neil looked puzzled and shook his head. 'Never occurred to me. I just thought he was getting moodier as he got older. I mean, we never knew who his dad was. Maybe he was a moody bugger. A case of like father, like son.'

Barry's phone rang. He stepped out into the hall to listen to Rae's information, then returned to the lounge.

'You helped out with the local youth club at one time. Is that right?'

'Well, I went along sometimes when Sarah couldn't make it. It was when Rosie, our daughter, wanted something to do on Friday nights. It stopped when she got a boyfriend with a car. She went out clubbing in Salisbury instead.'

'Was this at the same time as when Grant went?'

'You'll need to check with Sarah. She'll remember more. They might have been there at about the same time.'

'Would she remember Grant? Particularly with Sarah being Ms Kirkbride's close friend. Maybe the two youngsters did know each other a bit, with their mums being close.'

Neil shifted uneasily in his seat. 'Yeah, though Sarah's only Rosie's stepmum. She's my daughter from my first marriage. We had her here on occasional weekends. That's when she went to the youth club.'

He looked uneasy again. Maybe he was embarrassed at the fact he'd had to own up to a failed first marriage. Barry wondered why he would feel that way. It was common enough nowadays, wasn't it?

'Well, thanks for your help, Mr Wilkinson. If you remember anything else about Grant that might be useful, please get in touch. Or if you recall anything about Ms Kirkbride.'

Barry left the house and returned to his car. Fat chance of any significant help coming from that source, he thought. Neil Wilkinson gave the appearance of being slightly shifty. Maybe the word slightly was redundant. He was extremely shifty about something and, whatever it was, it was causing him to appear edgy, to Barry's eyes anyway.

* * *

'What?' Barry sounded surprised. 'He cheated at the annual angling competition?'

Tommy and Rae had discovered the scandal while talking to Billy Draper. Apparently it had been the main topic of conversation among the village's teenage boys when it had happened several years before.

'It's a wonder he still lives here,' Rae laughed. 'You can imagine the reaction in a small place like this. Billy said that Grant had taken it particularly badly. It's what caused the rupture in their friendship.'

Barry sat silent for a while. Did it add up? Would something like that explain Neil Wilkinson's edginess during their conversation earlier?

'The rest of the angling club refused to speak to him for months,' Tommy explained. 'And that would have included Grant. Maybe the "snake" he referred to at his mum's party was Neil Wilkinson.'

Barry was not convinced. Surely none of this could be the result of something as petty as catching a few fish illegally at a contest, if that was how he'd broken the rules? It was just too unlikely.

'I don't buy it. Something like that doesn't lead to murder. And four years have passed, from what you've said. What do you think, Rae?'

'Well, it was interesting hearing about it from the lad. But I think there's something much darker going on, even with Billy himself. He looked relieved when he thought we'd bought it as the main cause of problems in the village. But he was shaking like a leaf when we first nabbed him trying to escape via his back door. You don't get that level of tension from some four-year-old scandal about fishing. He's really scared about something. There's something else. Got to be.'

Barry put a hand to his head. There was something wrong in all of this. Grant's death may well have come first, a few days before that of his mother, but he knew in his bones that its tangle would be harder to unpick. It had been planned in advance, measured and considered in every way. Whoever had killed Grant hadn't been stupid. If it hadn't been for the discovery of Bridget's body a couple of days earlier, the son's death might well have been classified as an accident. Someone running in the rain, slipping on mud, cracking his head and falling into the river. But now the detectives were convinced it was no accident. It had all the hallmarks of a carefully planned attack, orchestrated so that it would yield few clues. In comparison, Bridget's murder had probably been more spontaneous and violent, her body dragged into the woods for a hurried burial. Someone had spotted the fog, watched her set off from her house for the footpath and made a quick decision. And it would have worked if it hadn't been for the chance in a hundred that had brought Duffy Edgington and her dog into the woods. Bridget's body would probably have lain there for months, maybe years. Would it then have been linked to the historic death of her son, out running on a riverside path more than fifty miles away in Gloucester? Probably not. This wasn't to do with some local feud over rule-breaking in an angling competition. This was in a different league, something much darker, much more sinister.

'Anything else of interest?' he asked.

'The vicar collared us on our way in just now,' Rae added. 'He wants to know whether we'd like him to come in each morning for a short prayer session and a blessing, maybe before we start the morning briefing.'

'What?' Barry sounded incredulous. 'Are you serious?'

'Yeah, of course, boss. Would I wind you up over something like this? Have you ever come across a suggestion like it before?'

He shook his head, looking bemused. 'No. But there's a first time for everything.'

It was Rae's turn to look shocked. 'Does that mean you're gonna take him up on the offer?'

He gave a short, cynical laugh. 'You must be joking. How did you reply?'

Rae laughed, looking relieved. 'I just said that I thought it might be deemed inappropriate but that I'd bring it to your attention. He seemed to accept that. Just said the offer was there if we wanted it.'

Barry shook his head in exasperation. ‘Have we stepped back in time somehow? Is this place some kind of time warp? I mean. Early-morning prayers? Every day? Just think of it. God.’

Rae grinned. ‘I expect she’d be there, listening in.’

Tommy looked blank. ‘Who?’

Rae’s grin widened. ‘God, of course.’

CHAPTER 16: MARITAL ISSUES

Sarah Wilkinson was in the kitchen of the Kellaways' house, elbows on the table and head in hands, trying to think through everything that had happened during the last few days, attempting to make some sense of it all. The trouble was, two large gin and tonics didn't exactly promote the kind of clear-headed thinking she needed.

'I don't know. I'm just confused by it all. What if Neil's somehow linked to whoever did it? You know how he crashes about like a bull in a china shop. He's so stupid when it comes to making friends with people. He always thinks, *What's in it for me?* without thinking of the consequences or the type of people involved. That's why he has all these shady contacts. Really, he's useless at reading other people's motives, but he won't admit it.'

Edie, considered by most of their friends to be the more self-possessed of the pair, glanced across at Minnie before speaking to Sarah. 'But surely the police will spot that he's not really the type of person to do any of this? I don't think you need to worry, Sarah.' She glanced at Sarah's empty glass and reached for the gin bottle, but Sarah put her hand across the top. 'I've had too much already,' she said. 'Alcohol goes straight to my head, particularly at this time in the morning. Anyone would think you wanted to get me drunk.'

Minnie looked momentarily at Edie with raised eyebrows. 'We wouldn't dream of doing that, Sarah. We know what a strain you're under. We just thought you looked as if a G and T might relax you a bit. We often have one mid-morning if we're feeling a bit low, don't we, Edie?'

'Absolutely,' her partner replied. 'A pick-me-up made in heaven. But we can get you a coffee if you prefer.'

Sarah glanced at the clock on the wall and made a decision. 'Thanks, but no. I'd better be getting back. I usually do some baking on a Thursday, but with all this going on I didn't get round to it. Rosie's calling in tomorrow afternoon to visit and there's not a cake left in the house. So I need to get busy today, even if it is a Saturday.' She knew her excuse sounded hollow, but she suddenly felt trapped by these two probing, waspish women. They'd been trying to coax information out of her. She realised it now. Why would they want to do that? She knew how friendly they were with Neil. He'd probably never realised that getting gossip out of people was the Kellaways' favourite hobby. How much did they know about Neil and his many weaknesses? It didn't bear thinking about.

She stood up, a little unsteadily, and picked up her coat from the back of the chair. 'See you next week, maybe.' She made it to the door and, once she'd sucked in several lungfuls of fresh air, felt more clear-headed. She realised her problem. She'd lost her best friend and was subconsciously looking for a replacement. One thing was for sure. Neither of the Kellaway girls would fill that particular role even if it was currently vacant. They had their own agenda and were probably following it assiduously. She was doing herself no favours by accepting booze from them, then answering their somewhat searching questions about Neil. Why were they so interested in her husband anyway? Did they have some kind of ulterior motive? She made a promise to herself not to fall into their trap again. God. She missed Bridget so much. Who else was there in the village who was anywhere near as trustworthy and sensible?

* * *

Minnie Kellaway-Brockhurst watched out of the window as Sarah walked away. 'Well, we didn't get as much as we wanted, did we? Even so, she's really worried about Neil. Do you think she knows something?'

'Doubt it,' Edie said as she joined her wife at the window. 'She's not the sharpest of people, is she? And why would Neil tell her anything? He'd have too much to lose. I think we should postpone our next couple of soirées though. Let the dust settle a bit. What do you think?'

Minnie nodded slowly and slid her arm around Edie's slim waist. 'Better to be cautious. We don't want things to reach the ears of those nosy detectives, do we, darling? They'd misinterpret everything and assume the worst.'

'I wonder why it was two blokes who interviewed us? There are women on the team, so I'm told. Do you think they've heard about us and wanted a peek? You know what men can be like. Tacky.'

'What, like Neil?' Edie laughed. 'Mr Tacky, *par excellence*! I couldn't believe it when he took off his trousers that time and waved his thingy around. I said to him, do you think you might have come to the wrong party?'

'He hadn't though, had he?'

Edie laughed even louder. 'No, but it made him squirm a bit in embarrassment. That was until you put him over your knee and gave him a good spanking. Shame Bridget's party wasn't as lively.'

They giggled some more and poured themselves another round of gin and tonics.

* * *

Sarah let herself in through the front door of the house.

'Are you in, Neil?' she called.

A grunted reply sounded from the kitchen, so she walked through.

'Busy morning?' she asked.

'I was hoping to get some work done but couldn't. That pesky detective was back asking me all kinds of stuff about Grant Kirkbride. How well did I know him? Why did I take him fishing? All that kind of thing.'

'It must be true, then. I heard Grant's body's been found in Gloucester. I'm scared, Neil.'

'No need. It's not as though we're involved, is it? So why should we be worried?'

Sarah knew that Neil was just being his usual arrogant, overconfident self. Full of bluster. He was worried, she could tell. Why did he have to be like this, displaying a couldn't-care-less attitude when she knew he was crawling with anxieties underneath? It was all down to his first wife, of course. Walking out on him and the twelve-year-old Rosie for a wealthier, younger, more flamboyant suitor. She, Sarah, had thought Neil was retrievable, but maybe that had been a false hope. Maybe his ego was damaged beyond repair. She couldn't say, in all honesty, that their own marriage had been the success she'd hoped for. She just hadn't been able to get through to him, no matter what she'd tried. But she knew they'd both gained from the stability the marriage had brought them. Until recently. Until that fishing competition fiasco. Until Neil had got in too closely with people like Dougie Dillon. Maybe even the Kellaway girls. There was something about those two that set her on edge, and it wasn't the fact that they were lesbians. She had several college friends who were gay, and she still kept in touch with them. No, something about Edie and Minnie didn't sit right with her. She knew Neil had been occasionally seeing them secretly, pretending he was in the pub. Only once or twice, mind. But he'd lied about where he was. Bridget had caught sight of him leaving the Kellaway house, distinctly the worse for wear. And she'd caught a whiff of perfume on his clothes. It didn't make sense though, with them being gay. Did anything make sense in this village?

She'd give Neil another couple of years to sort himself out. Rosie had left home for university and Sarah missed her stepdaughter's cheerful presence. What was there to keep her here now if Neil was going to get even more secretive, even more dubious in his activities? She wasn't his keeper, after all. That had never been part of the deal.

She realised Neil had asked her something. 'What was that?' she said.

'I said, what are the details? I got sod all from that detective.'

'His body was found in the river. That's the story that's going round.'

'Why do people think it was murder, then? He could have slipped and fallen in. Didn't Bridget say that he always went for a run in the mornings?'

Something in Sarah's head seemed to snap. 'Why are you so stupid, Neil? Do you really think the police would say it was murder if it wasn't? They must have evidence, for God's sake. You drive me mad sometimes, the way you always have to come up with some stupid objection to whatever's been decided. You're so full of your own self-importance.'

She left the room, slamming the door behind her. Neil sat with his head in his hands.

* * *

Paul Sutcliffe called to his mother just before he let himself out of the rear door of the pub.

'I'm just off, Mum. I'm picking Emma up and we're heading into Salisbury to do some shopping. Anything you need?'

Lisa appeared, drying her hands on a towel having just finished the morning cleaning of the bar area.

'Just find out what Emma would like for her birthday. Don't make it obvious though.'

Paul groaned. 'Mum, I don't even know what to get her myself and she's my girlfriend. And you're asking me for an idea for another present?'

'That's easy, Paul. You can get her some perfume. Chanel always goes down well. I can't get her something like that.' She paused. 'Okay, forget it. I'll get her a trendy scarf or something. How long have I got?'

'Till next weekend.'

'Thanks for helping out behind the bar last night. Enjoy your weekend and give my love to Emma.'

Paul made his way to his old car, left in the corner of the pub's parking lot. He'd be moving out soon, after almost ten years living in the rooms above the pub. When he'd broached the subject with his mother, he'd expected an attempt to talk him out of it, particularly since he'd been her main help as weekend bar staff in recent months. He'd been surprised when she'd greeted the idea with enthusiasm. He realised why now. It was because he and Emma planned to set up home together in Salisbury, where Emma lived and worked. That meant that grandchildren might be on the horizon, in his mother's mind anyway, even if they were living twenty miles away. It would be close enough for his mum. He knew that she doted on toddlers. To be honest, he didn't find the idea as off-putting as some of his pals. To them the notion of babies was an absolute no-no, but he quite liked the idea. Emma wanted a couple of years to themselves first though. She said that she needed more experience of full-time social support work before she could consider having children, with all the extra stress they would inevitably bring. Paul would be glad to get away from Millhead, if truth be told. There were too many secrets here, too many suspicions. He'd have to open up about them soon. Was it the right time now, with all these cops swarming around the place? He had a strong sense of duty and believed in justice. Something needed to be said about that poor guy Grant Kirkbride. But he needed to be sure before speaking to the cops. Finding any hard facts wouldn't be easy.

And there was that young guy, Billy Draper, to consider. He still looked shit-scared every time Paul saw him. He clearly needed someone he could talk to. Surely it was connected? How could it not be?

CHAPTER 17: SKETCHES

'Miriam Boateng's calling in mid-morning,' Barry said. 'She's got something for us, but she was a bit cagey about exactly what it was. She just said she hoped it might be helpful.' He glanced at his watch. 'About ten minutes.'

'It'll be interesting to see her, Barry. Who interviewed her originally? Didn't you say it was Rae and Stevie?' Sophie was perched on the corner of Barry's desk, glancing through a series of memos. She put them down. 'Rae was telling me about her conversation with the vicar a couple of days ago. That's a new one, isn't it? Offering us morning prayers every day.'

Barry grimaced but didn't say anything. He looked up as a uniformed constable approached. 'Sorry to interrupt, sir, ma'am. There's a Dr Boateng arrived to see someone.'

Barry pondered for a few moments. 'Put her in the interview room and ask her to wait a few minutes, please. Offer her a coffee.' He turned to Sophie. 'I'll get Stevie to join us. He's around somewhere. Do you want to see her too?'

'Oh, yes. Never turn down an opportunity to meet someone new, particularly if they sound interesting. That's my motto.'

Barry laughed. 'One of many mottos, as far as I can see.'

Stevie appeared, and the three detectives went to find Miriam Boateng in the somewhat pokey and rather misnamed interview room. He introduced his two senior colleagues. Miriam's eyes widened and she smiled.

'I am deeply honoured to be taken this seriously,' she said.

Sophie laughed. 'Just coincidence, Dr Boateng. I happened to be in this morning and I'm a bit of a nosy sod, to be honest. Added to which, we women have got to stick together against the dreaded patriarchy, haven't we? What have you got for us?'

Miriam drew a sketchbook out of her capacious shoulder bag. 'Sketching is one of my favourite hobbies. Well, along with walking. The two go together quite often. I did these. They're from memory, mind, and my memory can sometimes play tricks. But I think they're a good representation.'

She opened the pad and extracted two pencil sketches, each of a shadowy figure set against a misty background. Somehow Miriam had managed to convey a sense of eeriness in the drawings, along with some degree of emotional atmosphere. The first figure somehow looked vulnerable, glancing back slightly as if in fear.

'I didn't see any facial details,' Miriam explained. 'It was just too misty, and she was gone too quickly.'

'Did you think at the time it was a woman?' Sophie asked.

'I've asked myself that question. Clearly my recollections might have been influenced by the subsequent news. But I don't think it's entirely the case. The figure was slighter than the second one, and somehow scared. There was fear in the air, if I can put it that way. It was the way she was holding herself as she moved.'

Sophie passed the sketch across to Barry and Stevie, then examined the second one. Again, it showed a figure looming out of the mist, crossing right to left in front of the viewer. The stance was more aggressive, more determined. The person seemed to be hurrying, showing none of the hesitancy of the first figure, and was carrying a solid stick-like object.

Miriam explained. 'I didn't sense any doubt or fear this time. I know each glimpse was only a second or two, but there was a big difference in the attitudes of the two, if that makes sense.'

'Yes, it does make a lot of sense, Doctor—'

'Miriam,' she interrupted, with a smile.

'Yes, of course, Miriam. It makes sense. Many of us take a lot of clues from someone's body language and the way they move in any given situation. We don't even have to think about it.'

'So you see, Chief Superintendent—'

'Sophie,' came the interruption.

Another smile. 'Of course. Sophie. Well, my judgement is that this was a pursuer and prey situation. I may have only caught fleeting glimpses, but that's what I think. And I can remember feeling distinctly scared by the second figure, the pursuer. I'm glad he didn't spot me. He was too intent on what he was doing, tracking her.' She looked at her watch. 'Sorry, but I need to be off shortly. Thanks for indulging me so positively.'

'Do you want your sketches back right now?' Barry asked.

'No. I've taken photos. Anyway, I did them to help. They're yours.'

The group left the small room, with the three detectives heading for the incident room. They were joined by Rae and Tommy.

'Well, it fits, doesn't it?' Sophie said. 'We think it was some kind of heavy stick from the wound analysis. But they must be commonplace around here with so many people going out walking. Some of the slopes are quite steep.'

Rae spoke up. 'What showed up in the post mortem? Have they worked out the angles?'

'It's possible they were facing each other when the first strike was made. That doesn't mean she saw her killer clearly, though, not if the mist was as thick as Dr Boateng describes. My guess is that he either got in front of her or somehow got her to turn round. He was just on the edge of visibility, that's my guess. Then he hit her again, maybe when she was on the ground. What evidence there is suggests they were down in the valley by then. She might have been running away from him.'

'This all worries me a bit,' Barry said. 'It doesn't sound opportunistic, which is what Stevie and I thought at first. Someone's been far too clever. You know, the telephones being down so she couldn't contact anybody, then following her up over the hill. It all looks carefully planned to me. There was a bit of luck that the weather was so misty, but other than that, well . . .'

'The heavy mist was forecast,' Sophie said. 'In the late-night detailed forecast. Whoever her killer was, he knew the conditions would be right. There was no luck involved.'

Barry continued. 'I think we need to check with the immediate neighbours again. It looks so far as if she didn't see or speak to anyone the previous day. But can that be right? And when did her mobile phone go missing? Was it taken after she was killed, or did it go missing beforehand? Rae, can you contact her provider again to chase up her account details. We need to know when the phone was last used and to who. This is urgent.'

The team separated.

* * *

For once, Rae was pleasantly surprised at the speed with which the mobile phone service provider could supply the information she was looking for. Bridget Kirkbride's phone had not been used since the Saturday afternoon, two days prior to her murder, when she'd made a series of unanswered calls to her son, Grant. Well, he wouldn't have been able to answer, would he? He was already dead, lying in a reed bed at the side of the River Severn, up in Gloucester. There was no record of any activity after four that afternoon. Could that be the time when Bridget somehow mislaid her phone? Or had it been stolen? It would need to be checked. She tracked back through the other calls or texts that Bridget had made that day. Most were to her son, along with a couple to Sarah Wilkinson. And also a couple of unidentified numbers. And one that had called her at four thirty. The very last item on the list. Interesting.

CHAPTER 18: ASSAULT

Sunday

Eight o'clock on a Sunday morning was not Dougie Dillon's favourite time to be out and about, but he had good reason to be doing so today. He'd just collected a brace of illegally trapped pheasants from a pal and was making his way along a wooded path by the east stream, heading for home with the offending birds safely stowed in a rucksack that was slung across his shoulder. Even so, he kept a wary eye out for any possible challengers. He suddenly slowed, realising that there was some kind of altercation near the path ahead of him. Whatever was going on, it was half hidden by a clump of overgrown bushes at the side of the narrow track. He realised he was hearing the sounds of a struggle, accompanied by grunts and groans.

'What's going on?' he shouted, heading towards the undergrowth.

An old canvas newspaper delivery bag was abandoned beside the path, some of its contents scattered over the muddy surface.

'Are you okay?' he called to whoever it was, trying to sound as fierce as he could.

He could hear the scrambled sounds of someone hurrying away through the bushes. Dougie followed and almost tripped over a prone body curled up on the damp grass. He crouched down beside it. It was that young lad, Billy Draper. Blood was running from the side of his head. Dougie felt for a pulse. There it was, weak but present, accompanied by shallow breathing.

Dougie pulled out his mobile phone, hoping he could get a signal in this crappy little village. He was in luck.

* * *

The incident room was quiet at this time on a Sunday morning. Barry and Rae were the only detectives to have arrived so far, helped by a lack of any significant traffic on the roads coming from their respective homes. Barry was in the small office, poring over the latest forensic report. He was interrupted by a rapid knock on the door. Rae's head appeared.

'Boss. Something important's just cropped up. Billy Draper has been found unconscious up one of the side streets. Dougie Dillon phoned it in on a 999 call. An ambulance is on its way. It doesn't sound good.'

They hurried out to their cars. It wasn't often that the senior detective in charge of an investigation was one of the first police officers to arrive at the scene of a major crime. A solitary uniformed constable was crouched down beside the prone body, checking his pulse and breathing. Barry spread his coat over the young lad.

'I've just arrived, sir,' the officer said. 'It doesn't look good. This man found him and called in, and the control room passed it on. I'd just arrived for duty.'

'Well done for responding so quickly. Rae, can you head down to the shop and tell his mum.' He looked around at the scattered periodicals. 'It's the local free paper. He probably earned a few quid distributing it each month.'

Rae was back within ten minutes with Billy's distraught parents. Wendy even tried to get out of the car before it had come to a complete stop. A fast-response paramedic had just arrived and was carrying out some initial tests. The Drapers rushed across to their son. Wendy's face was as white as a sheet, her hands shaking.

'He's all we've got,' she gasped. 'He's our whole life.'

She almost collapsed. Rae put an arm around her and tried to calm her as much as possible. Barry was still talking to Dougie Dillon, having moved him further away from the immediate scene.

'I was just coming back down 'ere along the path,' Dougie said. 'I heard summat going on ahead, sounded like some kind of rough and tumble, but a bit more serious, like. I yelled out and someone scarpered sharpish. And young Billy's body was there, where it is now. Who'd do summat like that? He was no trouble to no one. He were a great young lad. I mean, look at that wound on the side of 'is head. It's bloody criminal.'

They were interrupted by the arrival of an ambulance nosing its way up the lane. Several more police teams were now present, with two of the officers marshalling the ever-growing crowd of onlookers. The vicar arrived, looking shocked.

'I heard the sirens,' he said. 'The vicarage is only a couple of hundred yards away. Is there anything I can do? It looks awful. Is it young Billy Draper? That's what people are saying.'

'We're not in a position to confirm anything, sir,' Barry replied. He wanted things to be under control when the super arrived and asked for an update. 'Maybe you can help by asking people to stay calm and go back home, vicar. They're not helping by being here, gawking.'

'How is he?'

'Like I said, if you want to help, move people back home, please.'

The vicar turned and spoke to the largest group of villagers. Some slowly moved away, but others were more reluctant to do so. In the end, one of the uniformed officers moved across and spoke to them more forcefully. The crowd slowly dispersed from the immediate area, but several groups reassembled in the village centre, next to the green. One woman, a late arrival, tried to get into the shop to buy some cigarettes but, of course, found the door locked.

'Bloody hell,' she complained. 'Can't even get fags when you need them.'

She was only partly mollified when the reason for the shop being closed was explained to her.

Billy was stretchered into the ambulance and he and his mother were driven swiftly off to Salisbury District Hospital, Rae following close behind with the father, Ian Draper, in her car. He'd wanted to take his own car but Rae had told him it wasn't a good idea, driving while under intense emotional stress.

'I'll get you back home whenever you want to leave,' she said.

Rae was already planning. Billy would need an officer on duty at the ward entrance as a precaution. Whoever did this had tried to kill him and might well make a second attempt on the boy's life. If he ever recovered.

Barry had his doubts about Billy's prospects. He'd seen head wounds like that before. They were usually fatal. He looked up as a familiar car arrived and Sophie Allen stepped out, looking sombre.

* * *

Rae was sitting with the Draper parents in a small family room, waiting for news from the medical team. Tommy had described Wendy as a cheerful woman with a pleasant, outgoing personality. She wasn't showing any of that today, understandably so. How must it feel to be told that your only child's life was hanging by a thread? Rae tried to imagine Wendy's inner feelings but had to admit defeat. She wasn't a parent. How could she be fully aware of the pain Wendy and Ian were going through?

They were all on their second coffee when the consultant, called in from his usual Sunday off, came into the room to speak to them.

'He's stable,' he reported. 'We've cleaned up the wound and he's on a complex drip. We'll keep him in a coma for several days until the trauma has subsided somewhat. I have to say, in the nicest possible way, that your son has a remarkably thick skull for someone of his age. I think it may well have saved his life.'

Wendy and Ian looked at the doctor, then hugged each other.

'We won't take that as an insult, doctor,' Ian gasped. 'He probably takes after me in that respect.'

'Look, the best thing you can do is to go home and get some rest. We'll call you as soon as there's any news or if anything changes.'

'Can we see him?' Wendy asked. 'I just need to touch him, hold his hand.'

'Of course. I'll take you along and leave you with the unit staff nurse.' He glanced at Rae.

'I'll need to see the hospital security chief,' she explained. 'We'll have an officer on duty here for a few days. I'll be doing the first stint.' She turned to the Drapers. 'I'll get Tommy to come and collect you when you're ready.'

CHAPTER 19: SHE'S THE ONE

She's the one he needs to treat carefully. Respectfully. He knew it when he spotted her earlier in the week. Something about her was vaguely familiar and rang some distant alarm bell, hidden in a long-forgotten part of his memory. Short blonde hair, perky nose, alert manner. He thought for a long time, nudging at the edges of his memory, to no avail at first. But he knew it would come, and sure enough it did. In the middle of the night. He hadn't been dreaming, not as far as he knew, but he realised instantly when he awoke. The memory had resurfaced.

It was more than a decade ago. He was hiding in a camouflaged cupboard upstairs in a Wolverhampton house, listening to the sounds of a police search team, watching them through a tiny crack in the cubbyhole's door. The room with the hidden cupboard had already been searched and his hidey-hole hadn't been spotted. He'd known that his whole future would implode if he were to be discovered, but he'd begun to relax, thinking that he'd got away with it. Then he'd heard the slightest of sounds and realised that someone had entered. She was standing just inside the door, her eyes slowly sweeping around the room, taking everything in. Of course, she was a lot younger then, maybe twelve years ago.

She had the same blonde hair and pert nose, along with that alert expression. At one point she'd looked directly at him. Well, that's how it had appeared. She'd looked as if she was about to step across and have a closer look at the panelling that hid him. He'd almost stopped breathing and could feel the dampness of perspiration breaking out across his body. Then a voice had suddenly sounded elsewhere in the house, barking an instruction. The woman turned and left. More importantly, she didn't return.

Here she was now, many years later. In his village, heading up a major crime unit. Would she know? Would she somehow spot the possible link? Would it have occurred yet to her or any of her squad? He doubted it. Not yet, anyway. He wished he could just make her disappear in some way. Maybe abduct her and sling her into a dark pit somewhere. One full of creepy-crawlies. Big spiders and cockroach-type things. God, how he hated women. Women like her even more so. Efficient. Organised. Careful. Observant. It was all too fucking much. He didn't even fancy them in a sexual way. He tolerated them, that was all. He knew they were necessary for the continuation of the human race, but that was all he'd admit to. The worst part of it all was the way he had to pretend to like them. It was a real strain the way he had to curtail the instinct to curl his lip in distaste whenever he met one of them. But they were everywhere in modern society. Fucking women. Or, more particularly, this fucking woman, with her keen eyes and alert manner. Why didn't she just piss off out of it?

He looked around. There were lots of people, all keen to see what was going on, many trying to watch as the lad was loaded into the back of the ambulance and driven off, his parents hurrying off to collect their own car and follow their son. He couldn't help silently cursing. It was all wrong. It should have been a hearse, with a dead body being stretchered inside, not an ambulance rushing off to hospital with a still-alive Draper boy tubed and wired up with all kinds of life-saving gizmos. His own future now depended on chance. Would the lad survive or not? Even if the boy died, were there still any loose ends that required more tidying up to be done? A messy business, but necessary. He had plans for his future and they didn't include spending the rest of his life in prison.

He backed away, nodding to a few of the locals, murmuring a few words of concern here and there when it seemed absolutely necessary, then walked home. A large whisky, that was what was needed. Nothing like a glass of scotch on the rocks to get those sluggish brain cells ticking over again.

Ten minutes later, he was back home, settling into a comfortable seat in a warm sitting room, with a large glass of iced whisky in his hand, sipping gently. He regretted the deaths somewhat, even though they'd proved to be necessary. It was a big step, killing someone. He'd never had to do it before this current mess. Threats had always been enough. When you thought about it, threats were good things. They kept events rolling along smoothly without anyone getting hurt. No bruises, slashes, gunshot wounds or blood. What's not to like? Why didn't people see threats for what they really were? Ways of keeping the peace. Allowing everyone to live their allotted lives without the need for unnecessary violence. If everyone just toed the line and did as they were asked things would be tickety-boo and no one would get hurt. It was society that got in the way, with its laws and regulations, all set up to look after normal orthodox people, along with the idea that intimidation was somehow criminal, that ordinary people shouldn't be on the receiving end of threats. Poor little lambs.

He sighed and took another gulp of chilled whisky. A plan. That's what was needed. Well, two plans really. One for if the boy died. Although, to be honest, nothing much would be needed in that case. Wasn't Billy Draper one of the last loose ends? He could tie things up in a leisurely way and get on with his life, maybe elsewhere. Start again? It certainly sounded tempting. But the world was a different place than a decade earlier. In the long run he might be better off heading abroad somewhere. The only flaw with this plan was if the Draper boy had told anyone, despite the threats. Who would he have talked to? Who would he have trusted? Track along that line of thought and decide who else might know something. He could see where it was leading.

Then there was the more urgent need. If the boy survived and started talking. And he would talk. How could he resist the pressure to do so, surrounded by detectives, counsellors, behavioural psychologists and the like?

It would all spew out, like shit from a sewer. His own days would be numbered then. They'd move in on him so fast he probably wouldn't see them coming. In that case he needed to be ahead of them, ready to go at a moment's notice.

Another gulp of scotch initiated another thought. He wouldn't have even a moment's notice, would he? As soon as the lad talked, they'd be on him straight away, well before they told the media of the boy's recovery. Could he find out from the hospital? Would he be able to tap into information sources there without raising any suspicions?

He thought again of that woman, the one heading up the police team. She might be too sharp. For all he knew, she might have already primed people at the hospital to notify the cops if anyone were to make any unexpected requests for information, however justified, whoever they came from. Normal cops were as thick as pig shit. But she wasn't. He'd followed that Wolverhampton case through the courts, sometimes even watching from the public gallery. He had to give it to her. Her court performance had been razor sharp. She'd made mincemeat of the defence counsel when they'd tried to suggest police incompetence. And his old buddy Corky had been locked up ever since. Well, until a few months ago. Corky had somehow managed to get out early on good behaviour. He could still remember the look of panic on Corky's face when he realised the game was up. None of the others had taken the time to look around that old house apart from him. Not even Corky.

'Christ, Jack, we're done for. It's time to start praying!' Those were Corky's last words as a free man.

He was the only one who knew about the secret cupboard. When Corky and the others ran for the stairs in a desperate attempt to escape out the back, he'd hurried the other way, upwards. Into the attic bedroom. Into the secret hidey-hole.

Had Corky spotted him in the gallery during the trial? Unlikely. He was in his usual disguise, after all. And Corky knew nothing of his real life. Nor did any of the others.

Another sip of scotch. His thoughts returned to the obvious problem. Might the Draper boy have talked to anyone? If so, who? And could something be done about it if he had? Too many problems. Too much to think about. Life had turned to shit.

CHAPTER 20: BLOODSTAINS

Monday

A wet day. Rain falling in that infuriating way that is so common in Britain's western counties: in a fine misty drizzle. Barry wished it would do one thing or the other. Either pour down in a sudden onslaught of fifteen soaking minutes or go away completely and leave everyone free to enjoy a dry sunny day. He poured himself a coffee and sighed. Why was he feeling so irritable? He knew, of course. His impending wedding to Gwen was now less than a month away and he was getting jittery. He wished it was all over and done with. He took a sip of the steaming liquid and settled down to face another day of relentless pressure. Two murders and a life-threatening assault. All in the space of eight days or so and all closely entwined. The press was pushing for quick results and the upper echelons within the police forces of the two counties were seeking the same. Even Home Office officials were making discreet inquiries about progress. The new unit was their experiment, after all. If it fell over on its first major case the home secretary would have a lot of questions to answer in parliament. Everyone knew it was her baby. Thank goodness he wasn't in overall command of WeSCU, just one of its two senior investigating officers. The other, Polly Nelson, was still across in Somerset, well out of harm's way. She'd phoned him last night. Although she was unable to offer any direct help, she could offer sympathy. Fat lot of use that was, although he'd been reassured by her concluding comment that he seemed to be doing everything right. No, the pressure was all on Sophie Allen, the chief super. And long may it stay there.

He looked up as the door opened and she came in.

'Morning,' she said breezily. 'Everything alright?'

He was about to reply in a mildly positive way when his phone rang. He listened and put a hand to his head. He replaced the phone slowly and deliberately.

'There's just been a 999 call,' he said. 'The vicar's home's been ransacked. He's gone missing. There are signs of a struggle.'

'Well, what are we waiting for?' the boss said. 'Let's get across there.'

Stevie and Tommy arrived just as they were hurrying out of the incident room.

Barry tried to sound authoritative. 'Tommy, you take charge here. Stevie, you come with us.'

* * *

Barry looked around him at the ransacked rooms in the vicarage. A bureau emptied, a couple of drawers hurriedly searched, books scattered from a shelf, prominent bloodstains on the hall floor. What was going on in this madhouse of a village? Two murders, a serious assault on a teenage boy and now this, the abduction of the parish vicar along with his home being vandalised. The vicar's car was still in the driveway, and there was no early-morning bus service out of the village. Was there another explanation, other than abduction? If so, Barry couldn't think of it. Dismay obviously showed on his face.

Sophie was watching him with a trace of a smile. 'Remember what that awful Corinne Lanston used to say, Barry? Every contact leaves a trace. Think it through. The more contacts, the more traces. This is our fourth crime scene. That means there's four times the likelihood of finding that all-important clue than if there was just one. It gives us a lot more to sift through and it'll all take time, but something will turn up, mark my words.' She looked around her at the notebooks strewn across the floor of the vicar's small office. 'And my guess is that this is the one. It's got the look of a rushed job, don't you think?'

Barry looked at her. 'You're right. It's just left me feeling a bit overwhelmed, that's all.'

'Do the usual. Forensics in here, going through everything. Door to door with all the neighbours. Who found it like this, by the way?'

'The housekeeper, Janet Rogers. She arrived at about eight to get his breakfast and start work. She's still around somewhere.'

'Well, you and Stevie see her. I'm heading up to HQ to see the chief constable and do some ego-stroking. We need some extra manpower. I'll probably be back later this morning.'

Stevie watched her leave and turned to Barry. 'Is she always like that? You know, that odd sense of humour.'

Barry laughed. 'It's usually worse than that. What's your chief constable like, here in Wiltshire?'

'A bit of a hardball, I guess.'

'Ha. He doesn't stand a chance. She'll breeze in and have him eating out of her hand before he realises what's going on. I'll interview the housekeeper. She's probably still in shock and desperate to get home. I'll send Tommy across to keep you company here.'

Janet was a short, dumpy woman with a decidedly pale complexion. Or maybe she was usually a bit ruddier and was just ashen-looking from shock. She was waiting in the back of a squad car, so Barry took her across to the nearby village hall, their temporary headquarters, to talk. He sent Tommy across to the vicarage and asked Rae, newly arrived, to make some tea. Rae joined them in one of the small rooms converted for interview use, carrying a tray of mugs. Janet had taken her coat off. She was wearing a dark top and trousers, but with a somewhat faded pale-blue apron covering them. Although her clothes looked a little shabby, they smelled freshly laundered. Her wavy brown hair was greying and looked unkempt. She glanced at the two detectives nervously, so Barry tried a reassuring smile.

'This shouldn't take long, Mrs Rogers. We just need some background information and a description of exactly what you found when you arrived this morning. Let's start with how long you've been the housekeeper in the vicarage.'

'About eight years.' Her voice was weak and quivering. 'When the vicar first arrived, he put an advert for a housekeeper in the village shop window. I applied and got the job. I've been here ever since.'

'That's useful to know. Does he have family living here? A partner?'

She shook her head. 'He's single. But very kind and thoughtful.'

'You get on well with him, then?'

'Yes. He's a quiet man. But I've got no complaints. He's good to work for.'

'You might know him better than anyone else in the village.'

'Probably.' She was wringing her hands but stopped when she realised what she was doing. 'I see him most days. Not weekends though. I cook him a couple of extra meals on Friday afternoon and leave them in the fridge for him to heat up when he wants them.'

'You arrive quite early in the morning?'

She nodded, a little colour returning to her face now she was engaged in something positive. 'Eight. I do some breakfast for him then get on with the housework. I usually finish midday, except Fridays, when I spend the afternoon getting the weekend food ready.'

'Is there very much housework to do?' Stevie asked. 'I mean, it's just him living here, isn't it?'

Janet seemed to take offence. She sat up straighter. 'He doesn't make any mess, but all the visitors do. Leaving dirty footprints on the floors. Grubby marks all around the place. That's what a vicar's life is, seeing people all day. He has so many problems to deal with. Other people's problems.'

'Let's switch to this morning,' Barry suggested. 'Was there anything different before you came in the house? Outside, maybe?'

She shook her head. 'Not really. I did notice a couple of scuff marks on the gravel path outside, but I can't be sure they weren't there last week. Nothing else was out of place.'

'Does he usually keep the door locked?'

'Yes. We all need our privacy, Inspector, even vicars. And people take advantage, don't they? People would get to know that he was living by himself, so he was free a lot of the time.'

Barry nodded. 'And it was locked this morning, as usual?'

She frowned. 'Yes. It was only when I got inside that I noticed things were strange. Stuff over the floor and those terrible bloodstains. It scared me. I phoned 999 and came back outside. Will he be alright? He's such a good man, always asking how people are.'

'The chances are good, Janet. But we can't be sure about anything. We just need to do our best to find him.'

Barry didn't say what he was really thinking. That the vicar might well be already dead, and hidden rather more effectively than Bridget Kirkbride or her son. Whoever the killer was, he wouldn't make that mistake again. Not if he had any sense. This time the body would be disposed of more carefully.

'Does he have any enemies? Anyone you know who might bear him a grudge?'

Janet looked shocked, as if the mere suggestion was an affront. 'Of course not. Gordon's a wonderful man, involved with far too much. He gives up his time without complaint, a bit different from the previous vicar. He was far too easily distracted and wasn't really interested in much outside the church. But Gordon really gets stuck in to local things. He's very popular.'

Stevie chipped in. 'So what else does he do? We need to consider any issue that might have led to this attack.'

Janet took a swig of tea. 'He's a judge at the flower show. He's chair of the local summer fete and has volunteered for most things, even if they haven't been taken up. He doesn't talk about it much, but he's also involved with the area child protection panel. You know, they discuss youngsters who might be at risk. He does a lot of work for them, partly because of his involvement with the youth club.' She paused, concentrating. 'Oh, and I think he's on the angling club committee. That's something I've never understood, because it's not as if he's keen on fishing. He did it to keep the peace between the two different factions, that's my guess. They were always at each other's throats. That's what I heard.'

Stevie was puzzled. 'What do you mean?'

'I don't know all the details but there was some kind of cheating going on a few years ago, and it split the club. Gordon went onto the committee to try and keep them together. That's what he told me. You'd be better asking someone who's a member. They'd know more.'

'Maybe Neil Wilkinson? He's a prominent member, isn't he?'

Janet snorted as if in disgust. 'That man? That would be scraping the barrel. He was the main cheat, that's what I heard. He got thrown out. His pals didn't like it and were threatening to quit but somehow Gordon kept them together. He deserved a medal for what he did. He stopped a real feud from starting. Oh, and he sometimes helped out with a bit of cricket coaching. That would have bought him back into conflict with that Wilkinson man.' She curled her lip. 'He's involved with the local cricket team too.'

She fell silent and finished her mug of tea.

Barry took over. 'Well, I think we have a clear picture, Janet, so thanks for your help. If you think of anything else, please contact us immediately.'

* * *

Rae cornered him as soon as he was free.

'Boss, I've picked up on something a bit peculiar. Whether it's relevant or not is a different matter, but you need to know.'

He looked across at her but couldn't read the expression on her face. 'Okay. The day can't really get much worse, so spit it out.'

'That Kellaway duo — have you noticed how people are slightly wary of talking about them?'

He sighed. 'Not really, Rae.' He wondered whether to say something a bit sharper if this was all she had. But he knew there'd be more. She was the one who often came up with the gold nuggets. 'Go on.'

'Apparently, they hold what they call *soirées*. A couple of times a year. You always imagine a soirée would be something refined. You know, with music, poetry, art. That kind of thing. But not these. They're kind of, um, sex parties, as far as the gossip is concerned. I've only picked this up from a couple of people, mind, and they're not entirely clear. It's hints and guesses.'

Barry put his hand to his head. 'Tommy and I interviewed them. I had no idea.'

'Well, you wouldn't, would you? The thing is, it might not be relevant at all, but it needs checking, don't you think?'

'Of course.'

'Can I do it? Maybe with Tommy to provide a bit of continuity? It's one of my favourite bits of the job, boss, shaking a tree to see what drops out. It's that ambiguity in my background. People find it unsettling without realising why. Useful.'

'Okay, go ahead. I don't know how much use Tommy will be though.'

Rae grinned. 'Camouflage.'

She collected the unit's junior detective and set off up East Street to the Kellaway house, an old low-ceilinged cottage with a well-tended front garden.

'You didn't tell me it was this pretty, Tommy,' Rae said. 'What a lovely place.'

As before, both of the women came to the door on hearing the mechanical clanging of the ornate bell. This time they were both dressed in tailored skirt suits, fifties style.

'Well, a second visit from the police,' Edie said. 'To what do we owe this pleasure?'

Rae didn't wait for Tommy to introduce her. She put one foot inside the doorway and said, 'I'm DS Rae Gregson. May we come in, please? I have a few questions for you.'

'Ooh, this sounds ominous,' Minnie said to her partner. 'Into the drawing room, do you think?'

'Why not? I'll get a jug of water for the officers,' came the reply.

Rae waited until they were all seated then spoke immediately. No point in delaying things.

'These soirées you host. Can you tell me about them? They might be relevant to our investigation.'

The two women glanced at each other. It was Minnie who spoke first. 'It's just a group of friends with the same interest in all things eclectic.'

Rae fixed her with what she hoped was an intimidating stare. 'Rather more, we've heard. Would you care to explain? Maybe describe exactly what goes on and tell us who attends?'

'We don't do anything illegal,' Minnie replied, with an innocent smile. 'It's nothing linked to these horrible attacks.'

'I'm not implying that anything illegal happens, Mrs Kellaway-Brockhurst. But we're investigating two murders, an attempted murder and an abduction. It's our job to decide what's relevant and what isn't, and we base that decision on evidence once we have the facts. I think you'll find I'm more of an expert on thugs, thieves and vagabonds than you are. And killers.'

'*Vagabond*,' Edie whispered, almost lovingly. 'What a lovely word. So romantic sounding.'

'*Killer* is the operative word here. So answer my question, please.'

'You're pushier than the other detective.'

'I know. But none of us like being given the runaround. I'm still waiting.'

Minnie took over again. 'We usually have about six to eight people, mostly from the village, but sometimes there might also be someone who's staying with us. We have some food, drink and a little entertainment. Maybe some singing and dancing.'

'Has anything ever happened that might conceivably have led to some kind of blackmail threat?'

Rae saw the flickered glance that passed between the two of them. So there was something.

'I suppose it's possible. But honestly, it's very unlikely. We only ask broad-minded people.'

'So what could happen that might make blackmail possible, as you put it?'

Another exchanged glance. Minnie took up the challenge. 'Well, for example, at the last one Edie and I put on a burlesque show. We were rather scantily clad, and we'd all had quite a few G and Ts.' She giggled. 'At one point my breasts popped out from the basque I was wearing.'

'And Neil Wilkinson somehow took that as a signal that he could do something similar,' Edie added. 'He dropped his trousers and offered to paint Minnie's nipples with lipstick. He, um, got quite excited, if you know what I mean.' She cocked her head and rolled her eyes.

Minnie joined in with the giggling. 'Edie put him over her knee and spanked him. I thought it would calm him down, but he got even more aroused, if that's the right word to use. Fred Golbie was there, and he was getting a bit hot under the collar too, partly because the woman he'd brought with him had disappeared into the guest room with our friend Guy, who was down from London. They were making a lot of amorous noises in there.'

'No sense of decorum,' Edie added. 'It's a bit of a problem nowadays, don't you find?'

Rae didn't answer. She was feeling gobsmacked. She hadn't expected this degree of detail to emerge so quickly.

Minnie continued. 'So we had two rather rampant males to cope with. And we were both wearing satin gloves. It all worked out in the end. Everyone left happy.'

Rae glanced across at Tommy, who had an astonished look on his face. He spotted her quick stare and managed to regain his previous po-faced look.

'Did other evenings of yours end up like that?' Rae asked, weakly. This wasn't proving to be the walkover that she'd expected.

'Only once,' Edie said. 'That was when Dougie Dillon deposited some . . . *bodily fluid* into a brandy glass. He added some vodka and tonic and went round offering everyone a taste. He said that he'd read it was packed with minerals, vitamins and protein. We banned him from our next soirée because of it.' She paused. 'See, we told you that nothing particularly naughty happens at our evening dos. Well, not to our knowledge.'

CHAPTER 21: CRICKET

'They're total fruitcakes, boss. Why didn't you warn me?'

'What, and spoil the fun? What happened to your idea of shaking the tree to see what falls out?' Barry was smirking.

Rae scowled. 'Yeah, well, if they'd been rational human beings, I'd have stood a chance. But they seem to have an utterly bizarre approach to life. Good job I was sitting down when they told me about their so-called *little soirées*. The thing is, boss, I can't see them as killers. It's possible they're both really good actors but I don't think so. When I finally got them to talk about alibis for the two murders, they provided chapter and verse. They were in London the morning that Bridget was killed and in Dorchester the weekend we think Grant was murdered. Both with a list of people who can vouch for them. Tommy's checking up on them now, but they sound reliable people. Bank staff and a doctor in Dorchester. A theatre director and a publishing editor in London. To be honest, despite some of the oddball characters who we've interviewed so far in this investigation, no one's given me the merest hint that there might be a killer lurking inside them.'

'Anything else of interest?'

'Well, there's one thing. The analysis of Bridget's landline phone record has arrived. The last call coming in on the

Sunday evening was from an unknown mobile number, at about ten o'clock. It's unidentifiable, an unregistered pay-as-you-go. The call only lasted for a minute. I'm wondering if it was the killer and she got spooked by something that was said. Could that be the reason she headed off via her back gate and the hill path the next morning? If that's what it was, then maybe we can discount Neil Wilkinson, if their house was where she was heading. She wouldn't head directly towards whoever was threatening her, would she?'

Barry scratched his head. 'It's not as clear-cut as that, is it? He could have lured her across under some pretext in that call. He'd know she'd come across the fields. It's by far the shortest way.'

Rae thought for a few seconds. 'But it doesn't match what Miriam Boateng spotted, does it? She felt strongly that the lead person — Bridget, as it turned out — was hurrying away from something that had scared her. And the second person seemed angry, determined and was following her. If it was Wilkinson, why would he be out on the open ridgetop, trailing her? Wouldn't he have waited for her somewhere down in the valley, hidden in the woods? And what was his motive? His name's already mud in the village. Everyone knows what he's like, but he doesn't seem to care. He's a dubious character with the morals of a rat. But something this serious? I just can't see it.'

Barry returned to the small office. He was tense and anxious. This was his first major case as SIO and they seemed to be grasping at straws. No leads, no witnesses and no real evidence. He knew he had the chief super's full backing, and he could talk things over with her at any time, but he would have preferred a more straightforward case as his first in charge, not this tangled mess. She was due across in the evening for an update. He just hoped that something useful had cropped up by then.

* * *

Stevie and Tommy were at the Draper home, the flat above the village shop, looking through Billy's room. It was surprisingly neat for a fifteen-year-old, with most of Billy's possessions stored carefully on shelves or in cupboards. Posters of Taylor Swift lined the walls, along with photos of Joe Root. There were no footballers to be seen.

'He was a cricket fan, then,' Tommy said to Stevie. 'Do you think he played? There are a couple of village teams, aren't there?'

Stevie opened the last cupboard, a narrow storage unit in a corner of the room. It held a cricket bat, pads and several cricket balls, along with a set of cricket books on a shelf in the cupboard.

'Looks like it,' Stevie replied. 'I'll ask his dad.'

Ian Draper was temporarily at home to collect a few things and give instructions to the stand-in shop assistant, drafted in to run things while he and Wendy were at the hospital, by Billy's bedside. The detectives descended the stairs in order to check with the boy's father. He was a short, thin man with dark, wavy hair.

'Yeah, our Billy's cricket mad. He plays for the village youth team. He's one of their star bowlers.'

'Right. That's helpful,' Stevie said. 'The season starts soon, doesn't it? Was he looking forward to it?'

Ian looked as though he was about to reply in the affirmative but then seemed to hold back. He frowned.

'I was gonna say, yes. He always looks forward to the first match. But he normally spends a lot of time in the nets, getting ready. I've just realised. He hasn't done that this year. Nowhere near as much as usual. He wouldn't tell us why though. Wendy even asked him about it, but he just shrugged. We just thought it was a phase he was going through. He's got an obsession with that singer, the one on his posters.'

'Taylor Swift?' Tommy suggested.

'That's the one. We also wondered if he'd got a girlfriend, but he wouldn't tell us anything. He just shrugged and left the room when we mentioned it.'

'Was that his normal response?'

Ian thought for a few moments. 'It didn't used to be. He was so cheerful as a lad. Always quiet, mind. I suppose he got a bit more withdrawn just last year. We've not really thought about it too much before.' He looked carefully at Stevie. 'Do you think it might be connected?'

'It's something we have to think about, Mr Draper. There may be any number of reasons why a teenager might become a bit withdrawn at his age, so it might not be linked. But we have to keep an open mind. We'll keep you informed of anything we do find.'

* * *

In Gloucester, Detective Sergeant Peter Spence was making progress at last. That's what he was beginning to feel, anyway. He'd spent some time with several forensic analysts looking at the riverside area where Grant's body had been found, examining photos and poring over the crime scene reports. At last they'd identified the spot where the assault had probably taken place, some ten yards upstream from where the body had been found, tangled up in a reed bed. A number of bloodspots had been found, two on a low riverside wall and three on some foliage close by. DNA analysis had shown them to be from Grant. The evidence tallied with the theory that someone had struck Grant with a heavy object as he passed by on his evening run, someone who'd hidden behind a bush that was next to the low wall.

Several scuff marks in the mud between the path and the river might be important. They were just at the place where someone might stand if they were hauling a body from the path into the water. Had the assailant hoped that the current would have taken Grant's body much further downstream? If so, they must have been disappointed by the short distance it had travelled before getting stuck. Or maybe they hadn't even noticed. It had probably been dark, and that section of the path was poorly lit.

Peter paid another visit to the scene, this time late in the evening. He worked his way through a possible sequence and realised that his supposition was probably correct. Once the body was in the water, it would have disappeared from view almost instantly. The downstream reed bed where it had become stuck wasn't visible from where he was standing.

The next thing to follow up was the report that someone had been seen around the college campus area a few days before Grant's disappearance. Someone well-hooded, with a dark scarf wound around their neck. Maybe the report was a bit vague, and the stranger involved had legitimate reasons for being where they were, but it needed checking. The stranger had been seen by at least two of the students, so maybe more probing was needed. If only there had been a witness in the vicinity of the riverside path at the time the assault had taken place. There was little hope of that though. The perpetrator wouldn't have gone ahead with the murder if there was any chance of a witness being in the vicinity, watching what was going on.

Even so, he felt that headway was being made. He'd whizz off a quick email to the Dorset team to let them know the latest findings. They must be under intense pressure to make some progress.

CHAPTER 22: NO SENSE

Barry was still looking sombre. 'None of it makes any sense. I mean, we're talking about two murders, an attempted murder and an abduction. It might end up as four murders if the boy doesn't make it and we find the vicar dead in a ditch somewhere. How can that possibly have anything to do with petty village feuds or the like?'

He and Sophie were sitting in the small office, late in the evening, each sipping at a cup of coffee.

'I agree with you, Barry. But nothing's surfaced yet to give us a lead, has it?'

'Ma'am, you're the one that said something was bound to turn up. That this latest one was a bit rushed. What was it you said? Every contact leaves a trace?'

Sophie grimaced. 'Maybe I was being a bit foolhardy. But surely that tells us something. Whoever's doing this isn't stupid, not by a long chalk. Which backs up what you've just said. It's not over something petty. So what is it about?'

Barry shook his head. 'I haven't had time to think along those lines. We're being inundated with stuff from Forensics, the house-to-house calls, statements and the like. It's a wonder I even have time to breathe.'

Sophie took another sip. 'So let's pick it apart logically and think about the four victims. Two are young men, teenagers. The other two are adults in some kind of position of responsibility. Bridget was Grant's mother. The vicar was involved with the youth club and a few other things. We know from talking to his teachers that Grant's personality changed when he was in his mid-teens. He became a bit morose. Didn't Tommy and Rae say that Billy Draper's been behaving oddly?'

Barry nodded but said nothing.

'So is there a match? Billy at fifteen might be behaving the same as Grant did at about the same age. Is that possible? And did they talk about what was bothering them? Grant to his mother and Billy to the vicar? Did both of those adults learn something and were then silenced?'

Barry looked worried. 'Are you suggesting what I think you are? Some kind of exploitation or grooming?'

'The thing is, Barry, it fits. Both of those lads might have mentioned something, and the adults were targeted as a result, before they could act on what they'd heard. Didn't you say the vicar was on an area child protection panel? If Billy Draper had mentioned something to him, the culprit would have had to act quickly. And it was pretty quick, wasn't it? The night after Billy was left for dead.' She paused. 'I was on an investigation into a child grooming gang once, when I was with the West Midlands. They were targeting a whole lot of teenagers at risk. Some were interested in girls, others boys. We struck it lucky, got some intel and raided an old house they were using as a base, keeping the kids there with the promise of booze, free clothes and drugs. It was totally sick. The court case was a hard one, but we won and got most of the gang locked up.'

'And you think this might be something similar?'

She shrugged and ran her fingers through her hair. 'I don't know. But what else makes any sense? We have to consider it, Barry. What I saw at that house and at the trial was really disturbing. Child exploitation always is. I swore to myself that

I'd never miss a chance to stop it happening. What's the latest report on Billy Draper, by the way?'

Barry frowned. 'No real change. The doctors won't commit either way.'

'So we just continue to do what we can in terms of Forensics, interviews and searches. Any ideas on why the vicar's place was ransacked? Is there anything obvious missing?'

Barry shook his head. 'It's not clear. There are still valuables left in the house along with some petty cash and his wallet. His passport's still there. They were looking for something, but what? We don't know. The housekeeper took a quick look around with us late afternoon, but she didn't spot anything obvious. It was paperwork, letters and files that were strewn about the place. It's possible they were looking for notes that might incriminate whoever's behind this. It ties in with what you said just now, doesn't it? The Draper boy might have gone to him for advice, and someone found out.'

Sophie sighed. 'It's logical, I'll give you that. What about the scuff marks on the pathway?'

Barry finished his coffee and put his mug down. 'Nothing that can be used for forensic evidence. But a parishioner we traced said they weren't there in the afternoon when they called. We think whoever took him got him out the back gate. The driveway is at the side. It comes in from a quiet lane and isn't overlooked. Anyone going in there for a few minutes is unlikely to be spotted, particularly at night. The forensic team hasn't finished yet but there's not much there, that's what they've said.'

Sophie remained silent for a few moments. 'I wonder how they did it. He's a tall bloke, and fit by all accounts. Do you think it was someone he knew?'

'Seems likely. A spiked drink and bob's your uncle. We've come across that kind of thing often enough.'

She stretched and yawned, then looked around her. 'You know, this place reminds me a bit of those early cases down Swanage way, before you joined the unit. Didn't we use a village hall in one of them?'

Barry gave a wry smile. 'In Studland. The smuggled girls. The first one I worked for you was Donna Goodenough. We used the old Swanage police station for that.'

'Those were the days, Barry. We used to chat late then, didn't we?'

'I learned a lot. I think you were secretly training me up.'

Sophie laughed. 'I never told you, did I? There was a DS lined up to join the unit, supposedly experienced, but he was a total crud. He paid a visit to HQ so we could meet but I bumped into him just beforehand when we were both coming out of the toilets. He obviously thought I was a receptionist or secretary. He said, "Well, if the staff here are all as gorgeous as you, darlin', I've come to the right place." Can you believe it? Even then, I was willing to give him a chance, but he must have spent those few seconds staring at my tits, not my face. That's the only explanation for the fact that he didn't recognise me fifteen minutes later at the interview. All I'd done was put my jacket on. I just couldn't believe it.'

'Did you enlighten him?'

'Barry, you know me. How could I resist the temptation of a few carefully chosen questions about how he'd view working with a woman boss and colleague? I'd already appointed Lydia by then. I kept him wriggling on the hook for several minutes before putting him out of his misery. Then you and Jimmy appeared for our first two big cases, and I realised the problem was solved.' She looked at the clock. 'Well, let's get home. We need *some* sleep, at least. Maybe one of us will have a brainwave during the night.'

Barry laughed grimly. 'Hah. How likely is that?'

He turned back to his desk on hearing his computer beep to indicate an incoming email. He glanced at the contents and seemed to relax a little.

'From Peter Spence, up in Gloucester. They're making progress at last. Several developments.'

Sophie leaned over his shoulder to take a look. 'See, Barry? I told you things would happen. He's obviously a good bit more optimistic now. We should be the same.'

CHAPTER 23: SPECULATION

Tuesday

Paul Sutcliffe arrived back in the village on Tuesday morning. He'd spent the weekend on a short break in Swanage with his girlfriend, Emma, staying in an upmarket hotel near the clifftop at the north end of the seaside town. They'd had the madcap idea of walking much of the way along the Jurassic Coast but doing it in manageable segments, a couple of days at a time. They'd managed the first section on Saturday, a six-mile stretch from Poole Harbour to Swanage, but then cold rain had set in. The plan was abandoned in favour of checking out the local shops, pubs and cafés. It was still March, after all. There was plenty of time to walk the remaining hundred and twenty miles later in the year.

Once he approached the village centre, he noticed even more police cars at the village hall and small groups of people gathered together, talking. Everyone was looking serious. Had something else happened? He steered his car into the pub's car park, hauled his bag out and walked towards the private rear door. He spotted his mother in the bar, wiping down the tables. She looked up as she heard his footsteps.

'Hi, Mum.' He dropped his bag and walked towards her.

She stopped what she was doing and hurried across, arms open for a hug.

'What's happened?' he asked. He could feel her trembling.

'Billy Draper's in a coma. He was attacked Sunday morning. The vicar's been abducted, sometime Sunday night, and bloodstains were found in his house. No one knows what's going on here. There must be a maniac on the loose. We're all terrified. I'm so glad you're home. I hardly slept a wink last night. Everyone's thinking, who'll be next?'

Paul was shocked. How could things have got so bad so quickly? And what were the police doing? Maybe he needed that conversation with them after all, and quickly. He sat his mother down, made them both a coffee and only set off for the village hall when she'd calmed down.

'Keep the door locked, Mum. Don't open the pub till I come back.'

He slipped out through the rear door, locking it behind him, and made his way across the green to the hall. Two uniformed officers were in the porch and looked him up and down as he approached.

'Is there a detective I can speak to? I have some information about Billy Draper.'

Paul was taken into a waiting area and from there to a small room that he guessed had become a makeshift interview room. It was only a few minutes before a tall, dark-haired man entered, giving him a probing look as he sat down opposite.

'DS Stevie Harrison,' he said. 'And you are?'

'Paul Sutcliffe. I live in the pub with my mother, Lisa. She's the licensee and owner.'

He held out a hand, taken in a quick handshake by the detective. Paul wondered why the door had been left open, but this thought was quickly answered as a middle-aged blonde woman slid into the room and pushed the door shut. She was the one who'd called into the pub for a light lunch in the middle of the previous week. She remained standing by the door, arms folded across her chest.

The detective sitting across from him cleared his throat. 'You have some information for us, Mr Sutcliffe. About Billy Draper?'

Paul nodded. 'I'd have been in sooner, but I've been away for a long weekend with my girlfriend. Only just got back and found out what's happened. How's Billy?'

'No change. He's stable. So what is it you want to tell us?'

'I used to be a member of the local cricket club and the youth club. I used to help out with both and got to know Billy when he was younger, before he hit his teens. I'm twenty-four, so a good bit older than him and even Grant. The thing is, I noticed the same thing happen to both of them, and at about the same age. They kind of withdrew into themselves.'

'Was it sudden?'

'Not really. To be honest, it was so slow that it could easily have been missed. I guess it was missed by a lot of people.'

'But you spotted it?'

'No, not with Grant. It's only been in the last year when Billy stopped chatting to me that I thought about it.'

'How come you noticed it? No one else has brought it to our attention in this way.' The detective seemed wary, as if he didn't know whether to trust what Paul was telling him. Paul could understand this. Why would you instantly believe what some stranger came by and said? They must have all kinds of nutters coming up with strange theories and ideas.

'Okay, I'll be open with you. There are all kinds of reasons why teenagers can seem to change their personalities for a while. But with Billy it was more than that. He seemed nervous and wary whenever I chatted with him in recent months. And since Grant disappeared, he's got a lot worse. He was terrified of something. But he never let on what it was.'

'Are you an expert on teenage behaviour, then?'

'Not really. But I know when something isn't right. My girlfriend, Emma, is a social worker in Salisbury. She does a lot of family support. When I told her she said it was a possible sign of abuse and that I needed to report it.'

'So did you?'

Paul shook his head. 'Not at the time, but it was only last week. I decided to wait and see. I should have pushed the issue with him. Maybe he'd have opened up.'

The woman standing at the door spoke. 'Or maybe you'd have scared him even more. You've done the right thing in telling us now.'

'The thing is, Emma told me that a lot of abuse is family related. But I can't help wondering if Grant went through it too, a few years ago. What if it's the same person? That could alter things, couldn't it? I know this is all speculation, but . . .' He shrugged and left the statement hanging.

Stevie answered. 'Well, leave it with us. We'll get back to you if we need more information. Contact us right away if you think of anything else. Meanwhile, keep all this to yourself. We'll be back in touch.'

CHAPTER 24: THE WATCHER

Miriam Boateng took another surreptitious peek out of the window, trying to stay hidden behind the curtains. That car was there again, parked on the other side of the road about twenty yards away. Why should it make her feel uneasy like this? There could be any number of reasons for it to be present in the avenue. She was sure she could make out the dark shape of a person in the driver's seat. But why was it sitting in that spot, allowing the driver a view up the hill and across her front garden to the house? It was parked against the direction of traffic flow. Surely that was unusual? And she knew it had been there for a short while the previous evening, in exactly the same spot. She'd never noticed the car in this area before, not on the street or in any of her neighbour's driveways. But she was sure that she had seen it before. Somewhere. And fairly recently. It was both puzzling and worrying, especially with Tom being away visiting his unwell mother for a few days. Normally she wouldn't worry about being alone for a spell. After all, she had her work to keep herself occupied, along with a wide circle of friends if she needed company. But recent events had unsettled her. That business out near Win Green seemed to have snowballed into two murders and some assaults, according to the press. It was all very disturbing.

She cast her mind back to that morning a week ago, shuddering at the memory. The figures in the mist. The distant screams. Then the return to the scene in the afternoon to convince the police officers that something worrying might have happened. And failing to do so, in the short term anyway. Miriam could still recall the suspicious and patronising look on the face of the woman constable. What was her name? Colleen Jackson? Yes, that was it. She'd obviously made some disparaging remark to the sergeant as they'd returned to their squad car. Miriam could picture the look on her face even now, a week later. And then Miriam froze. Hadn't there been a nondescript grey Ford in the car park at the time? With someone in the driver's seat? Or was she letting her imagination get the better of her?

Miriam went back downstairs to check that all the doors and windows were securely locked. When she returned to her bedroom and took another quick look outside, the car had gone. If it appeared again, she'd have to find a way of noting its registration details, just in case. The key issue now was whether she should tell the police. But was she just being paranoid? Why on earth would anyone want to watch her? Maybe she just had a stalker complex. No, she needed to wait for a while just to see. The police wouldn't thank her for wasting their time, not with all these murders and assaults to investigate. She'd stay alert and only contact them if she was sure.

* * *

The driver headed west and picked up the A30 on the outskirts of Salisbury. A half-hour drive and he'd be in Shaftesbury and the safety of his temporary hidey-hole, isolated on the edge of the hilltop town. He'd been lucky to find it, several months before. A short let from one of his friends, no questions asked. It was the end property in a quiet, tree-lined cul-de-sac, not overlooked by any of the neighbouring houses. No one would see most of his comings and goings. Not that he was there very often anyway, not in more normal times. And he wouldn't need it for more than a few weeks longer. A permanent, long-term move was very much in order when the time was right.

He slipped inside the porch and turned, checking for signs of nosy neighbours. No one about. Good. He let himself in, hung his coat and hat on a hook and made his way through to the living room, where he poured himself a glass of scotch. Not too large though. He needed his wits about him, at all times. You never knew when something unexpected would happen, requiring snap decisions. It just wouldn't do to have your thoughts clouded with the effects of booze. That could be fatal.

It had taken him several days to track down the identity of the woman he'd seen in the mist that day last week. He'd hardly noticed her on the morning in question. He'd been so focussed on following the Kirkbride woman that he was almost oblivious to other things going on around him. Not that there had been much to see. The thick mist had ensured that. Maybe that's why the problem had arisen. He'd been overconfident, too cocky. The fog that morning had lulled him into a false sense of security, sure that no one would be out on the hill, and if they were, they wouldn't see him. But the mist had swirled rather a lot, creating thin spots, and he'd worried that one such clearer patch had occurred at just the moment he'd passed her. Good job he was so cautious and had driven back in the afternoon to check. The sight of a police car had been a real shock, even more so the sight of the two cops talking to her. And it had been her. He realised once he'd taken a quick glance through his binoculars. Her red walking jacket was the same colour as the one he'd glimpsed earlier, and her height, head shape and skin colour confirmed it. If only he could have heard what was being said, his worries would have either been confirmed or laid to rest. Not possible though, not without showing his face to her. He'd been somewhat reassured when he saw the facial expression on the woman cop as she returned to her squad car. She'd been shaking her head as if in protest at having her time wasted. He could have left it at that, but a niggling worry had caused him to check the black woman out. That's when he'd discovered who she was. A surgeon, influential in nearby Salisbury. An art-lover and concertgoer. She'd know people. She might not be satisfied with the fob-off she'd probably got from those two lowly cops. She might press things further, particularly with those pushy detectives egging her on. He needed to stay alert.

Miriam Boateng. That was her name. She lived with her husband in a creeper-clad house in a leafy suburb, and she was relatively easy to track. Particularly with her other half seeming to be away for a few days. What to do with her? It was probably safer at the moment to leave her be. There was enough police activity to monitor in the village and up in Gloucester. He'd need to keep an eye on her though. Things could change at any moment.

God. Why did people have to be so uncooperative? Why did they have to stick their shitty little noses into things? Infuriating do-gooders with their stupid wish for a neat little world where everyone's always *nice* to everyone else. It makes you sick. It makes you enraged. It makes you wonder about sticking a knife into some of them and watching them squeal.

He immediately chopped this line of thought off. Rage wouldn't get him anywhere. He needed to stay on top of things, maintain control, think things through logically. That's what had kept him out of trouble so far; he'd been more cautious than his fellows. Too many of them had ended up with long prison sentences, their names dragged through the mud, their identities logged on various registers, all through a lack of logical thinking. He wouldn't make that mistake.

CHAPTER 25: BUTTON

Peter Spence, the Gloucester detective who was liaising with WeSCU, was feeling quietly pleased. News of the details surrounding Grant Kirkbride's death had got out and was seeping through the student population. Grant had obviously been quietly popular, someone who had proved himself to be reliable, even amiable once his initial shyness had been overcome. So people started coming forward, willing to share their thoughts about him with the police. Members of the running club identified his favourite routes around the city and along the river. He'd signed up for the college cricket club and had been looking forward to the opening match of the season. In preparation he'd been a recent regular at the training area, improving his skills as a bowler. He played guitar and had joined the college folk music club, exchanging views on music with the other members and attending occasional gigs in local pubs.

Some of the most useful information had come from Nikki Orlando, the woman student who had fallen for him a few weeks prior to his murder. She was on the same course as Grant and, apparently, had spent several weeks making gentle overtures to him, all seemingly ignored. She told Peter that she'd all but given up before she made the final attempt to land Grant. She was still distraught at what had happened to him. It was Nikki he was speaking to now, chatting to her in a quiet room in the college.

'I read the account you gave to the Dorset detective, so we don't need to go over that aspect again, not unless you've thought of something else,' he said.

'Maybe I said too much,' she replied. 'I suppose I was in shock.'

'No, not from our point of view. Your suggestion that he was so taken aback at first was a puzzle. The squad investigating his mother's murder found it really useful. Do you still think he was a virgin when it happened? Sorry, this might seem very intrusive but there's a reason I'm asking.'

'Well, that's the strange thing. Yes and no. I can't really explain what I mean. He seemed both inexperienced and experienced at the same time. Sorry, but I find it really hard to talk about it.'

Peter shook his head gently. 'Don't worry. I can always find a female detective to talk to you if you'd find it easier. It was the senior detective from Dorset who spoke to you before, wasn't it?'

'I think she sort of tricked me into opening up. She was very empathetic and gently nudged me into thinking along those lines. I guess it was all very clever.'

Peter smiled. 'She's well known for it. We worked together on a case some years ago and she used it on me. But she can also be as hard as nails. I suppose we're all a bit like that, as detectives.' He decided to change tack. 'Is there anything else about Grant that we might find useful, from the couple of weeks you spent together?'

Nikki frowned as if concentrating hard. It was obvious that she was picking her words carefully. 'It was as if there was a shadow lurking over him. I can't really explain it. Maybe some brooding secret that he couldn't escape. He never really let his guard down. There were a couple of times when I felt he was about to tell me something, something really important. But he drew back at the last moment.' Tears once again appeared in her eyes. Her voice dropped to a near whisper. 'I was falling in love with him, you know. I feel awful. All the time. Why would someone want to kill him?'

'That's what we intend to find out. I'll be back in touch, Nikki.'

* * *

A Gloucester police forensic team had been at the riverside for several days now, completing a detailed sweep of the surrounding area and taking careful measurements at the site where Peter had found the suspicious marks on the bank. Whoever had attacked Grant had been careful but not quite careful enough. The marks in the mud gave them an idea of the perpetrator's shoe size, even if there was no discernible tread pattern.

'What do you think? About a size eleven?' David Greenaway, the local DCI suggested.

'Looks like it,' the forensic technician said. 'But more than that, it gives us an idea of the shape of the shoe. It's not a trainer, more of a traditional leather construction.'

Peter, listening in, felt pleased. Maybe it was only a minor piece of evidence, but when they found their man, they might be able to find a pair of shoes that matched up. It would never be conclusive enough for court evidence, not unless some traces of residual riverbank mud were still present, but everything helped to build a picture. As his boss often said, solving a crime was not that dissimilar to completing a jigsaw puzzle.

'Then there's this.' The forensic chief held up a small plastic bag. It was difficult to make out its contents.

Peter moved closer. 'What is it?'

'It's a button.'

'Is it relevant?' David said.

This was met with a shrug. 'Could be. Let's hope so. It was found between the spot where we think the assault took place and where the body was dumped into the water.'

'So, you're thinking it might have been torn off in a struggle?'

'It's possible. What we can say is that it hasn't been there very long. It wasn't covered in mud. The question is, how did it come to be there?'

Peter turned to his boss. 'The post mortem showed the possibility that there were two blows to the head. That could suggest a blow followed by a struggle of some kind, then another blow.'

'Can you send a report of this down to the WeSCU team?'

Peter nodded. 'Of course. I'll phone them as well.'

* * *

Back in the Gloucester incident room, Peter set to work on a possible timeline for Grant's death. They were now fairly sure the assault and subsequent drowning had happened on the Sunday morning when the young student was out for his usual early-morning run. His phone record had shown activity up to the previous evening, one of the last calls being one he'd made to his mother at about six. What had been discussed? Had one of them said something that had set the whole sorry sequence of events in motion? If that was the case, someone had reacted very quickly, killing Grant the next morning and Bridget the following day. If it was the same person, they'd made a sequence of very rapid decisions and done a lot of driving. That kind of rushed reaction would normally mean a few mistakes being made, but none had shown up so far. Had Grant made a decision about something important and opened up about it to his mother? Had she deliberately or even inadvertently warned the assailant?

Peter had been kept up to speed on the most recent developments in Millhead St Leonard. He speculated on what the atmosphere must be like in the village, with two residents dead, one seriously assaulted and one missing, presumed kidnapped. The locals must be terrified, wondering who might be struck down next. He'd grown up in just such a village in Gloucestershire. He knew how familiar people could get, how closely small village life revolved around gossip and perceived social status. They'd all be looking at each other and wondering. Even when these murders were solved, would life ever return to its pre-tragedy norm?

CHAPTER 26: ROSIE

Barry was expecting the door to be opened by either Sarah or Neil Wilkinson, but instead he found himself facing a woman who looked a few years younger than Sarah. There was a facial resemblance though. He found himself under close scrutiny.

'Yes?' she asked, warily.

'I'm DI Barry Marsh. This is DS Rae Gregson. We've called to speak to either Sarah or Neil. Are either of them in?'

The woman spoke sharply. 'Sarah is. As for that good-for-nothing husband of hers, well . . .' she snorted. 'I've no idea where he is and, to be honest, I couldn't care less.' She turned and called back into the house. 'Sarah, it's for you. It's the police.'

She turned again to face Barry. 'You haven't come with good news, like he's been found dead in the river or buried in the woods, have you? He's a dickhead of the first order and deserves whatever's coming his way.'

Sarah appeared behind her. Both women were dressed casually, in jeans and loose tops. 'You'd better come in. This is my sister, Jenny. She doesn't like Neil very much.'

Rae pushed the door shut behind them and followed her boss and the sisters into the living room. Sarah seemed somehow different this morning. She was pink-faced but looked more determined, as if she'd sorted something in her mind.

'I only called to check up on a few points to do with the youth club, Mrs Wilkinson. But has something happened?' Barry sat down.

Sarah sat up straight. 'I asked him to leave, yesterday. He was ruining my life with all his carryings-on. I couldn't think straight. I was spending all my time worrying. Then, yesterday, I found out about some more stuff he was up to, when I spoke to people down in the village. It was all too much.'

Jenny took over. 'She phoned me and I hotfooted it across last night, intending to have it out with him. But he'd already gone. Good for Sarah. It may have been a couple of years too late, but she made the right decision at last. That pig never deserved her. Do you know he made a pass at me once? Disgusting creature.'

'So where is he?' Barry asked.

'Couldn't care less,' was Jenny's immediate response.

'He's staying with Dougie Dillon,' Sarah sighed. 'That's what I heard. I couldn't sleep and got up early to walk down to the shop. Apparently, they were in the pub last night, getting drunk as usual. Some people never change.' She glanced at her younger sister, who responded with an exasperated look.

'I told you that years ago,' Jenny replied. 'But I have to give you full marks for trying. In fact, you deserve a medal for commitment. I could never have lasted as long as you with him. It's what Alec, my own husband, says. It's the minority of men like Neil who let their whole gender down. The "take what you can get and bugger the consequences" brigade, as he calls them. Sorry, sis, but it's true.'

Barry was perturbed by the news about Neil. He excused himself and headed for the hallway, where he made a quick phone call to Stevie in the incident room, asking for someone to verify Neil Wilkinson's whereabouts. The investigating team couldn't afford yet another local to disappear into thin air. He then returned to the lounge in order to question Sarah about signs of fraught relationships in the local youth club, but Rae had already started the conversation.

'I never noticed anything odd,' Sarah said. 'The youngsters generally got on well together. But I can't claim to be an expert on teenage behaviour. I wasn't there every week, anyway. I helped out when Bridget was on the rota, just as an extra pair of hands. But it wasn't very often because I didn't want Rosie, my stepdaughter, to think I was keeping an eye on her. It can be a bit tricky, the relationship between stepmum and stepdaughter. I felt I had to give her some leeway.'

'Did Rosie know Grant at all well?'

'Well, sort of, I suppose. I don't think there was ever anything going on with them. More pals than anything else.'

Barry broke in. 'Maybe we should talk to her. Can you give us contact details?'

Sarah scribbled a phone number onto a slip of paper. 'She's at university, in Bournemouth. Her mother lives close by, so it made sense to go there.'

'Anything else you can remember about the youth group? We've heard there was no detailed organisation and no written records of any type. Is that right?'

Sarah pursed her lips. 'That wouldn't surprise me. Not in the years that Neil chaired the committee. Though maybe the word "committee" is wrong. It was more a group of people that met in the pub, over drinks. I mean, the Kellaways were sometimes there. What did they have to do with the youth club? Nothing at all. Basically, they just sat in, joining in with the boozing, as far as I could tell. It was ridiculous.'

'Tell me more about Rosie. She lived here with you until recently?'

'She's a really nice young woman. Very caring. She had a bad speech defect as a child though. That meant she came in for some bullying when she was younger, as far as I know.'

'Why did her parents break up?'

Sarah shrugged. 'I don't know the full details. I never bothered asking. They'd been separated for some time when I met

Neil. Marie was an alcoholic and was incapable of looking after a youngster. I think she's recovered now though. From what Rosie told me, she's held down a job in a local shop for a few years now. They've rebuilt their relationship during that time. Rosie always felt abandoned by her when she was growing up and it took some time for her to get over it and start again. I think they're much closer now. Rosie stays on campus but sees Marie a lot.'

'What's she studying?' Rae asked.

'Medical stuff. She's training to be a paramedic. Her speech has improved a lot in the last few years.'

Barry took over again. 'What might your future be, Mrs Wilkinson?'

Sarah shrugged, her eyes damp. 'I haven't thought that far. It's over between Neil and me, I can tell you that. Whether I stay in the village or not? Well, probably not. I'll sell up and move to somewhere bigger. Maybe Shaftesbury or Salisbury. It's my house, you see. I was here before I got together with Neil. I've kept it in my name.'

Jenny broke in. 'That's probably my fault. I never trusted that man. He caught Sarah on the rebound. She couldn't see what he was really like, not then. I told her to hang back on doing anything with the house ownership until she was totally sure about him.'

Sarah sighed. 'I was ever hopeful. And stupid.' She paused. 'The story of my life, really.'

* * *

Rae had arranged to meet Rosie Wilkinson in her room on the university campus.

'You're lucky,' the young woman said. 'I'll be off campus for the next four weeks, attached to a paramedic team as a trainee. It would have been a lot harder to meet up.'

'We'd have found a way,' Rae responded. She looked at the young woman facing her. She had curly brown hair, olive-green eyes and freckles and was wearing jeans, a loose jumper and trainers. Rosie had an expressive face and was using hand gestures as she talked. Maybe that was linked to her childhood history of having a speech defect, when animated hand movements might have helped to clarify meaning. She certainly had an outgoing personality, if her initial greeting was anything to go by.

'You wanted to talk about Grant Kirkbride?' Rosie said. 'Anything in particular?'

'Well, to start, did you know him at all well?' Rae asked.

'It ebbed and flowed a bit. I got to know him a bit better when we were in the sixth form. We both did A-level biology and were in the same class. Sometimes we worked together on assignments, and that was a help. Neither of us were very academic. It was hard, so sharing stuff made it easier.' She paused. 'There was one time when I got a bit drunk at a party and tried to get off with him. It wasn't any good though. He was always so distant when it came to any emotional stuff. It's like he kept himself kind of caged up. That time I felt he was almost going to drop his guard a bit, just for a moment. He didn't though. He backed off. I ended up saying sorry to him.'

Rae thought for a few moments. 'Did he ever give a clue as to what was bothering him?'

'I thought he might be gay or something, but later on I realised it might not be that. Something was bothering him, something big. That's my guess. He wouldn't let anyone get close, not even his mum, and she's really nice.' Rosie realised her mistake and put a hand to her mouth. 'Sorry. I meant, was. I keep forgetting.' She pulled her fingers through her curls and wrapped one lock of hair around her index finger. Her eyes had dropped. 'It's all so awful,' she whispered.

'Can you think of anything he said or did that might be a clue as to what was troubling him?' Rae asked.

Rosie looked up again. 'I've never said this to anyone, but I wonder if he might have been abused at some point.'

Rae waited but no explanation was forthcoming. Rosie looked deeply troubled. 'Can you explain, Rosie? We need to know, even if there proves to be nothing in it.'

'It was in the summer a couple of years ago. We were at a party and some of us were out in the garden 'cos it was so warm. We got chatting and I told him my mum had hit me across the face once when she was blind drunk. That was when I was about twelve, when she was at her worst. I'd bottled it up for a long time and not told anyone. I don't know why I told Grant. Maybe I was looking for sympathy. Well, I didn't get any. He just looked at me and said, "You think that's bad? It's nothing compared to what I've been through." Then he seemed to soften and looked at me more like a human being. He suddenly hugged me and said sorry. He said, "You didn't deserve that. We all need understanding, abuse victims." He walked off. I asked him about it later, but he just shook his head. "I'm not ready yet," was all he'd say. It made me think. I mean, I told him about me being bruised for days from that punch from my mum. So whatever it was he was talking about must have been a lot worse, don't you think?'

'That's what we're trying to find out. He never gave you any clue as to who it might have been?'

Rosie seemed to think long and hard. 'Not at the time, no. But there's something I can tell you. It's only occurred to me in the last few days, since I heard the news about him. He stopped talking to men. I mean, completely. He was still close to his mum, and to Sarah, my stepmum. And to other women, as far as I can remember. But he seemed to be more distant with men. Like he was distrustful. It wasn't obvious but it was there.'

Rae thought through possible explanations. 'Could it have been linked to that angling club scandal that involved your dad? Grant was close to him at one time.'

Rosie shook her head. 'Nah. He's just a bit of a moron. I know what happened there upset Grant, but it wasn't that. I reckon it was something much darker. And it wasn't Dad, I know. Grant told me another time that Dad was just a harmless idiot. And that matches my view of Dad exactly.'

'I know this isn't strictly relevant, Rosie, but how do you feel about your dad and Sarah breaking up?'

Rosie frowned again. 'It's no real surprise. It had to happen sometime. Dad really misses my mum, but she's found someone else. He's just floundering around, really. Sarah's a lovely person but she allowed him to walk all over her and that was the wrong approach. He needs someone strong, someone who'll keep him in line. And that's not Sarah, no way.'

CHAPTER 27: LAPTOP

The detectives were grouped together for their evening meeting, assessing progress made during the day. Barry had shared the discoveries made by the Gloucester squad, listed in an email from Peter Spence and summarised in a phone call made during the late afternoon. Rae had reported on the interview with Sarah, along with the thoughts that Rosie, Neil's daughter, had supplied.

'Were there any clues in Billy Draper's bedroom, Stevie?' Barry asked.

'Nothing that would help us directly, to be honest, boss. He had some posters up on his wall. The usual stuff. A couple of singers and some famous cricketers. Taylor Swift on stage. His mum said she was his favourite girl singer. But if you were hoping for a diary or something written, then no. He wasn't a great writer, according to his mum. No sketches or drawings either. She said he wasn't very artistic either. My guess is that he bottled things up and that's why people said he looked miserable recently. He was troubled but didn't have an outlet. His mum said he looked up to Grant though. There had been some talk that Billy might follow in his footsteps and go to agricultural college. It was early days though. He's still only fifteen.'

'His teachers think a lot of him,' Tommy added. 'He might be quiet, and he wasn't very academic, but they all said he was reliable and trustworthy. A good kid, that's what they said.'

Barry ran his fingers through his ginger hair. Still no breakthrough despite everyone's best efforts. What did that mean? Someone had been very thorough. Whoever the killer was, they might not have prepared the whole sequence of events, but they surely had some of the various component parts pre-planned and ready to activate. If this happens, I'll do that. If that happens, I'll do this. Just like a sequence in a computer program. So how many other actions were being held in reserve, ready to set in motion if needed? And did this idea mean they could strike some names off their list of suspects? Surely people like Neil Wilkinson or Dougie Dillon could never put together a complex plan such as this?

Or was he, Barry, just reading too much into recent events? He knew his boss, Sophie Allen, thought that chance may have played a big part in the awful sequence of incidents in and around the village. In this idea, only Grant's murder in Gloucester had been pre-planned, with the other assaults making use of opportunities that had arisen naturally. Once again, the self-same awful thought struck him. Was he losing his touch? Did he ever have the touch to start with or had his career rise, in reality, been made on the back of his boss's talent?

This was no good. It wasn't a productive line of thought. He realised that the others were looking at him.

'Let's call a halt for today. We're all tired and could do with some sleep. The super will be back in tomorrow and we could do with some fresh thoughts. The forensic report from the vicarage should be with us, so let's hope something shows up.'

* * *

At home an hour later, Barry opened a bottle of Chardonnay that had been chilling in the fridge while Gwen, his partner, was checking to see if the casserole that had been cooking in the oven for the past ninety minutes needed more seasoning.

'Surely it has to be someone local,' she said. 'Or *someones*, plural. And more than that, it has to be someone who knew those woods. What did you say? The woman's body was some fifty yards away from the footpath? That doesn't imply to me that it was someone just getting rid of the body quickly. Whoever it was, probably knew the best place to hide her, surely.'

Barry looked up. 'But there's an alternative explanation, Gwen. Maybe Bridget headed off into the trees, in an attempt to lose whoever was following her. But it didn't work. That's why she was so deep in the woods.'

Gwen decided that the food was ready, so she started spooning it onto the plates.

'I hope it's sorted soon,' she said. 'Our big day's only two and a half weeks away, Barry. I want you all to myself then, not you still worrying about this case.'

He put his arms around her. 'Don't worry. The boss has got it all arranged. That's why she wasn't around today. She was across in Taunton seeing Polly Nelson. The local case Polly was working on is coming to an end, so she's ready to take over from me if things haven't sorted themselves. Are all the replies in?'

Gwen nodded. 'Almost everyone is coming.' She rolled her eyes. 'It'll be one helluva noisy reception. What with a load of off-duty cops and all my Welsh relatives. You can guess what they're like when it comes to a singsong. It'll be "Land of My Fathers" at least twice. You'll be expected to lead them, Barry.'

'What? You never told me that!'

'I was frightened you'd do a runner on me. It's too late now. You'd better learn the words.'

'Oh, God. What have I let myself in for?'

Barry didn't sleep well that night. And when he finally drifted off, his rest was disturbed by dreams of drunken people singing loudly and gatecrashing the wedding, along with the troubling image of Gwen's brothers turning up for the ceremony wearing muddy rugby kit.

* * *

Surprisingly, he felt more positive the next morning when he arrived at the incident room. Maybe it was the fact that Sophie was due to spend today with the team. Her presence invariably cheered him up. Barry summarised the latest forensic report, detailing the findings from the vicarage. The report was thin.

'They didn't find much, did they?' Stevie said when Barry finished.

'I don't think we expected much,' Barry replied. 'We didn't spot much when we went across on Monday morning, did we? You were there, Stevie.'

'I know. But we'd normally expect more than that at a break-in, wouldn't we? We've all been at enough break-ins over the years.'

'But this is different. It wasn't a burglary, not as far as we know. Our guess is that it was always planned as an abduction.'

Stevie shrugged. 'So why was the place turned over? I mean, either it was an abduction or it was a burglary. Why are there signs of both?'

'We don't think there was any theft involved. Remember that the focus seemed to be on the vicar's office and paperwork. It was that kind of stuff that was strewn about, not cash or valuables.'

It was a good hour after the end of the meeting that Stevie came back to speak to Barry.

'I've checked through the receipts he kept in the desk drawer. There's one for a laptop from two years ago, a black Lenovo. But there wasn't one anywhere in the house. I've double-checked.'

'That's interesting. Go and find the housekeeper. See if she ever spotted one.'

CHAPTER 28: HIDEOUS THOUGHTS

Wednesday

The Kellaway-Brockhurst duo were on a morning ramble, hoping to enjoy the sunshine that was forecast for the first part of the day. They were both kitted out for an early-springtime country walk. Edie was wearing a cherry-red walking jacket, jeans and a red bobble-hat, while Minnie was in matching olive jacket and trousers, with a pale green baseball cap perched jauntily on her head. They'd walked down to the village green and were now heading back uphill along West Street.

'I never thought the interesting people in the village ever lived on this side,' Minnie said as they passed the church and the now unoccupied vicarage. 'All the people with any appeal were over in East Street, by us. Maybe I was wrong.'

Edie giggled. 'That's an evil thought, you naughty girl. But it's true. Bridget and Grant both dead. Does that make them interesting?'

'In a peculiar sort of way, yes. Then there's Gordon, the vicar.'

'Was he ever interesting before? Gordon the Godly?'

'Gordon the Gaunt!'

'Gordon the Gatekeeper, preaching to everyone about how hard it was to get into heaven,' Edie added, mischievously. 'He was always going on about it.'

Minnie looked askance at her. 'How do you know? You hardly ever set foot inside the church.'

Edie raised her eyebrows. 'I'll have you know that I was there several times.'

Minnie snorted. 'Yes, for funerals and that one wedding. And I was there too.'

'Ah, but I stayed awake when he clambered up into that pulpit. The pews were so bloody hard I couldn't drop off like you. You've got a fleshier bum and managed to snuggle yourself into a snoozing position, leaning against me. I had to stay awake and listen to him droning on about redemption and all the other assorted stuff. I used to stay awake by winking at him.'

Minnie suddenly slowed down in surprise. 'What? You never told me that!'

'I'm entitled to some secrets, you know. He'd occasionally look up and scan over the congregation. When I thought his eyes were passing over me, I'd give him a big wink, just to try and unsettle him.'

'Did it ever work?'

Edie sighed. 'Not really. I think he might have spotted me once and stopped looking my way. Peculiar man. Why wouldn't he want to look at me? Or you, even? I mean, what's not to like about us?'

They slowed as they passed the Kirkbride house. The driveway had crime scene tape secured across the gateposts and a uniformed constable stood in the porch. Minnie called to him.

'I don't suppose we can use our normal shortcut through the garden to the back gate? It saves us about thirty yards from our walk. Bridget never minded.'

He kept a straight face but shook his head.

'Worth a try, just for a quick look-see,' Minnie added quietly.

They walked on. Beyond the Kirkbride house the road deteriorated into a track and they found themselves ascending a steeper incline towards the distant ridge.

'You see, that's what I don't understand,' Edie said. 'Why on earth would anyone want to abduct Gordon? I mean, what use could he be to anyone? Awkward-looking, bony, holier-than-thou. What would you do with him? He'd be no fun.'

'You could use him as a prop in the garden. Or a bean-pole. It'll be summer in a few months, Edie.'

'Ah, that's it. A scarecrow! That would be right up his street. In the middle of a field, yacking on about all kinds of religious stuff to a load of cabbages. Just like his weekly sermons.'

They came to a fork in the path. The main track went straight on in a steady ascent towards the height of Win Green Hill, whereas the right fork would take them across the lower ridge, then loop eastwards towards the next vale, with its path heading downhill back into the village.

Minnie voiced concern. 'Is the path open, Edie? The police might have it closed it off if they're still doing forensic work where Bridget's body was found.'

Edie shook her head. 'We're fine. They reopened the path yesterday, according to Dougie. I wouldn't have suggested this route otherwise.' She threw her arms wide. 'Isn't it lovely today? Summer is on its way!'

They walked for another twenty minutes to the top of the high ground then started to descend. Minnie checked her watch.

'Time for a rest,' she said, unhooking her backpack. 'I've got a rug and a flask of coffee.'

'That's why I married you,' Edie replied. 'You're so domesticated. And organised. And cute.'

Minnie spread the rug. 'Flattery gets you everywhere, as you well know.' She poured the coffee and started sipping at her cup. She pointed downhill. 'See that little dell down there? The one with the bushes around it?'

Edie followed the direction of the outstretched hand and nodded.

'I think I saw someone down there once.' Minnie paused. 'Being naughty.'

Edie frowned. 'Who? And what do you mean, *being naughty*?'

'The sun was in my eyes so I couldn't be certain. He was kneeling in the grass. Might have been wanking. I think there was someone with him.'

Edie sat up. 'What? Are you sure?'

Minnie shook her head. 'No. I can't be sure. It was just before I got new glasses. Things were a bit fuzzy.' She was frowning.

'Didn't you try to get closer?'

'No, absolutely not. I felt scared. Anyway, it might not have been anyone we knew. It could have been a couple out having a good time, down from Win Green.'

'God. But I can just about imagine a few men we know doing it outdoors. Especially if they had a few drinks inside them. Neil? Dougie?'

Minnie took another sip of coffee. 'No, I don't think it was them. You know I don't usually get bothered by it, Edie. We've been to our fair share of exotic parties. We've even joined in. But something was out of kilter that time.' She was looking worried and didn't elaborate any further.

'Did they see you? Whoever it was?'

Minnie shook her head. 'No. Too involved with what they were doing, I guess. Anyway, I backtracked. Very carefully. Went back home the long way. Had a large G and T to calm myself. Not pretty thoughts.'

'No. Bloody horrible ones.' Edie took a hip flask out of her bag. 'See. I came prepared as well. Do you want a slug of scotch in your coffee? Take away those hideous thoughts?'

Minnie held out her cup. 'I was scared, Edie. I thought it was a bit sinister. Don't know why though. I mean, why should I have thought that? We've had our share of outdoor passion, after some of our picnics up here. I must have picked up on something that made me feel so uneasy. It was all a bit weird.'

'Who was it? Could you tell?'

'I've got some thoughts but I'm not really ready to talk about it yet, Edie. It's a little unsettling.' She turned to her wife and whispered a name into her ear.

They remained for a few minutes longer, observing the line of the ridge that stretched eastwards towards Salisbury, and the valley that dropped down towards Millhead and home.

'Is it worth telling the police?' Edie said quietly, as they packed the rug away.

'Maybe we should ponder on it for a while,' Minnie replied. 'I can't be sure of anything. That's the problem.'

* * *

Twenty miles away, in the intensive care unit at Salisbury District Hospital, a nurse was checking the medical equipment beside Billy Draper's bed. She called a doctor. Billy's parents were both in a nearby lounge having a coffee break. One or the other of them had been beside Billy's bedside for much of the past few days. They looked up as the doctor came in. She didn't waste any time.

'Things are looking up slightly,' she said. 'There's been a change for the better, just in the last hour or two.'

'Oh, thank God,' Wendy said. She hugged her husband tightly.

'I need to stress that it's still early days,' said the doctor. 'But we're in a better place than yesterday. You can go back through to his bedside, if you want.'

Wendy spent the rest of the morning holding tight to her son's hand and talking quietly in his ear about family holidays they'd all enjoyed together when Billy was younger. 'We'll do it again this summer,' she said. 'When you're better. Off to Tenby. You always liked Pembrokeshire, didn't you? Those fantastic beaches with the surf? What do you think, Billy? No need to answer now. Just think about it for a while.'

On the opposite side of the bed Ian was squeezing his son's other hand. He had tears in his eyes.

CHAPTER 29: SLUG

Thursday

Neil Wilkinson was feeling angry and confused. Why had this happened? How had it happened? His life had turned to shit. Was Sarah being serious when she said their marriage was over? It was that pesky sister of hers, stirring her up, filling her head with resentments. And the result? Here he was, having to kip down on Dougie Dillon's sofa rather than being in a nice comfortable bed with a warm body beside him when he woke up each morning. Instead, he was greeted with the smell of old cigarette smoke, spilled beer, stale food and unwashed clothes. He put his foot down on the floor. Ugh. What was that? Something cold and slimy under his right toes. He took a look. It was a small black slug. For Christ's sake, what was that doing in here? He used a finger to flick it back onto the floor. When was the last time this room had been cleaned? Thank goodness Sarah had never wanted to go to Dougie's place. She would have had a fit. There wasn't even a fully functioning hot water system, for pity's sake. Dougie had been complaining about it for what seemed like months but still hadn't got it sorted. Didn't he care?

Neil made his way to the tiny kitchen and put the kettle on. He looked in the fridge for some milk. None there. This was the pits. He got dressed, put on his coat and shoes, and slipped out to buy a few groceries at the village shop. Maybe he could ask other friends to see if they'd help. After all, that's what friends were for, wasn't it?

His first port of call was to the Kellaway girls, where he tried to talk them into renting him a room for a few weeks, but that conversation didn't go the way he'd expected.

'No, Neil,' Edie said.

'Absolutely not,' Minnie added. 'We're a married couple, Neil. We love our life and our home just the way it is. You'd completely throw us out of kilter.'

'I thought we were friends,' he protested.

Edie looked at him as if he was a naive young child. 'We are, Neil. But not that kind of friend. You're fine for a giggle on Friday nights. Anyway, don't you work from home?'

He nodded.

'So you'd want to be here in the daytime as well?'

He nodded again before he realised that this admission wasn't going to help his case.

'Certainly not,' came the reply. 'Impossible. Try your friend Dougie Dillon.'

They shut the door on him. Firmly. Was he really stuck in Dougie Dillon's little hovel for the foreseeable future? The situation was intolerable. How could he get any work done there? What with the smells, the perpetual cold and the lack of hot water, it was as far from being a comfortable workplace as it was possible to be. He couldn't even find a convenient electrical socket in which to plug in his laptop, let alone his printer and scanner. And as for broadband, well. He might just as well go and whistle. No. Time to face up to it. This was a disaster, and one of his own making.

Maybe Wendy or Ian would know of someone with a room to let. Sod it. He remembered that they wouldn't be there. They'd still be across at the hospital, by their lad's bedside. Their shop was being staffed temporarily by some cretin from a couple of villages away who seemed to know nothing about what was going on. Though she did have a very attractive bust. There was a thought. Maybe she had a room to let. He'd ask her. What was there to lose?

He got nowhere. Instead she glared frostily at him, particularly when he praised her figure. Why on earth did she take offence at such an innocent remark? It was a compliment, for God's sake. Why were people so touchy nowadays? He tried to think of other people to ask. Maybe he'd better return to Dougie's, get some work done and think about it a bit more. Something would turn up, surely. Maybe a visit to the pub was in order. Someone there might be able to help.

* * *

The Archers was busy, not unusual for early Thursday evening soon after opening time. Locals often popped in for a quick drink on their way home from work.

'So what's wrong with Dougie's place?' Fred Golbie picked up his pint glass and downed another large gulp of beer.

Neil rolled his eyes. 'Have you ever been in it, Fred? For any length of time? It's bloody disgusting. I don't think it's been cleaned for months. It smells of putrid food or something worse. Would you believe I put my foot on the floor this morning and stepped on a slug?'

Fred pulled a face. 'That can happen if you've got a log burner, Neil. The little buggers creep into the log pile. You bring in some logs and all kinds of creepy-crawlies come in with them. It's nothing unusual.' He finished his beer.

'Well, that might explain the slug but not the other things. It's all messy and smells of drains. I just can't live there any longer, Fred.'

'Well, don't look at me. I haven't spent a fortune on doing up my place for me and Roxy, only to have the atmosphere spoiled by another guy living in. No way.'

'It'll only be for a short while, Fred. I'd be gone before you know it. I'd soon find somewhere better.'

'Well, you can just find somewhere better right now. The answer's still no. Haven't you twigged there's a killer on the loose? It could be anyone. We can't help you. Thanks for the beer though.' He looked at his watch. 'I'd better be off. Roxy's expecting me back and she won't be pleased if I'm late.'

He got up and left. Neil remained in his seat, his head in his hands. Paul Sutcliffe came across from the bar to collect the two empty glasses.

'Cheer up, Neil. It might never happen.'

Neil stood up, angrily.

'Fuck off,' he said, and stormed out of the pub.

* * *

Ten minutes later Neil was back.

'Sorry, Paul. I didn't mean to be as rude as that.' He was looking sheepish. 'Umm, can I have another pint, please?'

'Sure,' Paul replied. He wasn't at all sure what Neil was up to. First the return to apologise after the insult. Then the fact that he'd used the words please and sorry. He'd never heard Neil say please before, not even when he was in the pub with his wife, or any other women. He'd once been heard to boast that saying please was a sign of weakness. Apologising, even more so. What was going on?

Paul soon found out.

Neil took a gulp of his fresh glass of ale. 'Ah, Paul. I was just wondering. Would you have a room to let in the pub? I'm in a bit of a difficult situation at the moment. Sort of homeless.'

Paul decided to gently milk the situation. 'I thought you were staying with Dougie Dillon? That's the rumour.'

'Yeah, well, it was only a temporary measure. See, I need somewhere with broadband so I can still run my business. And a bit of space to work. Along with some peace and quiet.'

'And you can't get those at Dougie's?'

Neil didn't say anything. He just shook his head and stared into his glass.

Paul looked at him levelly. 'I'll need to ask Mum. She's the boss, after all. How soon would you want it?'

Neil looked sheepish again. 'Soonish? Like, now?'

CHAPTER 30: ROOM WITH A VIEW

Friday

Sophie arrived from county headquarters late in the morning.

'Fancy some fresh air?' she said to her second in command as she stood in the doorway. Barry looked careworn.

He gave her a puzzled look. 'Should I be worried?'

'No, of course not. Not yet, anyway. I just feel a bit sluggish this morning and could do with a few minutes to clear my head. There's a cool breeze outside and the sun's shining, in case you haven't noticed. You probably haven't, have you?'

He shook his head.

'These things are important, Barry. I know you want to keep on top of everything, but you've got to keep some distance as well. Step back and give some perspective to things.'

Five minutes later they were sitting on a wooden bench, overlooking the village green. The only signs of activity were a delivery van outside the village shop, the driver unloading boxes of groceries, and a solitary dog walker, watching her pet as it cocked its leg against a tree.

'You're doing everything right, Barry. I just wanted a few minutes to give you that reassurance. Think about it. It's only a week since we were called in and look how much we've uncovered.'

He sighed. 'It's the fact that some of it has happened right under our noses. The assault on the Draper boy. The vicar going missing and his house ransacked. The place was crawling with cops and forensic people, yet someone still felt confident enough to go ahead and do them. That's what I'm bothered about. It's as if we weren't here, swarming over the place. Someone is very confident.'

Sophie shook her head. 'You're wrong. Someone is panicking. And badly. The attack on Billy Draper was botched. He's still alive and he's showing signs of improvement. And I'm wondering if the same kind of thing might have happened with the vicar.'

Barry seemed to relax a little. Sophie knew how important it was for the senior officer in a case like this to have opportunities to freely air their thoughts. When she was SIO in the past, she'd always used Matt Silver in that very way. It was equally important for Barry to feel he had someone to whom he could open up. She listened as he went on.

'You mean the fact that he was abducted rather than killed? I've been wondering about that too. The only thing I can think of is that he's got some information that the killer needs. Otherwise, why spare him? There's nothing to gain, is there? Not with two people already dead.'

'The other thing to remember is that if our killer's keeping the vicar somewhere, his hands are full. He can't really be holding on to a live kidnap victim and making plans for what's going on here, despite what TV thrillers would have us believe. He'll need to be monitoring what we're doing, trying to second-guess us. It'll be hard.'

'So you think he might make more slip-ups?'

'Well, he's made some already, hasn't he? Every time. The things that have come to light in Gloucester. The fact that Miriam Boateng spotted him up on the hill here. Having to leave young Billy still alive.'

Barry sat silently for a few moments. 'No real clues at the vicarage though. Not yet. The back door was very insecure and could have been forced open without a problem. Or maybe it was someone the vicar knew and he let them in.'

Sophie smiled. 'Give it time.'

'The vicar's laptop is missing. Stevie's checked with the housekeeper and she confirmed he had one. Nothing else appears to have gone.'

They both sat for a few moments longer before standing up.

'That's puzzling,' Sophie finally said. 'Other valuable stuff was left, wasn't it?'

'Looking for information, we think. Maybe something incriminating the killer.'

* * *

Rae and Tommy were back at the vicarage, having another look around, this time with the forensic report to hand. It was an old building, dating from Victorian times and probably worth a fortune if it ever came up for sale on the market, Rae thought. It had somehow escaped the ecclesiastical trend to either sell off such buildings and replace them with much smaller units for the local priests, or to split the buildings into apartments. It could be a worthwhile property purchase if it ever happened, but not one she'd opt for, even if she had the money available. This village was just too claustrophobic, too full of oddball people. She smiled to herself. In most people's eyes, she would come under that classification. Maybe she shouldn't be so condemnatory of others who lived their lives outside of society's somewhat over-rigorous norms.

Tommy was checking his way through a list, so she walked through the large porch, with its ornate umbrella stand, and outside into the garden. It had already been thoroughly searched, of course. It would have been a mistake of gigantic proportions to have reported the vicar missing, initiated a countywide search and then found his body hidden in the garden's undergrowth.

The church and vicarage were situated on a slight rise to the side of West Street, safe from the dangers of flooding. The back garden gave a view up the western valley to the grassy ridge beyond and she could just make out Win Green Hill in the distance. Turning through ninety degrees, she could make out the village cricket ground on the far side of East Street. Then, further round and along the river valley, she could see a gap in the trees where a small lake was situated, the one at the centre of the angling club row of a few years ago. No wonder there was an angling club. The village was fortunate enough to have trout fishing in the river and coarse fishing in the lake. She'd better not mention this fact to her boyfriend, Craig. He'd most definitely be interested in moving here, given such opportunities to wield a rod.

Rae went back into the building and checked on Tommy's progress. He was on the first floor, peering into the bedrooms, contents list in hand. She left him to it and climbed up a narrow set of stairs to a set of small rooms on the rather barer upper floor, probably servant accommodation in former times. She looked inside a small box room that appeared to function as a storage space. It was tidy, with most of the items stored in cupboards. One held several cameras. A single piece of amateur artwork was hanging from a hook on the wall. It was surreal and slightly unsettling, composed of strangely disarticulated limbs. She tried to decipher the signature at the bottom but it wasn't entirely clear. 'Corky', maybe? She wandered across to the window. It looked northwards, towards the high ground, but it also gave a view up the length of West Street. There was a gap in the trees, allowing her to make out the last few houses, including Bridget Kirkbride's cottage.

She looked at the neighbouring properties, close to the vicarage. A middle-aged woman was climbing out of a car that had just driven into the driveway of the next house. That building was also old and sprawling. Probably worth a pretty penny, Rae thought. These country villages tended to show the stark difference between the haves and have-nots of society, maybe more so than in many urban areas. The rural poor could often be at the bottom of the country's social heap.

Rae returned to the ground floor and spoke to Tommy, who'd completed the check of the vicar's valuables.

'Pay a visit to the housekeeper again, Tommy. There's a small room on the top floor that has a collection of optical kit. Cameras, binoculars. Even a telescope. Most are inside a cupboard, but I want to know if she ever saw anything left out for more regular use. Maybe a camera or binoculars that he took with him if he went for a walk. There are bird books on his bedside table, so I'd have thought he might have a good set of scopes.'

'Sure.' Tommy left and Rae wandered into the back porch before locking up. It housed a rack for walking sticks, although just a single solitary pole stood in it. Rae looked at it thoughtfully, then made her way outside. Instead of returning directly to the incident room in the village hall, she turned the other way and walked up the driveway of the neighbouring house. Her ring on the doorbell was answered by the well-dressed woman she'd spotted from her high viewpoint in the vicarage. She looked at Rae quizzically.

'DS Rae Gregson. I've just been in the vicarage checking things and I saw you drive in,' Rae said. 'I wonder if you could help by answering a couple of questions. It should only take a few minutes.'

'Of course, although I've already been questioned by one of your colleagues a couple of days ago. You'd better come in. I've just popped home to check the plumber has finished. He's been working on a bathroom conversion this week and messaged me to say he'd cleared up and gone. I want to check while there's still time to call him back — if it isn't right.'

'Please go ahead. I can wait a minute or two.'

Rae looked around her as they walked through the hallway. The walls were all wood panelled, with matching doors. It was simply stunning.

Left alone in the spacious kitchen, Rae listened to the sound of footsteps on the stairs. She looked out of the window. As expected, it gave a good view of the upper windows in the neighbouring vicarage, although the ground floor was obscured by the high hedge. She was still at the window when the woman returned. She'd brushed her dark hair, not that it had been untidy before. Rae noted the clothes she was wearing, practical but expensive.

'Everything's fine. He's a good, reliable tradesman,' she said. She looked relieved. 'I'm Sue Gazzard, by the way. As I mentioned, I've spoken to a couple of your detective colleagues, but only in passing. I own the local sawmill and timber yard and they came to interview one of my employees, Dougie Dillon. I think it was a DI?'

'DI Marsh, my boss,' Rae replied. 'I'm not following up on that. I wanted to ask you about the vicar, the fact that you live next door. He's got a nice collection of cameras and binoculars. I wondered if he ever goes out birdwatching or anything like that. Would you know?'

Sue frowned. 'He isn't the easiest person to get to know, to be honest. Like many church ministers, I suppose. They have a lot of responsibility, don't they? Worried parishioners and so on. They must get fed up with all the personal problems they have to deal with. So maybe a lot of them are as guarded as Gordon. I'm not a churchgoer so I don't really have many dealings with him. But I know that the people in the village who go to church think a lot of him.'

'So you don't know? About the birdwatching or rambling, I mean.' All Rae wanted was a quick, straightforward answer.

'Well, I did see him several times heading out with a backpack and walking gear. I guess he liked an occasional ramble.'

Rae pointed to the vicarage. 'There's a room there, high up, on the top floor. Do you know if it was ever used very much?'

Sue thought for a few moments. 'Not really. I caught sight of what could have been a figure in there on a couple of occasions. I can't be sure though. Even if it was, it could have been the housekeeper. She's well known for being a bit nosy.'

'What did you think of the vicar? On a personal level, I mean.'

There was a pause. 'He's fine as a neighbour. He keeps himself very much to himself. They're a breed apart, aren't they? Church ministers, I mean. He's okay on the grand scale of things.'

'And his housekeeper?'

Sue smiled wryly. 'Janet Rogers? She calls herself the housekeeper and so does Gordon, but she's no more than a glorified cleaner, really. She cooks him the occasional meal and makes sure his laundry's done.'

Rae wondered why this woman had offered more information than she'd been asked. Was some personal animosity at work? 'You said she can be nosy. Is that through personal experience or is it just village talk?'

Sue suddenly looked guarded. 'I don't get involved with local gossip, if that's what you mean. No, I've spotted her looking over here on many occasions. And she often peers in as she walks by.'

'Well, it is a lovely house, Mrs Gazzard. I can imagine lots of people feeling envious and wanting to take a look.'

'I come from a local farm-owning family, officer. I liked this house even as a girl. It was owned by my great aunt. She knew I loved it and left it to me when she died, knowing that I'd cherish it. I'm not rich but I get by on what the timber yards bring in, along with some investments I made when my husband died.'

Rae was on high alert. 'Sorry to hear that. So you own more than one yard?'

'I have another across the other side of Shaftesbury. There's not a lot of money to be made in the business, but, as I said, I get by.'

Rae pondered for a few seconds. 'Did you know Bridget Kirkbride?'

Sue spoke quietly, her voice controlled. 'Yes, although we weren't close friends. Circumstances, I suppose. She came to visit soon after my husband died to offer sympathy. He was in the navy and died in an accident during a yachting race, and Bridget heard about it. She seemed very pleasant, and I was grateful for someone to talk to, but we didn't really click. Different backgrounds, I expect. She was pleasant enough. I must say, it's a tragedy what happened to her and her son. Appalling. I only hope you catch whoever is responsible.'

'Oh, I'm sure we will,' Rae replied. She stood up. 'Thank you for your help.'

They walked back to the hall and Sue suddenly spoke. 'By the way, I know you haven't asked, but I would like to say that I don't believe Dougie Dillon was involved. I have no illusions about him. I know he's a bit of a rogue and likes the drink rather too much. But murder? No, not him.'

Rae walked slowly back to the vicarage. Was she any the wiser? Not really. But Sue Gazzard had been very guarded throughout their conversation. Was she always like that or was there a reason?

CHAPTER 31: SUSPICIONS

The WeSCU team was gathered together in the incident room for their late-afternoon briefing when Sophie Allen appeared, fresh from a meeting with the local forensic chief. She was holding a thin sheaf of papers, which she placed on the table in front of her.

'You were right, Barry. It was a probably a heavy stick of some kind that was used to kill Bridget Kirkbride. One of the guys from the forensic unit thinks it might have been one of these traditional walking sticks made of ash. I'm not sure why, though.'

Barry looked thoughtful. 'But it ties in with what our witness, Miriam Boateng, claims she saw. Someone hurrying after the first figure, carrying a pole of some sort. That probably makes me more confident that the rest of her story is true.'

Stevie spoke up. 'Do you think she needs another visit? Maybe she's remembered something else since we saw her last.'

Sophie felt pleased with the way the team were handling things. WeSCU was shaping up nicely. 'Good thinking, everyone. We're getting closer. Three things: Keep chipping away at the evidence, the stuff we have already and whatever comes in from Forensics and Peter in Gloucester. Keep looking for possible links. And do keep thinking outside the box. There's something here, somewhere, that's a bit odd. None of us can put our fingers on it yet. But it'll happen, trust me. If you have a brainwave don't be afraid to speak up about it. I'm heading back to HQ but I'll be in tomorrow for a longer session. Don't you just love it when you've got a problem as knotty as this?'

She slipped into her coat, waved and left.

Rae, open-mouthed, looked at Barry. 'Really? Love it? Not the best choice of words, surely?'

Barry shrugged. 'She is who she is.'

'Yeah, but you and I know full well what she's like, boss. Even Tommy, to some extent. As for you Stevie, welcome to the strange world of our boss's brain.'

Stevie grinned. 'But it seems to work, doesn't it? I never thought she'd manage to get more people out of our chief constable, despite what you said. Another eight arrived earlier, so we've nearly finished the house-to-house already. How did she manage it?'

Rae laughed. 'A bit of eyelash fluttering and bum wiggling, I expect. I've seen her in action. She rarely fails. It even works on other women. I couldn't believe it.'

Barry was looking irritated. 'Let's just concentrate on the case, shall we? Do we need another trawl through the forensic evidence, Stevie?'

The unit's most recent recruit shook his head. 'I don't see the point. Tommy and I went through it with a fine-tooth comb and crosschecked with each other. We didn't miss anyone or anything.'

Barry was trying to reason his way through a dense fog of competing thoughts, not helped by the usual sense of tiredness. 'Has anyone spotted a heavy walking stick when you've been carrying out interviews? What kind of person would it be? Motives? Think back. Has anyone let anything slip when we've interviewed them that we missed somehow? Mull it over and we'll discuss it again tomorrow morning. And we've still got the vicar to find. How does that fit in? Is he still alive somewhere, held captive or what? It makes no sense.'

Rae wondered whether to voice her somewhat vague thoughts. Was it the right time or should she wait until the next morning? In the event, the decision was made for her when Stevie spoke. 'That's the bit I can't make sense of either. What's the connection with the vicar? He was at the party Bridget threw, the one just before Grant was killed. But he must have stood out like a sore thumb in that group. The Kellaways? Neil Wilkinson? This Dougie Dillon character? And that ex-darts pro. I mean, a vicar in the middle of that lot?'

Rae made her move. 'To be honest, boss. I'm a bit suspicious too. I was at the vicarage earlier, with Tommy. I went up to the top floor, up in the roof space. There's a room with a side window that looks up the valley. Guess what you can see from there? A perfect view of the Kirkbride house. And you can see Bridget's back garden with the gate out onto the footpath. The cleaner told Tommy that there was often a pair of binoculars kept on a shelf by that window. And there's a rack for walking sticks in the back porch, but only a single lightweight pole in it. Do you see where I'm going with this?'

Barry scratched his ginger hair, his usual response to new, potentially worrying ideas. 'Are you suggesting what I think you are?'

'Think about it, boss. It fits. I might be completely up the wrong alley, but it does fit. And very little else does.'

Barry pulled out his phone. 'I'll call the boss back in. She'll hit the roof if we leave her out of this.'

* * *

Gwen, Barry's partner, noticed a difference in him that night. For the first time in more than a week he didn't have the look of a man with the weight of the world on his shoulders. He opened a bottle of wine. He smiled and chatted over their meal. He actually listened to what she was saying, even when it was about final plans for their forthcoming wedding. The evening went downhill after that though. Barry fell asleep after stacking the dishwasher and only awoke in order to make his way to bed, where, once again, he fell into a deep slumber. She wondered about disturbing him but decided against it. She knew how fitfully he'd been sleeping in recent nights. This was just what he needed, a night of undisturbed rest. She'd leave him be. Gwen suspected that the investigation had just opened up. She knew her partner and how his mind worked. Passion could wait for another night.

CHAPTER 32: SLEEPOVERS

Sarah Wilkinson wearily rose from her chair and moved to the window. It was approaching dusk, and the last gleam of sunlight caught a clump of daffodils in the front garden, seeming to set their petals aglow. What a difference a month could make. At this time in February the weather had been bitterly cold, but she'd had an apparently functioning marriage and, in Bridget, a close friend on whom she could rely. Here she was, just a few weeks later, bereft after the shock ending to that wonderful friendship and having made the momentous decision to end the constant stress of her relationship with Neil. Really, she should have known it would end up like this. He wasn't the man she thought he was when they'd tied the knot a decade earlier. She'd soon realised that after he'd moved in with her all those years ago. Had it always been a case of wishful thinking on her part? Probably. But her close relationship with her stepdaughter had made it tolerable. And now, with Bridget dead and Rosie away at university, what was there?

She pulled one of the curtains across and was reaching for the second when she saw a figure opening her front gate. A woman. Wearing a bright red jacket, black jeans and boots. She had shoulder-length dark hair, but her face was turned away, looking down the lane. She also had a capacious bag across her shoulder. The figure turned up the short path and rang the doorbell. Sarah finished pulling the curtains and made her way to the hall, where she engaged the security lock on the front door before opening it. Better safe than sorry. Or was it paranoia on her part?

A soft smile greeted her. 'Hi, Sarah. It's me, Sue. Sue Gazzard. I thought I'd pop up to see how you were.'

Sarah's puzzlement must have been obvious to her visitor because she quickly said, 'I'd better explain. I know I have a reputation for being a bit of a recluse but it's unintentional. I heard that you might be going through a hard time, so I thought I'd pay a visit.'

Sarah looked out along the lane. No car. She returned her gaze to her visitor. 'How did you get here? I don't see your car.'

'I walked. It's not a cold evening. It's a bit unusual, I'll give you that. For me, anyway. But these awful things that have happened have made me have a rethink. About my place in the community, I mean. I should be more involved rather than being viewed as the village widow, keeping myself always to myself. It's not a healthy state for me to be in, not in the long term.'

'Isn't it a bit dangerous walking up here by yourself? I mean . . . well, you must know what I mean.'

Sue smiled and held up a solid-looking ash walking cane. 'I've got my trusty stick,' she said. 'And a safety alarm that sounds like a ship's foghorn when it goes off. Oh, and I've also got some highly illegal pepper spray in my pocket. See? Nothing to worry about!'

Sarah slid the chain away and opened the door wider. 'You'd better come in.'

She hadn't been expecting any visitors, but a call like this was preferable to being stuck in the house alone for yet another evening. She took her visitor into the lounge, where they both sat down.

'I heard about you and your husband splitting,' Sue said.

'I don't really want to talk about my marriage. Or at least the ending of it.' This was true. She might be lonely, but the constant comments from other villagers hinting that taking Neil back might be a sensible move were beginning to annoy her. It was as if a woman choosing to be alone was still some kind of abomination, even though there were several men living by themselves in the village. Did they get the same kind of unintentionally patronising comments? Of course not.

'But you are missing your friend Bridget, aren't you?'

Sue's expression looked kindly enough, Sarah thought.

'We were close,' she said.

'I could see that. Look, I don't want to replace Bridget in your affections. That would be wrong. But I'd like to lay my cards on the table, as it were. I'm also a single woman, a widow, living alone. And I need a friend. That's what I've come to realise.'

Sarah looked at her for a few seconds, then relaxed. 'Do you want a cup of tea? Or coffee?'

'That would be lovely. Coffee please. And this is for you. Or maybe us.' She reached inside her bag and pulled out a bottle of white wine.

'I like your thinking,' Sarah said. 'Let's go into the kitchen while I make the coffee.'

Sue followed her through and waited while the kettle was filled. 'Tell me about your friendship with Bridget.'

Sarah repeated the story she'd told the police. That the duo had become firm friends while serving on the youth club committee together.

'See, that's where I missed out,' Sue replied. 'Childless. So I missed out on those kinds of opportunities. It had benefits, mind. My husband was away a lot. He was in the navy, so it gave me plenty of time to concentrate on running my business.'

'You own the timber yard, don't you?'

'That's right. It keeps me busy. I enjoy it, really. I'm what's known as an independent woman. Alan died in a yachting accident some eight years ago. I still miss him. He was a good man. But life must go on. I threw myself into my work even more and expanded the business. No kids to look after, you see. I had to do something to keep my mind off it.'

'Well, I'm not a mother, not really,' Sarah said. 'Rosie's my stepdaughter, Neil's child with his first wife. She's a lovely kid. She's what kept us together, really. But now she's gone, well . . . I'm really fond of her, but Neil himself?' She shrugged. 'Shall we take our coffee back through?'

The two women settled into comfortable chairs and sipped at their cups while they chatted. As the minutes passed Sarah somehow felt her mood lifting. She'd been in a dark place since learning of Bridget's death and, at last, this conversation with Sue had somehow lifted the mental clouds.

'Wine?' she suggested.

She went back to the kitchen and poured some of the chilled liquid into two glasses, replaced the bottle in the fridge, then tipped a packet of cheesy nibbles into a dish.

'Do you have any thoughts about what's been going on?' Sue asked after her first sip of the chilled Vouvray.

Sarah shook her head. 'Absolutely none. I knew Bridget better than anyone, I think. And what happened to her leaves me feeling at a complete loss. None of it makes any sense. Not to me, anyway. You?'

Sue sipped her wine slowly. 'I'm a bit like you, I guess. But I suppose I can take a more detached view of it. I didn't know any of them that well. Something deep's at work here. It's got to be, hasn't it? Something really nasty and intimidating. Something that's been kept hidden from everyone, but it's finally surfaced and all this is the result. Two young men. Bridget, the mother of one of them. Gordon, the vicar.' She took another mouthful, larger this time. 'You want to know what I think might be behind it all?'

She reached out for a few nibbles as Sarah watched her, her lips apart.

'Abuse of some kind. Involving those two boys.'

'God.' Sarah was horrified. It made some kind of sense. But the idea was too awful to contemplate. 'But Bridget would never have harmed Grant. She doted on him.'

Sue shook her head. 'Not her. She wouldn't have known.' She swallowed her small snack. 'No, I mean Gordon. I never liked him. There was always something there, something lurking in him.' She took another sip. 'I always kept my distance. He gave me the shudders.'

Sarah sat open-mouthed. Gordon had organised occasional sleepovers for the village teenagers under the guise of weekend bible-study breaks. Held at the vicarage. Rosie had gone several times. Could it be true? She suddenly felt sick.

CHAPTER 33: NO ONE HOME

It was back. The slightly grubby grey Ford, parked in the same spot. With someone inside, facing her way. Miriam went round the house, closing the curtains and checking that all the locks were secure. Should she tell Tom? Probably best to leave it. He'd take things into his own hands, go out and have it out with whoever it was. Not a good idea, not if Miriam's thoughts on the matter were correct. She'd just take a heavy poker to bed with her and ensure her mobile phone was fully charged and under her pillow when she turned in for the night.

When she'd completed her security check of the house, she glanced back outside through a gap in the curtains. The car was moving off. She phoned the police.

* * *

It was time to make his escape, he could feel it in his bones. Maybe it hadn't been a good idea to visit the Boateng house again. He'd had doubts during the half-hour drive across, but for once curiosity had got the better of caution in his mind. A bad sign. He'd caught a glimpse of someone peeping out through the curtains, only a few minutes after they'd all been closed. That meant only one thing. He'd been spotted. Now he'd have to get rid of the car, once he'd made it well away from the area. If she had access to binoculars, she might have seen the car's registration.

How long did he have? In the worst-case scenario she'd call the cops right away. It was late evening and things would necessarily take longer than in the daytime. Maybe half an hour to get the information to someone who'd take it seriously enough to act on it? Maybe another half hour for them to check the details, get stuck into the various databases that cops had access to, find the address of the place in Shaftesbury and get things in motion. Then another hour to get a squad together in the right kit for an armed response. Two hours, at best. More likely to be three or four. But it would happen, he was sure of it. No time to waste. Good job he was packed and ready. Half an hour to get across to the house, ten minutes to get the car loaded. He'd be away within the three-quarter-hour mark. And then a couple of hours to get to Birmingham. He'd unload, ditch the car somewhere out of the way and then make his way back to his hidey-hole on foot. A different county with different cops. Problem solved.

In the event, he was back in the loaded car well inside his allocated forty-five minutes, heading north. Shame. He'd have liked to get even with the Boateng woman, but it was just too dangerous. He'd made a serious slip-up with the Draper boy. He couldn't afford to make another one.

* * *

'Shit.' Barry was not pleased. He was standing in the tiny hallway of the small maisonette on the outskirts of Shaftesbury. Greg Buller, the snatch squad leader, smirked, and Sophie laughed.

'These things happen, Barry. I thought you'd have got used to it by now.'

'I suppose he might still turn up. I'll organise a watch on the place.' He looked at his boss, as if seeking her approval.

'Sensible,' she said. 'But I don't think he's likely to be back, not in the short term. Not here, nor back in Millhead. At least the villagers can relax a bit.'

'So it was the vicar all along?' Greg commented.

Barry nodded curtly. He was still angry. 'If only we'd had a few more hours,' he said. 'Everything happened at the same time. We had a phone call from Dr Boateng who'd spotted him outside her house, then one from Sarah Wilkinson. They both tied in with what Rae suggested earlier this evening. I could kick myself. If we'd acted sooner on Rae's hunch, we might have got him.'

Sophie thought Barry needed some reassurance. 'You made the right call at the time, Barry. Rae's hunch was exactly that. A hunch. It needed further checking before acting on it. Don't beat yourself up about it. I think he probably spotted someone at a window in Miriam's house. According to her, he drove off while she was looking out. He must have realised the game was up. If he'd done his homework on her, he'd know the type of organised person she is and that she'd act on what she saw. He's gone to ground somewhere else, probably well away from here, and we've got the job of tracking him down. We'll do it, Barry. Now we know for certain who he is, we'll go back to all the people who knew him and crosscheck every little detail they recall. And get Rae and Tommy busy on his back story, Barry. First thing tomorrow. His history in the church. And before. Something will give. It's bound to.'

'Who's the car registered to?' Greg asked.

'William G. Wentworth,' Barry replied. 'He dropped the William in all his church work. Everyone knew him as Gordon. Even the few church documents we've seen so far. He compartmentalised his life. Often the sign of something troubling. He registered the car to this address. It looks as though he led a kind of double life.'

Sophie looked at her watch. 'Three thirty. An hour before we get back home. Maybe a couple of hours' sleep if we're lucky. Will nine be okay for the debrief, Barry?'

'Sure. Not that I'm likely to sleep, not after this.'

'Try my trick. Hot chocolate. With a large slug of rum in it. It does wonders for me.'

'Hah!' Greg sounded put out. 'It was me that gave you that idea. Now you're claiming it as your own.'

Sophie laughed. 'It's one of my only vices, pinching other people's ideas.'

'Pull the other one,' came Greg's reply. 'I bet you've got loads of vices. I've been with you on some of your pub crawls.'

* * *

In one of the single-bed observation rooms in Salisbury District Hospital everything seemed quiet, apart from the gentle hum of the monitoring equipment with its banks of blinking lights and glowing displays. A soft light cast a somewhat eerie glow over the sleeping patients. A nurse wearing soft-soled shoes finished checking the last of the machines and made her way back to the desk in the main unit outside, ready to make the all-important coffee that would help to keep her alert through the rest of the night shift.

The patient seemed to be unchanged, still in a deep coma. But deep in his brain things were subtly altering.

There was no awareness, not at first. Was it just something vaguely visual? Or did that need some kind of cognitive recognition before it could exist? A slight greyness, in an all-encompassing nothingness of velvet black. Then a movement of sorts, not real motion, more a sort of swirl, even though there was nothing there to swirl. But it was there all the same. And a vague coming-together, even though there was nothing there to come together. But it was doing it anyway, like an empty eddy of thin air. Except that it was black and heavy and suffocating. But there was a misty greyness present, and it was still swirling. It wasn't black, not anymore. Indigo was there. And some violet. But there was still nothing there to be indigo or to be violet.

Then a softness. Some pinkish red. And this time it was something more tangible. What was it? There were no words, no sounds, no recognition, no awareness of anything. Not yet. Softness. Now it was here. Pink softness, pulsing. Throbbing gently. These words named the phenomenon. It began to coalesce. Like . . . petals. Or cushions. What are they? Things. What are things? What are these colours and swirls and pulsings? *Why* are they?

The pinkness forms into a sort of roundness, stretching. A gentle thing. A caring thing. What are these . . . words? Labels for things. Colours, shapes, mists.

Drifting. Floating. Watching. Watching the shape, the pinkness transform into something clearer. Mum's face.

What is that? What is *Mum's face*? Mum. She cares. Who? Mum. She floats. Her face floats then recedes. Another. It's Dad. Dad cares. Mum and Dad. They are saying things to him but he can't hear them. They fade. They're gone. He feels lonely, scared. Who is that? He can't see. It's black. Someone is there, beyond his vision, beyond sight, beyond reason. Someone. Someone who brings fear. Terror.

His mum's face returns, bringing soft red, soft indigo. She brings calm. He knows Mum. And Dad. How? They are his. They bring calm and safety. Not the other. Who is the other? The one who brings threats, like a snake. He's the one who rears up, about to strike. About to lash out, about to strike him with that . . . that . . . that club thing.

Who? Who? Who? The face. The evil face. Him. The snake. The serpent watching him, threatening him, scaring him. Him. The one who watches everyone. Who knows everything. The one who should know better. Him.

Eyes blink open. Dim lights in a pale room. He gasps. He murmurs. He groans, then screams.

CHAPTER 34: GAUNT FACE

Saturday

It was Barry's last day before a short break. Sophie had tried to talk him into taking a few days off a fortnight before his wedding, just to give him time to ensure everything was as it should be in terms of planning. He'd resisted, of course. In the end she'd secretly phoned Gwen and had a quick discussion. Barry was up against the two most important women in his life, and he quickly realised he had no room for manoeuvre. What was it with women and weddings? He finally gave in but insisted that he wanted to be present when Billy Draper was visited, a compromise that his boss thought was acceptable. So here he was, at Billy's bedside with Rae, Billy's parents waiting outside in the small family room. The lad was still looking extremely unwell, his features pale and sickly in the artificial light of the ward. He was extremely lucky to be alive, Barry thought.

'Billy, we won't be here long,' Barry said. 'Your doctor has given us just a few minutes. She says you really need several days of rest before you should try and remember too much. She doesn't want you getting too upset. But just a couple of comments from you might help us with our investigation. Are you okay with that?'

Billy nodded, his eyes only partly open. He was sitting up, leaning against a wedge of pillows. He reached out a trembling hand, taking a tumbler of water from the bedside table and sipping at the liquid through a straw. He then glanced at Rae.

'Yeah, I'm okay, I s'pose,' he said.

'That's good. I'm DI Barry Marsh, by the way. I'm the SIO on the investigation, which means I'm running things. You've met my sergeant, Rae Gregson, before, haven't you?'

Billy nodded again, then yawned widely. 'Sorry.' He looked sheepish.

'Don't worry. You've been through a tough time. And you've survived it all. We're really pleased about that. I need to ask you a tricky question. Can you remember anything at all about when you were attacked?'

Billy's eyes dropped. 'It was him. The vicar. He came up to me when I was on my paper run. I just came out of a garden. He was waiting.'

'Did he say anything?'

Billy shook his head. 'I don't think so. He just hit me with something.'

'Do you know why he did that, Billy?'

Billy said nothing.

'You see, he might have attacked other people: Grant, and Grant's mum. Did you wonder if it was him that killed them? I mean, before he attacked you?'

Billy kept staring at the bedclothes but nodded. Finally, he spoke. 'Yeah. I guessed.'

'Why, Billy? What made you think that?'

'He was doing nasty things to Grant, back years ago. He tried it with me.' Billy started sobbing.

'Thank you, Billy. That's all we want to know for now. I'll get your mum and dad in. Sergeant Gregson here will be back in to see you again, maybe later today or tomorrow. Whenever you feel ready to go on.'

The teenager looked up at him. 'Have you got him?'

Barry shook his head. 'Sadly not. Not yet. But he won't escape us. We've got every police force in the country looking for him. And you're safe here, by the way. There's an officer outside day and night, and another keeping an eye on the hospital entrance. No need for you to worry.'

'When do we publicise all this?' Rae asked as she drove her car out of the car park and looked for a road that would take them towards the A30 and Millhead St Leonards.

'Not yet. We have to leave Billy out of it anyway. But a couple of days won't go amiss. It'll give you a bit of time to dig around and see if Wentworth's left any clues anywhere. Once the locals realise why we're really looking for him they'll be at us with all kinds of stuff, most of it completely irrelevant.'

Rae wasn't convinced. 'I know it sounds a bit cheeky, boss, but are you sure you haven't decided that because you'll be away for a couple of days? Don't you trust us?'

'Of course I do!' he exploded. 'You should know that. The super agreed with me. Two more days to go through everything we have access to in the vicarage and elsewhere. Then we get the locals involved. That's the time to come clean with our suspicions.' He glanced across at his junior. She was looking shell-shocked at his outburst. Should he apologise or would that be construed as a sign of weakness? In the event he was beaten to the mark.

'Sorry, boss. I was only joking.'

He gave her a rueful grin. 'I overreacted.'

Rae smiled. 'The wedding's getting close, isn't it?'

He nodded but chose not to say anything. His phone rang, disturbing his chain of thoughts. It was Miriam Boateng.

* * *

Stevie and Tommy were interviewing villagers they'd identified as being particularly well acquainted with the vicar, although they were conducting the enquiries cautiously. They were not to publicise their suspicions about his actions, even though this made certain lines of questioning difficult. Stevie could see the sense of the decision. He'd been involved in cases where high levels of public involvement had delayed progress on a case like this. They were currently interviewing Janet Rogers, the vicar's housekeeper, again, in her home.

'That Sunday morning a couple of weeks ago, Mrs Rogers. Did you see the vicar then?'

She narrowed her eyes at Stevie, as if she was weighing him up as a potential gossip rather than a police officer on a murder enquiry. 'Not at the vicarage, no. I don't do Sundays. I keep my eye on the time, though, and if I can't see any sign of movement at the manse or the church, I give him a call. We can't have him not turning up for the service, can we?'

'Does that happen often?'

She shook her head, guardedly. 'Only once or twice. And that's in nearly ten years. Anyway, he was up and about that morning.' She frowned, as if trying to recall details.

Stevie waited. He didn't want to appear too curious.

'I think he'd been out for a walk. His shoes were a bit dirty.'

Stevie smiled conspiratorially at her. 'Well, that's not unusual for men, is it? Particularly in the country.'

She looked offended. 'Gordon is always meticulous about his appearance, something I approve of. Cleanliness is next to godliness, after all. Anyway, I clean the church as well as the vicarage. I don't see why people with grubby shoes should make my job harder.'

She wasn't an unattractive woman, but Stevie noticed that she'd perfected the kind of disapproving look that bordered on being sour-faced. She was wearing just such a look now. He needed to follow it up.

'Surely it wasn't that bad? A few specks of dirt, maybe?'

'It was more than a few specks, officer. And when I checked the vestry later, there was more. It usually only takes me a minute or two to clean in there. That time I had to take the hoover to it. Though he did apologise when I told him.' Janet only looked partly mollified. 'He had grubby marks on his trousers as well.'

'So you think he came straight into the church from his walk? He didn't go to the house first?'

She gave Stevie a hard look. He could see what she was thinking. A sudden realisation that she might have said too much, that all might not be as it seemed.

'Maybe. I couldn't say.'

Janet clammed up after that, so Stevie thanked her. The two detectives left.

'Well done, boss,' Tommy said as they walked the few yards to the vicarage. 'It fits, doesn't it? Late getting back and muddy shoes. He could have been in Gloucester at the riverside. Where to now?'

'We'll look through his coats and jackets. In particular, for one with a missing button. That would be the real clincher. Though he might have dumped it. I wonder if it's worth checking the local charity shops?'

* * *

Rae silently cursed as she turned her car around. They'd only just managed to extricate themselves from the traffic queues on the south side of Salisbury city centre and here they were having to return along those self-same roads in order to see Miriam Boateng. If only she'd called a few minutes earlier, when they were still in the hospital. Rae kept her eye on the road signs more carefully this time, checking that she was in the correct lane at each junction, ensuring that the short trip back to the hospital was rather less problematic than their arrival an hour or two earlier.

Miriam was waiting for them in her office within the spinal unit. It was functionally furnished, although there were several brightly coloured prints hanging on the walls. Rae thought they had a West African feel to them.

'I had a flashback,' Miriam explained. 'This morning, soon after I woke up. I saw his face. More clearly. So I sat down and added a bit more to the sketch I did for you. His face was thinner than I thought, a bit more gaunt. His eyes were more piercing.'

Barry frowned slightly. 'Are you sure though? If it was a dream, your imagination could be playing tricks. You know, merging features with someone else from your past.'

She looked guarded, upset even. 'No, it wasn't a dream. I was already awake. I'd had a shower. It just came to me from nowhere when I drew the curtains back at the window where I spotted him last night. I thought you'd want to see the sketch.' She sounded hurt.

Rae took over. What was up with the boss? He was so jumpy this morning. 'Of course we do, Dr Boateng,' she said, smoothly. 'Everything helps. Do you have it with you?'

The two detectives looked as the pencil image was pushed across the table top. It showed subtle changes to the original, with more detail in the cheekbone shading. Miriam had been right. Though the changes were not great, they made a significant difference to the character of the subject. Determined. Highly focussed. Angry? Cruel? Staring out at them from the sketch was the face of Gordon Wentworth, the vicar. Barry had been right to take the two phone calls of the previous evening seriously.

'Sorry for doubting you, Dr Boateng,' Barry said. 'You've been a great help.'

They were about to leave when Rae turned back into the office and had a few quiet words with Miriam.

'Don't take it personally,' she whispered. 'He's getting married in two weeks.'

Miriam smiled broadly. 'Ah. Explains a lot. I hope it goes well.'

'Oh, it will. I know his fiancée. She's lovely.'

CHAPTER 35: BILLY'S STORY

Sunday

Rae and Tommy settled down at Billy's bedside. The boy's mother was already sitting in a bedside chair, holding his hand. Rae thought that the lad looked a lot better than on the previous day. Perkier, with eyes that were less dull.

'How are you feeling, Billy?' she asked.

'Okay. I had bacon and eggs for breakfast today. The nurse said that was a good sign.'

Rae rolled her eyes dramatically and laughed. 'I can understand that. You must be on the mend if you can cope with that kind of food. You look a lot better than yesterday. You've already met my colleague Tommy Carter — think of him as a younger, much more handsome version of the DI.'

Tommy grimaced. 'Thanks, boss. We've come in to see if you've remembered anything else. Whether you've got your thoughts in order. But we don't want to pressure you, Billy.'

The teenager frowned, as if trying to concentrate. 'Sort of. It was stuff I didn't want to think about. You know, Grant and what happened to him. I was trying to forget it all, pretend it wasn't real.'

'That makes sense,' Tommy said. 'That's how most people would have reacted. It was only natural. When did it start?'

'About two years ago. I joined the cricket club about a year before that. He sort of helped out. The vicar, I mean. I didn't have that much to do with him at first. He did bowling and I'm no good at it. I got into wicket-keeping. But he kind of watched me. I didn't know what was going on, not for a long while. But he said nice things about my playing whenever we met. He had a way of making me feel good with what he said.'

Rae was listening closely. Classic grooming technique, she thought to herself. A gentle start, always positive and encouraging, gaining the confidence of the youngster, then, when things were right, moving in closer.

'Then he said I'd make a good all-rounder. He offered me some bowling practice. I didn't see the point, but he kept on till I gave in. He bought me stuff.'

'What kind of things?' Rae asked.

Billy shrugged. 'Cricket books. T-shirts. Trainers. He said he had a friend who could get stuff cheap. So he never wanted anything for it. Chocolates and sweets. Then he got me cans of cider. That was later, when I was at his home. He told me he had some good films and stuff.' His eyes dropped.

Rae spoke quietly. 'What kinds of films, Billy? Take your time.'

'It was normal stuff at first. Action. Fantasy. But then he gave me some cider and asked if I liked girls. I didn't know what to say. He put on a film with teenage girls, you know, in bikinis. Then they took them off.' His voice trailed off and he looked at his mother.

'Would it be easier if I left for a few minutes?' she said, tears in her eyes.

Billy nodded, so she went outside.

'It was sort of teen porn, was it?' Rae asked.

Billy nodded. 'He was sitting next to me and he put his arm round me and said there was nothing wrong with it. It was natural.'

He was looking increasingly tense and awkward.

'Are you alright to go on?' Rae asked. 'We could come back if you'd prefer.'

Billy shook his head. 'I don't really want to talk about it. But if he killed Grant, I've got to tell you. Grant tried to warn me. That's why he got killed, I reckon.'

He took a sip of fruit juice and closed his eyes for a few seconds as if preparing himself.

'He had his telly connected to his laptop. I went round other times and the films got . . . you know. And he put his arm round me a lot. I shouldn't have done it but he always gave me cider and it made me feel a bit drunk. Then he said we ought to try touching each other, just to see how it felt. So I'd know how to do it proper with a girl, later. And tell her how to do it to me. It didn't make any sense, not really. But I was kind of fuzzy.' The teenager was clearly struggling with his emotions at this point.

Rae saw the turmoil on his face and broke in. 'Billy, it's probably better if you stop. We're not experts at what he did to you, but we've got contacts who are. We need to come back with someone who can take you through this and get the details from you. But I want to reassure you that none of this was your fault. And what you experienced needs to be told, for your own benefit. Is it okay if we break off just now and take it up later? Can you tell us about Grant instead?'

Billy looked relieved.

'I'll go and get your mum back in,' Rae said.

Rae went out and had a short chat with Wendy. She was clearly still emotionally fraught afterwards but followed Rae back to the bedside, and grabbed her son's hand, squeezing his fingers reassuringly. This must be the pits for a parent, Rae thought. No matter how much reassurance she and her colleagues gave to parents in this kind of situation, they'd inevitably feel that they'd somehow failed in their duty of protection, that their cherished son or daughter had suffered an anguish that they, the parents, should have foreseen and guarded against in some way.

‘So how did Grant come into this?’ Rae said.

‘He’d been through it before me, that’s what he said. He told me that he’d spotted the signs and realised what was going on. That was back at Christmas, when he was home from college. He came to find me. He told me to steer clear of the vicar. He told me we should start to plan what to do. That we needed to tell someone but it had to be done carefully. But he got attacked before we could decide.’ He paused. ‘I was so scared. I knew he’d come for me.’

Billy looked totally miserable again and started to sob. Rae had an inkling of what was coming next. ‘None of it was your fault, Billy,’ she said. ‘That man is evil. He manipulates people.’

‘But it was,’ Billy cried. ‘It was my fault. He went after Grant because of what I said. I couldn’t help it.’

Wendy said, ‘What do you mean?’

‘I just stopped seeing him. It was what Grant told me to do. I avoided him. I crossed the street if he was ahead of me somewhere. But he waited for me at the bus stop one day. I tried to get away, but he grabbed my arm. I wasn’t going to tell him anything, but he guessed. I told him to stay away from me. He guessed that I’d been talking to Grant. He’d seen us together, talking. I didn’t say it was Grant, but he knew. I could see it. I thought Grant would be okay. He was a hundred miles away. But then I heard what had happened. I was caught in a nightmare.’

He sank back onto his pillows and closed his eyes.

Wendy looked aghast. ‘So was that why Bridget was killed? Do you think she found out?’

Rae spoke quietly. ‘It looks like it. And, somehow, she must have let slip about her suspicions. Neither of them realised just how violent he really was. Is, I should say. He’s still out there, somewhere. But I can offer you some reassurance. We don’t think he’ll be back this way. We’re finding out all we can about him, trying to trace his current whereabouts.’

‘But he’s a vicar. How does any of this make sense?’ Wendy was shaking her head, as if she couldn’t believe what she'd discovered since her son regained consciousness. 'How could he do all that? He was well thought of.'

'Camouflage,' Rae said. 'It's what practising paedophiles do. Work themselves in to a position where they can gain access to young people and get their trust. Maybe he believed in the work he did for the community. Who knows? It's not my job to speculate. We've just got to find him and get the evidence to put him on trial.'

'He was in the army for a short while. He told me.' Billy had been listening intently.

Rae looked at him with interest. 'Now that's something we didn't know. Well done, Billy. Another good lead for us to follow up.'

CHAPTER 36: MAP

Monday

Sophie Allen had been looking forward to this morning. Her new role heading up WeSCU currently involved far too much time spent on forward planning, talking to various chief constables or their deputies, and liaising with civil servants at the Home Office and the Ministry of Justice. She could cope with the former. She wasn't so keen on some of the civil servants though. Too many seemed to be ultra-cautious in their approach to new projects, and a few diehards seemed to still have a somewhat patronising manner towards women go-getters like her. It worried her. If this was what it was like with the home secretary, Yauvani Anand, on her side, what would it be like with someone rather more hostile? Though maybe that was part of the problem. It was very likely that Yauvani had ruffled a few feathers with her confrontational attitude and Sophie was facing the consequences. But here she was, back in one of the roles she loved, running a complex murder investigation, if only for a couple of days while Barry got his wedding plans sorted out.

Rae appeared with a mug of steaming coffee for her, pushing it across the table as she sat down, a broad smile on her face.

'Welcome back to where you belong, ma'am,' she said. 'If only Barry were here as well, it would be like old times.'

'Change is the only constant in life, Rae. Got to get used to it.'

'I think I know that better than most.' She took a gulp of coffee and spread some papers out in front of her. Tommy and Stevie did the same.

'I guess it's obvious we're on a new line in this case,' Sophie began. 'So the purpose of this meeting is to shape the way we go about it. Our aim is to find and arrest Gordon Wentworth, along with getting enough evidence for a conviction. It won't be easy. These people are adept at hiding their tracks and erasing evidence. He seems even better than most, judging from what Barry's been telling me. So we split our approach and spend the next couple of days getting the lowdown on him. We'll go public when Barry's back on Wednesday. Some of the locals have already guessed, so it won't alter things much in the village. Rae and Tommy, you get stuck into Wentworth's background. Follow up on that comment Billy Draper made, that he might have been in the army at one point. Track back through his church career. We need a complete timeline of everything he did since he left school, along with where he was. Stevie, you and I are going back to speak to all the locals again. We need to bully them into giving us every single little bit of information, no matter how irrelevant it seems to them. We'll use a couple of local cops to help us — the designated team for this area. They might have some snippets of insider knowledge that will save us time. You take that sergeant, Mark Riley. He seems a responsible sort and you said you got on well with him. I'll take his sidekick in hand. What was her name again?'

'Colleen Jackson.' Stevie didn't look enthused by this second suggestion.

'It's okay, Stevie. She needs a bit of a kick up the rump, from what I can make out, but I'll be subtle about it. It'll be my personal present to Wiltshire Constabulary.'

He looked relieved. 'Should we prioritise who we see first? Some of the team have picked up on bits of the local gossip.'

Rae broke in. 'Put the Kellaways at the top of your list. They looked distinctly worried — shifty, even — when I said hello to them late yesterday. Definitely worth a visit.'

Sophie was feeling pleased. It was always a good sign when the more junior team members made suggestions. 'You do that one, Stevie. Then move on to Sarah Wilkinson and Wentworth's neighbour. Oh, and the cleaner. I'll take Bridget's neighbours and some of the church regulars. Maybe I should do the people at diocese level, but we can make that decision later. If possible, I'd like to have a fairly complete picture in two days, ready for our Wednesday briefing. The other thing is this: we want any documentation relating to his work that contains personal details — who supplied references for him, who might have recommended him for the job here. There might be a bigger picture here, like in other places where rogue priests were quietly shunted sideways into rural backwaters rather than their crimes being brought to our attention for possible prosecution. That's mainly you and me, Stevie. Okay, everyone? Let's get busy.'

* * *

Stevie found a moment to sidle up to Rae before setting out.

'I hadn't thought of that last bit at all. I was so focussed on the goings-on here that I hadn't even considered the bigger picture.'

'Join the club. That's why she is where she is. Better get used to it, Stevie. You think you've got something sussed then she says something that opens up a whole different perspective. I reckon she's got two other targets in her sights. The people in the church who might have pushed him down to this parish just to get him out of their hair, hoping that he'd become a reformed character — out of sight, out of mind — and other predators who he might have links with. Don't be surprised if she brings in some specialists or taps up some of her ex-colleagues. You're seeing her at the top of her game. She's remorseless when she's on a mission.'

Stevie headed off to find Mark Riley, leaving Rae deep in thought, recalling earlier cases in which the super had somehow managed to wrench a case back from the brink of failure. The obvious parallel was with one of the first cases Rae had been involved in. The one with the skeletons of the two young children found buried under a bush in a back garden in Dorchester. Another case that had involved child abuse, albeit of much younger victims. Maybe it was that aspect that pushed the boss into finding an extra gear. Rae herself had contemplated suicide during the investigation, having been bullied mercilessly by a senior officer, but Sophie Allen had rescued her from a deep pit of despair. She would never forget. How could you forget someone who'd probably saved your life without realising it? Or maybe the boss did realise it, deep down.

Rae found Tommy, and together they started work on the task in hand: painting a detailed picture of Gordon Wentworth's life. Trying to identify some key turning points that would give them a start on tracing his whereabouts. It wouldn't be easy, not if he'd hidden his tracks as well as it appeared.

'Well, Tommy, have you made any progress?' Rae said, teasing her younger assistant. She was somewhat astonished by the reply.

'He was in the army but not the regulars. He was a reservist with the territorials. Twenty years ago. But not for long.'

'Tommy, you're brilliant. How did you find that out so soon?' Rae pulled up a chair and sat down, listening attentively as Tommy explained his methodology.

* * *

Meanwhile DS Stevie Harrison had collected Mark Riley and explained the task they'd been allocated.

'Our first port of call is this duo the Kellaway girls. They've managed to bemuse just about everyone who's seen them so far. Have you come across them?'

Mark laughed. 'Oh, yes. They were in a nasty RTA last year and I was first on the scene. I called in on them a couple of times to check they were alright. They seemed off the wall, but harmless. That's what I thought then. Should I change that view?'

Stevie shook his head. 'No reason to, not yet. We've seen them a couple of times because they knew Bridget Kirkbride and most of the other locals. To be honest, I'm a bit intrigued. They've managed to wrong-foot the other three at various times.'

'I can understand that,' Mark replied, and laughed.

In fact, the interview proved to be both orderly and efficient, with the two women seeming to go out of their way to be helpful.

Edie answered the door and listened attentively as Stevie explained the nature of the call. 'You want to know about Gordon? You'd better come in. There's something Minnie might want to tell you.'

She called through the house. 'Minnie? You're needed. It's the police again. That nice one who looked after us last year, after the car crash. They want to know about Gordon.'

Edie ushered the two officers into the lounge. 'We're beginning to get quite used to this,' she said. 'Detectives coming to visit. Different ones each time. Is that usual?'

'It depends on where we are in the enquiries. Things have moved on a lot since you were last seen.'

Minnie came in and sat down next to Edie but said nothing. Stevie noticed that she gripped her wife's elbow.

'You're both looking well,' Mark said. 'No long-lasting effects from the crash, then?'

'Not really,' Edie replied. 'A month or so of whiplash but a load of painkillers helped that. We did feel a bit drugged-up though, didn't we, Minnie?'

Minnie nodded but said nothing.

'We liked the warm, fuzzy feeling the painkillers gave us. Like brandy but different.'

Stevie decided to dive straight in. 'We're trying to find out a bit more about the vicar, Gordon Wentworth. So we're on a second trawl through the people who knew him.'

Edie stared at them; Minnie stared at the floor. Her hand tightened on Edie's arm. Finally Edie spoke.

'We didn't like Gordon very much.'

Stevie sensed tension in the air. 'Why was that?'

'There was something about him. We didn't really trust him, did we, Minnie? I don't mean the way we didn't trust Dougie Dillon or Neil Wilkinson. They're rogues. We know it and they know we know it. But Gordon. It was something very different. He's the vicar. But . . .' She let the sentence hang.

Stevie waited but the silence continued. 'Can you be more specific?'

Edie moved her arm and gripped Minnie's hand, squeezing it gently. 'Time to tell them, Minnie.'

Minnie recounted the incident she'd witnessed on the hillside some months earlier.

'But you're not absolutely certain it was Gordon?' Stevie asked.

Minnie shook her head. 'It was just before I collected my new glasses, so it was slightly fuzzy. But the man was kind of gaunt looking. That's why I thought it was Gordon.'

Mark broke in. 'Do you have a map? Could you point out where it happened?'

Edie pulled a walking map out of a nearby cupboard and spread it across the low table in front of them. Minnie traced the footpath with a finger and finally held it still.

'About there.'

Mark looked across at Stevie. 'That's where our witness said she'd seen the man with the walking stick.'

CHAPTER 37: MARTHA

'Come in.' Sophie didn't look up as the door opened.

'Ma'am, I got a message from Sergeant Riley that I was to report to you.' Colleen Jackson was looking nervous.

'I need some local expertise with me. We're going to do some more interviewing but this time with a bit more focus. We need the lowdown on the vicar and what people really thought of him. I'm standing in for DI Marsh for a day or two. You and Sergeant Riley probably know the locals better than most. I want to find out about any history he had with Bridget Kirkbride, so let's start with her neighbours. Ready?'

Colleen looked surprised. 'Yes. Ma'am.'

They made their way out to Sophie's car. 'We'll start with Martha Marshall. She lives right next to the Kirkbride house. She'll have spotted most of the comings and goings. And the vicar's difficult to miss.'

Colleen looked at her. 'Really? Do you mean they were . . . involved?'

'No, I don't mean that. But we think he might have been there more often than he admitted to us, and this neighbour might have spotted something. She's been living there alone since she was unexpectedly widowed a year ago. Do you want to try your hand at some questioning?'

'If you're sure, Ma'am.'

Sophie smiled to herself. Colleen looked on edge, clearly unsure why she'd been selected for this task. Let's see how this pans out, she thought.

Colleen rang the bell. The door was opened by a late-middle-aged black woman. Colleen stood stock still, seemingly unable to speak. So far, not so good, Sophie thought. She stepped forward quickly.

'Good morning, Mrs Marshall. I'm Detective Chief Superintendent Sophie Allen. I think you've already spoken to my colleagues, if briefly. We're trying to flesh out some background so we have a few questions to ask you. May we come in?'

Martha looked at her shrewdly. 'Of course. You're a bit senior for a house call, aren't you?'

They followed her in, ending up in the kitchen, full of the smells of cooking.

'I've given the DI a couple of days off. He's worked non-stop since we were brought in and he's getting married in a couple of weeks. He needs some planning time. Anyway, I like to keep my hand in. That smells delicious.'

'Jerk chicken. A couple of friends are coming in for a meal tonight. I'm preparing as much as possible in advance.'

'Very wise. PC Jackson here needs to ask you a few questions. Can we go somewhere we can sit down?'

Martha checked the contents of a few pans. 'Okay. Nothing's in danger of burning. Shall we sit round the table in here? How can I help?'

Once they were seated Sophie indicated with a nod that Colleen should start.

'Um, Mrs Marshall, it's about visitors to Mrs Kirkbride's house. Did you see many?'

Martha frowned, as if the question wasn't entirely clear. 'Did she have many visitors? Not really. The village is a quiet backwater, and up here is a quiet part of the village. Not many people come up here.'

'What about local people?'

Again the puzzled look. 'Almost all her visitors were local. She only had a small family. One sister, I think. A niece and a nephew. They came once or twice a year. Usually Easter.'

'What local people came most to see Bridget?'

'Ah, I see what you mean. Sarah Wilkinson was her closest friend. She was here a lot. Wendy Draper from the shop, but she's always so busy, so not so often. Lisa from the pub sometimes, but she's very busy too. How's Billy Draper, by the way? Has he recovered? That's what the rumours say.'

Sophie broke in. 'Yes, he came to yesterday. He's still very shaky, but the doctors think he's on the mend.'

'That's good. I was a nurse, you know. I trained back in Jamaica and came across to join the NHS, working in London. My husband was a dentist and I retrained as a dental nurse in his practice. He set up in Shaftesbury until he retired five years ago. He died last year.'

'I'm sorry to hear that, Mrs Marshall. It must have been a hard time for you if you'd planned for retirement together.'

Martha looked down at the table top. 'Indescribable, really. I still don't know what to do. Stay here or head back to London, where my family lives. I'll probably sell up and move back. Most of the villagers are okay but some aren't, if you know what I mean.' She looked Sophie in the eye again. 'When Richard was here it was fine, but I feel so alone now. And vulnerable. I feel like I'm on display all the time. It didn't matter when Richard was here, but it does now, particularly with Bridget gone. She was so supportive.'

Sophie waited to see if Colleen would spot the opportunity, but the PC remained silent. So she asked the obvious question herself.

'Did you get help from the vicar? We heard you're one of the more regular churchgoers.'

Martha gave a wry smile. 'That's not one of Gordon's strong points. He's a bit sort of . . . emotionally constipated. He doesn't show much empathy, really. And when he does it feels forced. Well, to me anyway.'

Colleen at last posed a good question. 'Did Bridget get on well with him?'

Martha thought for a short while before replying. 'She never said so. But he came up to visit her. Quite a lot recently. She joked once that he might be making a play for her. You know, wealthy single woman. Quite a catch, really. It was only a joke though.'

'Are you sure?' Colleen asked.

Martha looked at her shrewdly. 'Yes, trust me. She didn't like him, not deep down. Same as me. Same as some others who had a bit of insight. He's too . . . forced.'

'Could you explain?'

'It's just a feeling, really. Haven't you found him yet? It's nearly a week since he disappeared.'

Sophie shook her head. 'We're hopeful, though. So if Mrs Kirkbride wasn't interested in him in any personal way, why did he call so often?'

Martha shrugged. 'We couldn't work that out. It was a bit of a puzzle.'

'Did you see her in the two or three days prior to her death?'

Martha shook her head. 'I was in London for a family wedding. My niece. It's what's given me the idea of moving back. I felt I kind of belonged there in a way I don't here, not since Richard died.'

'Don't rush your decision, Mrs Marshall. Most of the people in the village think highly of you. That's what we've picked up on. And the ones that don't . . . well, their view really isn't worth considering, is it?'

Martha didn't respond, so Sophie decided to shift the topic back to Gordon Wentworth. 'Did the vicar ever talk about his background?'

'Not really. He always seems to be in-role, if that makes sense. He's a very guarded man.'

Sophie glanced at her watch. 'Time we were off. Thanks for your help, and if you do think of anything that might help us, please give us a call.'

Martha showed them to the door. Sophie sensed that the woman was intrigued by the focus of their questions but had held back from asking why. Maybe that would come later.

Colleen was silent as they walked back to the road.

'Think of this as an opportunity, Colleen. One with no comeback for you. You don't work for me. You're employed by Wiltshire Constabulary. You did a reasonably good job of interviewing Martha back there. You can do it when you try. So why do you have this reputation? What's the problem?'

Colleen shrugged but said nothing.

'If I had to line up the villagers and put them in order of usefulness to the local community, she'd be near the top. And the same for Dr Boateng across in Salisbury. And quite often the same for other people I know who are from ethnic or other minorities. What does it matter if someone's black or gay or was born in Greece? If they're contributing to society, they deserve respect. And they deserve to be treated by us, the police, in the same way as anyone else. I've seen what can go wrong when that doesn't happen. If the situation is tense enough, just a single misplaced word or action on our part can trigger something really nasty. I know what the future of policing is, and there's no room for prejudice of any type. There are enough thugs, thieves and hooligans out there. We don't pick needless fights with innocent people. What would be the point? We're stretched enough as it is. We need decent people on our side, not against us.'

Colleen's cheeks were pink but she remained silent. Sophie turned to face her.

'Everyone has prejudices of some kind, Colleen. It's part of the human condition. What we have to do, though, is to ditch those harmful ones when we put our uniforms on. Understand?'

'So this was a stitch up? This whole exercise?'

'If you see it that way, it illustrates the problem you have. I just told you, I've no axe to grind. After all, you don't work for me, you're just on loan. You can view me as an outsider and we can talk informally. I can tell you some truths, like the fact that people are worried about you. They think you have a self-destructive streak. They're concerned about your future, like what you'd do if you overstepped the mark sometime and lost your job.' She paused. 'At least give what I've said some thought. Now, let's head across the road and speak to the Baileys, then this Fred Golbie character. Which one do you want to take the lead on?'

* * *

Fred Golbie and his new partner Roxette, a buxom brunette with a throaty laugh, offered no new insight other than the obvious one. That the vicar must have had the hots for the attractive and relatively well-off Bridget Kirkbride to explain his frequent recent visits. He probably wasn't getting anywhere though, Roxette suggested. He was rarely invited inside Bridget's house and, even when he was, his stays rarely exceeded the length of time it took to drink a mug of tea or coffee.

'Not long enough for any hanky-panky,' she said with a laugh. 'And I'm a bit of an expert at these things!' She glanced at her partner. 'Well, me and Fred both are.'

'Did you get to know the vicar?' Colleen asked.

Fred stayed silent but Roxette laughed again. 'You must be joking! Church? Us? God, no. Weddings and funerals only. We can't be wasting time on that stuff, can we, Fred? Life's too short.'

'I s'pose he's okay as a vicar. Goes through the motions, like. That's what I've heard. Hard man to read, that's what they say.'

'Who's they, Mr Golbie?' Sophie asked.

Fred shrugged his broad shoulders. 'Well, the other locals. Village gossip, I s'pose.'

Roxette giggled. 'It's such a bloody dull place that the locals wet themselves over the tiniest thing. The vicar's eligibility. How many of the local cows are pregnant. That kind of stuff.' She rolled her eyes.

Fred didn't look particularly pleased. 'I like it here,' he said.

Roxette looked at the two officers. 'See what I mean?'

Sophie decided that they'd got all they would out of the pair, so they moved on to the final set of neighbours. The Baileys lived in a newish bungalow directly opposite Bridget's cottage. The owners had worked hard to make it blend in with the neighbourhood, with a carefully landscaped garden full of shrubs and perennial plants.

They didn't add much to the picture at first. Although retired and obviously middle class, they explained that they were both committed humanists.

'I can't cope with all that religious nonsense,' Valerie explained in a brusque, slightly schoolmarmish manner. 'Don't have time for it. Never did. Never will. Common sense. That's what we all need. Not some strange being in the sky who never seems to do what he should. And it has to be a he, doesn't it? Can you imagine a woman making a mess of the world like this? Pah!' She shook her head impatiently as if she had no time for any airy-fairy nonsense of any kind.

'So you can't really tell us anything about the vicar?' Colleen went on.

Valerie looked at her. 'Tall, thin, gave the impression of living a spartan existence.'

Sophie's ears pricked up. 'Gave the impression of?' she said. 'What do you mean?'

'Saw him once coming out of Tesco in Shaftesbury with a case of scotch. Doesn't add up, does it? See what I mean about the deficiencies of men? Can't stay away from the drink, can they?' She glared at her husband, who shrank back his chair looking sheepish. Sophie guessed that he indulged himself with a tipple rather more than his wife approved of.

'You saw him across in Shaftesbury?'

'That's what I said. I was there with some ex-work colleagues, celebrating someone's birthday. About a year ago.'

'You're sure it was him?'

'It was either him or a doppelganger. I remembered it because it didn't seem to add up. He preaches about the evils of alcohol during his sermons, apparently. That's what other people in the village tell me. I'm not surprised though. So many of them are hypocrites, aren't they? Maybe not as bad as politicians, but even so.'

Sophie handed over a contact card before leaving. She turned to Colleen as they drove back to the incident room. 'Well, maybe that was worthwhile after all. How did you find it?'

The PC looked a little sheepish. 'Okay. I'll think about what you said, ma'am. I don't know what I'd do if I wasn't a copper. Thanks for being honest with me.'

As they climbed out of the car at the incident room they were met by Tommy Carter. 'A coat with a missing button has turned up, ma'am. In a charity shop in Shaftesbury. It matches the description the vicar's cleaner gave us and the man who took it in sounds like him. I've asked them to hang onto it. Should I go across and collect it?'

'Of course. Take a photo of Wentworth with you. Good stuff, Tommy. It was worth pursuing.'

* * *

After the morning spent with Colleen Jackson in the village, Sophie experienced a rather more difficult time probing Gordon Wentworth's background within the church. In terms of their willingness to be helpful to her, the staff she spoke to fell into two main camps: those who openly expressed a sense of shame about the church's history of hushing up cases of child abuse — and, consequently, were only too willing to give her the help she needed — and those who still seemed somewhat reluctant to be frank. The latter spoke very guardedly and picked their words carefully. They came across as being defensive, as if it was the institution of the church that was being investigated rather than a single vicar, and that its reputation had to be defended at all costs. Couldn't these people see that was the worst line to take? This split was unpredictable. It didn't seem to be related to either age or gender. All Sophie could tell was that some people she contacted were extremely helpful and others were markedly less so. In the end, though, she got the information she wanted.

The younger Gordon Wentworth had trained for the ministry in Coventry and had, at the same time, signed up as an army reservist. As far as the college training tutors were concerned, he'd balanced the two conflicting demands extremely well. Most of the army training had taken place during college holiday periods. It rarely caused a clash with his studies.

The single most interesting point to come out of Sophie's probe into his training years was the option Wentworth had chosen during the third year of his studies. He'd elected for a course on 'Young People and the Church'. Had all of this been carefully planned in advance? Or had the teenagers he'd come into contact with during those sessions awakened a hitherto dormant malignancy? Nothing in the official records of his training hinted at an unhealthy interest in teenagers, but Sophie never expected any such comment to have been recorded. It would have made the tutor writing the notes somehow complicit in serious subterfuge. No, if there had been any suspicion of deviancy, he would surely have been required to leave the college. Of course, this had all happened before many of the wider scandals came to light in the media. The churchman who had severely beaten teenage boys in a grotesque distortion of the idea of 'finding God through suffering'. The sexual abuse of teenagers, targeted at vulnerable youngsters within the care system, often orphans and abandoned children. Sophie felt a sense of fury just thinking about the schemes these twisted people came up with, the care with which they went about identifying and grooming potential victims. How many adolescents had been mistreated in such ways? Hundreds? Thousands? She remembered the first time she and Martin had gone to see the film *Spotlight*, the story of the *Boston Globe* investigative team who had uncovered rampant abuse within the Catholic Church in the USA. They'd come out of the cinema in shocked silence. Sophie because she felt that some Boston police officers must have known about the exploitation that had been going on, and Martin because, as a senior teacher aware of the vulnerability of many young people, he felt so much sympathy for the young victims and so much rage against the perpetrators, whatever positions they held in society.

CHAPTER 38: WEDNESDAY BRIEFING

Barry arrived back in the incident room in a much lighter and more positive mood than before he'd taken his two days' leave. Sophie saw the change in him right away. He actually smiled, then cracked a joke with Stevie and Tommy about the perils of wedding planning. He and Gwen had obviously managed to get most things sorted. Sophie saw him glance across at her, so she gave him a wink. He smiled back, a somewhat shy look on his face that was vintage Barry.

'I'm heading up to the West Midlands,' she said. 'My old boss, Archie Campbell, will be retiring soon. I want to pick his brains a bit. He was on an investigation with me some ten years ago when we cracked a child abuse case. I wasn't directly involved but there was an overlap with some witness intimidation I was investigating. He might have a clearer memory of it than me. He's checking out some of the files for me. With you back, Barry, I can afford to disappear for a couple of days. I might call in to Gloucester on the way and check on the state of play there.'

Barry took over the meeting. 'Any more information about Wentworth's background?'

Tommy was the first to answer. 'Three things. We're pretty certain the coat taken to a charity shop last week was his. It's in for analysis. And we also found he was an army reservist when he was a lot younger. That ties in with what Billy told us.'

'Well, that's useful to know,' Barry said. 'See if there's anything on his record that might be relevant. Anything else?'

Stevie continued. 'He'd planned his finances very carefully. His accounts have all been cleared out. It looks like he made big transfers in recent weeks to an online bank and from there made conversions to cryptocurrency. He's probably changed it back by now and has an account in another name. Whether we can ever trace it is doubtful. Sorry. Bad news, I know.'

Barry listened carefully as the unit members recounted summaries of their interviews with locals. The story Stevie told about Minnie Kellaway's recollections of the incident on the hillside was particularly interesting.

'It's a shame she can't be sure it was him up there,' Barry said. 'No clue as to who he was with?'

'None at all,' Stevie replied. 'It might have been a youngster but there's no way of knowing. By the way, a couple of residents in East Street think they saw the vicar walking past their homes on the morning Bridget Kirkbride was killed. In the downhill direction, heading back to the vicarage.'

'Any news on the walking stick, the one Forensics think was used to hit Bridget?'

This question was met with shaking heads all round. It hadn't turned up in any search, either of the vicarage or the small maisonette in Shaftesbury. Barry wondered if that meant Wentworth still had it with him somewhere. Surely not. Wouldn't he have got rid of it? Squads had searched through every disposal bin in the village, but the offending cane hadn't turned up.

'Did anyone have any idea as to his possible whereabouts now?' Barry asked. 'That has to be the focus of our efforts from this point on. We've got to find him. And time's running out.'

'Just the one,' Sophie said. 'Valerie Bailey, Bridget Kirkbride's neighbour. She claimed to have spotted him once in Shaftesbury. Carrying a case of scotch out of a local supermarket.' She shrugged, as if she was unsure as to the reliability of this information.

Rae shifted in her seat. 'Ma'am, there were a couple of bottles of scotch in the vicarage. Not in the drinks cabinet downstairs, where you'd expect them to be. These were in the top-floor loft room, the one with the good view up the valley towards the Kirkbride house. One was open. There was a single tumbler in the cupboard as well.' She raised her eyebrows.

'What are you saying, Rae?' Barry asked.

'Well, it kind of suggests things, doesn't it? Did he sometimes sit up there watching Bridget's house through the binoculars and sipping a glass of scotch? Why else would the whisky and the glass be there?'

Sophie broke in. 'In which case, the purchase in Shaftesbury might be significant. You need to know what I found out about his ecclesiastical training but I'm in a bit of a rush. Barry can fill you in. I brought him up to date earlier. Can I suggest that Tommy tries to find out a bit more about Wentworth's time as an army reservist? There might be something there that gives us a lead of some kind.' She paused and glanced at her watch. 'I'd better be off. Great stuff, everybody. We're getting there but we need to bear something else in mind. We've been assuming that he's been acting alone. But that isn't always the case with predators like him. He could be working in league with others. And ask yourself this: why did he end up in this village? Why here, specifically? Wouldn't an urban environment give richer pickings for someone like him? What if he was working in league with someone else here? We need to consider it, even if it is an awful thought.'

With that she turned and left.

* * *

It was lunchtime before Sophie found herself in the reception area at the West Midlands police headquarters. She looked up as Archie Campbell appeared through a door. Sophie thought he was beginning to look his age. He must be close to retirement, surely? He'd been her boss during her stint as a DI in the West Midlands Serious Crime Squad and they'd got on extremely well. Neither of them had forgotten the great team they'd built up in those productive years. He almost skipped across the gap to the row of chairs where she was sitting, a wide grin on his face. His face had thinned since she'd seen him last, at her father's funeral some five years earlier, and his sandy-coloured hair was sparser. He flung his arms around her.

'You're like a ray of sunshine on a dark day, Sophie. I thought we could go out to lunch. Okay?'

She laughed. 'Being wined and dined is right up my street, as you well know, Archie. I think I can stretch the length of my visit to include a nice lunch. Do you still use that little Italian place? What was it? The Amalfi?'

He nodded. 'It's still there. And the food is still as good as it was back in the day. It'll be a nice change. I don't get out of the office much, as a rule. I thought we could talk more freely there.'

'Well, that's one excuse. I'm sure you've got a string of them.'

It was only a five-minute walk to the small, family-run restaurant. Sophie couldn't believe that she was welcomed at the door by the same manager as when she'd worked in the West Midlands unit a decade earlier. 'Luigi?' she said, tentatively. 'Have I got the name right?'

The manager stepped back, a broad smile on his face. He bowed, somewhat dramatically. 'You remembered! Now, let me show you to your table. We haven't changed the Bolognese recipe since you were here last.'

Sophie laughed. 'I'm amazed! No need for me to see the menu, then. You know what I'll have.'

'And your husband? How is he?'

'He hasn't changed, Luigi. Not really. He's still got the same sense of humour. He's a deputy principal now. But we're both getting older. We really need to talk about our futures, but we never seem to have time.'

They were shown to their table and started the serious part of their meeting once the restaurant manager had withdrawn.

'I've looked over the file you asked for,' Archie said. 'You know that my gut instinct is that someone got away, that day the house in Wolverhampton was raided. Several of the victims gave us detailed statements about their abusers. And it didn't quite add up, not in terms of the people we had under lock and key. Do you want to go back and see the place after we've finished here?'

This took Sophie by surprise, and it showed on her face. 'What? Hasn't it been sold or something? I imagined it would be someone's home by now.'

Archie shook his head. 'It became too notorious. It's due for demolition sometime but the developer wants to do the whole block in one go. So we still have access to it. I don't know how relevant it'll be to your current case though. What are the chances that the same person was involved? We are talking ten years ago, after all.'

Sophie took a sip of water and tucked a loose strand of hair behind her left ear. 'Greater than you think. He was a local curate at the time and lived only a couple of miles away.'

CHAPTER 39: HOUSE OF EVIL

Sophie shivered, wrapped her coat more closely around herself and took a moment to get her bearings. The vague memories began to coalesce. Yes, she remembered that unusual stairway now. She'd forgotten about that peculiar kink in the stairs halfway up, along with the colour of the paint, a dingy shade of sludge brown, and the mustard-coloured wallpaper, even more faded and grubby after the accumulation of ten years of dust.

She turned her mind back to the bend in the stairs. She'd been standing on this very spot a decade earlier, having just arrived. The abusers had already been taken away. As she'd stood at the bottom of the stairway, looking upwards, a silent group of empty-eyed teenagers appeared, led down the stairs by two paramedics, and followed by a doctor. The youngsters had blankets around their shoulders. She heard a noise behind her and turned in time to see a line of wheelchairs being brought into the hallway. She stood back against the wall, to allow the group to complete their slow trek down to the waiting line. She could never forget the expressionless faces of those young people. They'd been drugged, of course. Maybe kept drunk as well. They looked pale and empty, totally washed out. Was that the state of their minds too? They filed past, not speaking, and allowed themselves to be lowered into the waiting chairs, then wheeled out to the ambulances.

She came back to the present. Where were they now, those seemingly lost souls? Had they made new lives for themselves? Had they managed to complete some semblance of an education? Did they have jobs, relationships, even families of their own? Or had their experiences inside that house of evil scarred their futures so deeply that no normal life would ever be possible for them? Some of them, but certainly not all, might have responded well enough to therapy. Sophie remembered the emotion she'd experienced during those few seconds. She'd rarely felt so helpless during the whole of her career, not before and not since.

She and Archie climbed the stairs to the upper floor. She turned to him. 'This place shouldn't still exist,' she said, her face pale. 'It should have been flattened already. Wiped from the face of the earth. I can still feel it, that sense of evil. It's still lurking here.'

Archie nodded. 'I understand how you feel. Looks like you'll get your wish eventually.'

They were now standing on the landing at the top of the stairs. A dim light came through a small, grubby window covered by a torn net curtain. Archie pointed to an open doorway halfway along the landing. 'This is what I wanted you to see.'

Sophie walked slowly towards it, pushed the door open wider and stepped inside.

'I was in here!' she gasped. 'I came in and looked around. I remember. There was something strange about it. What was in here?'

Archie opened the file he was carrying and took out a photo. 'A bed against the right wall. A wardrobe opposite. A chest of drawers by the door. But it wasn't that I wanted you to see. Look at that shadowy area nearly hidden by the wardrobe.'

Sophie walked across and examined the surface carefully. 'It's a covered recess!' she said. 'Does it open?'

'Apparently so.' He looked again at the notes, then moved forward and gently tugged on a hook that was attached to the panel surface. The whole face swung towards him, revealing a narrow space behind. 'We wonder if someone was in here, hiding. If so, he got clean away.'

'I only came part way in,' Sophie whispered. 'I stood just inside the doorway and looked around. I was going to have a poke around in here, but someone shouted from a room further along that they'd found another victim, a young girl. I was the closest female officer so I went to help. She'd been hiding under a bed, scared out of her mind by all the noise earlier on, during the raid.' She stopped for a moment. 'I never came back in here.'

She took a closer look at the moveable panel. 'There's a hole at eye level. Was someone in here, looking out?'

Archie nodded grimly. 'We think so. The team that was running the raid think there was one more man here. One of the abusers let it slip under questioning but then clammed up.' He held up the file. 'It's all in here.'

'So whoever it was, they were watching me.' Sophie shook her head as if trying to clear her mind and allow her to focus better on this one set of events. It didn't work. No more memories or thoughts appeared. After all, what else was there? She hadn't been on the team running the investigation, and Archie, in his senior role, hadn't been directly involved. This was the extent of it. A dingy house in a rundown side street, but one with a shocking history. A police file that contained a summary of all the relevant evidence that the detectives involved in the investigation had discovered. And the memories of the victims, their lives probably altered forever, maybe ruined forever, by their experiences.

'Let's get out of here,' Sophie said. 'I've seen enough. I'm finding it difficult to cope with, Archie. The fact that I was here, in this room. So close. So unbelievably close.'

They left the room, returned to the ground floor and walked out of the front door onto the street.

'I don't want to come back here again,' Sophie said. 'Not ever.'

'But has it been useful?' Archie questioned, watching her closely.

'Christ, yes. I feel sick with anger. You know the problem, Archie. When you're in charge you've got to stay slightly distant, stay in control in order to keep everything together. You keep the rawness at bay. You've got to, otherwise everything would go to pot. But just sometimes it's good to get that anger back, that feeling of utter fury that people can behave like that towards others. And it's worse when it's kids on the receiving end. They were all vulnerable, were they?'

Archie nodded. 'In one way or another. Broken homes, poverty, isolation, feelings of powerlessness. Just like all the other cases up and down the country. The kids don't realise they've been carefully targeted. They take the clothes, the booze and the drugs, thinking someone cares for them.' He paused. 'I don't have to tell you this. You know it already.'

Sophie stayed silent, thinking hard, as they closed the door of the house and walked back to the car. She waited until they were back in the ACC's office at police headquarters before speaking up.

'Archie, I think the case needs to be reopened. You won't get an official request from me until I've had time to study the file. But unless the material inside tells me I'm on the wrong track completely, that's what I'll be angling for. I think there's a chance he's our man. We're still collecting evidence back at my place, but when we put it all together, if we think there's a connection, that's what I'll do. Put in an official request. It's better if you know now.'

'Okay. It means I can start thinking about how we do it. Are you sure though?'

'No, I'm not sure. How can I be? But it all fits. As I said earlier, Wentworth was here as a curate, at the right time. He was involved with youth work. We think he's learned to watch and wait before acting. He's a meticulous planner. He has an uncanny knack of getting away just before the net closes in on him, just like your missing guy from that raid.' She tapped the file. 'There may be stuff in here that gives me more confirmation. And you don't have to worry too much. It'll be me up here, in charge, if you agree. I'll bring someone from my team with me. Best of all, I'm still getting Home Office funding. If I do the planning right, it might not cost you a bean. What's not to like?'

Archie laughed. 'You scheming scoundrel, you! But I like the sound of it. Let's go and get a coffee.'

* * *

Sophie decided to pay a visit to the area of Wolverhampton where Wentworth had worked for several years as a parish curate, based at St Oswald's Church. It was an area she didn't know well, even though she'd spent nearly a decade working in the West Midlands. It was in a semi-rural area situated to the south-west of the city and had always experienced a much lower crime rate than much of the urban sprawl to the north and east. She parked her car near the church and took a walk around. She guessed that Wentworth might have had accommodation in one of the old, terraced buildings nearby. Some had been owned by the parish, according to the information Rae had messaged to her.

The church building itself dated from the seventeenth century. Old, but not archaic. It seemed to be relatively peaceful, although the usual urban hum of traffic provided a constant backdrop. The church was empty apart from a woman setting out some flowers near the entrance. Sophie decided a chat was in order.

'Lovely flowers,' she said, walking over.

The woman, short and dumpy, looked up in surprise. 'Oh, I didn't hear you. It's an age thing, I expect. They're nice, aren't they? The local florist is quite generous. Some of the blooms they've got left over are kept for us. I collect them early in the morning and set them out here. We don't get a long display from them but it's better than them going to waste.'

'Have you been a volunteer here for very long?' Sophie asked.

The woman pulled a face. 'Longer than I want to admit to. I'm local. I've never lived anywhere else.'

Sophie thought carefully. She needed to do this right. 'I'm a police officer. I'm investigating the disappearance of a vicar, Gordon Wentworth. He used to be a curate here many years ago. Did you ever come across him?'

The woman frowned. 'The name's familiar. It's hard to remember though. Was he tall with sandy hair?'

'That sounds like him.' Sophie waited as the woman stood deep in thought, her face screwed up in concentration.

'See, curates only stay a few years. It's hard to remember them all. The vicar might know more. I remember him, but he wasn't easy to get to know. A bit distant, if you know what I mean. I think he left under a bit of a cloud, but I never found out why. He was here, and then he was gone. Really sudden, like. That's if I've remembered right. Why?' She was frowning again.

'As I said, we're just trying to trace him.'

That seemed to satisfy the woman. 'Mebbe the vicar can remember more. He ought to, eh? He works with the curates.'

'What's your name?' Sophie asked.

'Dolly Knightley. Everyone to do with the church knows me.'

'Well, thanks for the information, Dolly. Maybe I'll check with the vicar.'

On her way out of the churchyard entrance, Sophie stopped at the ornate information sign to study its contents more closely. The vicar's name was Marcus Dunn and, according to the gold-lettered text on the blue notice board, he'd been the minister for fifteen years. The current curate was Lillian Beckton. She walked on to the vicarage, situated two houses along from the church, and rang the doorbell. It was answered by a grey-haired woman in her fifties who said she was the vicar's wife. In answer to Sophie's question, she explained that both the vicar and the curate could be found in the parish office, next door.

In fact, the vicar wasn't there. Lillian, a youthful-looking, dark-haired woman in her twenties, explained that he'd popped out for ten minutes on a short errand but would be back forthwith.

'What do you want him for?' Lillian asked, a look of curiosity in her eyes.

Sophie kept her explanation short, as before. There was no need to provide more than the minimum of information. 'I'm trying to trace a vicar who's gone missing. He was a curate here about a decade ago.'

Lillian didn't look entirely convinced. 'But you're rather senior for that, aren't you? To come here all the way from . . . Dorset? Isn't that what you said?' She waited.

'We think he's an important witness in a murder investigation. Does that help to explain?'

Lillian's expression relaxed slightly. 'Sort of. But not entirely. It doesn't quite fit with crime dramas on the telly. Don't senior officers usually stay in their offices?'

Sophie sighed. 'Okay. I'll come clean. I used to serve here, in the West Midlands Serious Crime Squad. I've been to visit some ex-colleagues. I thought I'd kill two birds with the proverbial single stone.'

Lillian returned the smile and seemed to relax. 'Now that does make sense. I know the feeling — having to juggle things to make the best use of time. Who's the person you're interested in? I can maybe find some records for you. The personnel stuff is kept in a locked filing cabinet in the inner office.'

Sophie was surprised. 'Do you have access to it? Isn't your own record through there?'

'No. Everything's computerised now, but ten years ago things were still kept on paper. It should be going through a rota of being scanned into the system then shredded, but the authorities haven't got round to us yet. We're a bit out in the sticks here.'

Lillian led Sophie through a locked door into a large cupboard containing several filing cabinets. She opened one, searched through a drawer and extracted a thin file.

'Well, that's a surprise. There isn't much.' She turned and showed Sophie the contents. A single sheet of paper.

They were interrupted as a middle-aged, grey-haired man came into the room. Lillian waved a greeting. 'This is our vicar, Marcus Dunn. Marcus, this is Chief Superintendent Allen, with the police. From Dorset. She's looking for a personnel record from ten years ago. One of the past curates, Gordon Wentworth. But the file's almost empty.'

Sophie had always thought herself to be sensitive to people's shifting emotions. She didn't need to be sensitive on this occasion. It was as clear as day that the parish vicar, Marcus Dunn, knew something. His face went as white as a sheet and he sank down onto the nearest chair.

* * *

It was late in the evening before Sophie arrived home. She pulled her car into the driveway, switched off the engine and sat for a few moments, exhausted, resting her head against the steering wheel. Back in Gloucester she'd debated whether to stay the night with her grandparents, but that would have meant a late arrival in the incident room the next morning, and there was so much to do. So she'd set out on the two-hour drive back to Wareham after sharing a hurried meal with them. Here she was, feeling drained, as if she'd already plundered her last reserves of energy.

She sensed, rather than heard, a slight movement and looked up. Her husband Martin was at the front door, peering out into the gloom. He walked across to the car and opened her door.

'Come on, you. Out. It looks like you need a pick-me-up and a warm bath. I can organise both.'

Sophie allowed herself to be led inside, hung her coat up and sank into a chair in the lounge. Martin placed a glass of iced Amaretto in her hand.

'Drink up,' he ordered.

She sipped at the soothing drink for ten minutes, then made her way to the bathroom, where, as promised, a bath of luxuriously warm water was waiting. As she lay in the warm suds, she reflected on the afternoon's events.

Marcus Dunn, the minister at St Oswald's, had finally opened up about the worries that had haunted him for many years. There had never been any direct evidence that Wentworth had broken any child protection guidelines during his two-year stint as parish curate. But Dunn had felt uneasy about several episodes he'd witnessed in which Wentworth seemed to have struck up a close relationship with a couple of teenagers from a foster home in the town. Dunn had been walking his dog in the local park and had spotted his curate behaving in a manner that he described to Sophie as being rather provocative, at the time totally different to the way the man behaved towards teenagers in the church youth group. The vicar had pushed the thoughts to the back of his mind. Some months later he'd watched a church-based football session organised by Wentworth and had spotted the same kind of behaviour. The curate was just that little bit too physically close, too touchy-feely with a couple of the boys. Marcus had gently mentioned his concern to the curate and had been surprised by the sudden flash of venom in his reply. It had only lasted a few seconds, but he'd seen a different and entirely unexpected side to Wentworth's character.

Dunn had chosen not to report the incident in any official way. He'd had an off-the-record chat with a senior figure at diocese level and been told not to put anything in writing. Maybe the best option was to shunt Wentworth off to another region entirely when he'd completed his training. And that had been exactly what had happened. Wentworth had applied for the newly vacant vicar's role at Millhead St Leonard, had been given a glowing reference, most of it truthful, and the problem had disappeared.

Sophie took another sip from her glass. But, of course, it hadn't disappeared, not in reality. The problem had merely shifted elsewhere, where it had festered and grown until it resulted in the tragic events of recent weeks.

An hour or two later, in Gloucester, Peter Spence, the detective investigating Grant Kirkbride's murder, had offered several more items of news to add to the picture, although none were ground-shaking. The thin scars on Grant's arms were probably three to four years old and fitted the well-known pattern of self-abuse through cutting with a sharp knife or razor blade, so common in abused teenagers. Sophie had told him that the timescale fitted with their own theory, one of sexual abuse as a fifteen-year-old at the hands of Wentworth.

Sophie was worried on another front. Child abuse was exactly that: abuse of a young person, boy or girl. Yet any news of such abuse of boys by older men carried with it a double risk where the story might be deliberately twisted by elements of the media that were hostile to gay people. No wonder her gay friends were so edgy about such events and tended to react even more strongly than the general public. People like Wentworth did so much damage to the public perception of gay people. Maybe a phone call to Benny Goodall, Dorset's senior pathologist and a close friend of hers, was in order tomorrow. He was gay and hated such scandals because of their negative impact on social acceptance. Although, knowing Benny, he might well make a joke of it.

She finished her drink and lay back in the warm, soothing water. The next thing she knew was the sound of Martin's voice.

'Wakey-wakey, sweetheart.'

She opened her eyes. 'Goodness. I must have dropped off.'

'You don't say.' His eyes twinkled. 'It wasn't for long, though. I thought I'd come by and check on you when I stopped hearing the sounds of dolphins splashing.'

Sophie flicked a few drops of water over him. 'Cheek! But thanks. I'd better get out before I drop off again. Hot chocolate?'

'Ready and waiting.'

She dried herself, wrapped a robe around her body, then returned to the sitting room.

'I'll be heading back to the Midlands for a couple of days, Martin. There's a good chance he's gone to ground there. It's his old stomping ground, and my guess is he'll start to feel safe.' She took a sip from the mug of soothing drink, savouring its smooth warmth, and took a bite of flapjack. 'We found a discarded bottle of hair bleach in the rubbish from the maisonette he rented in Shaftesbury. Buried deep in a plastic bag that he'd double-tied. He'll be feeling cocksure, convinced he's made a clean getaway, thinking no one will recognise him. But we'll get him.'

CHAPTER 40: OUT OF LUCK?

Thursday

Sophie and Rae had booked into a motel in Wolverhampton, situated conveniently close to both the local police station and St Oswald's Church. After depositing their bags, the two women visited a nearby café for a light lunch. They were dressed to blend in: jeans, faded jackets and trainers. Woolly hats, scarves and gloves. They differed in their chosen colours, though. Sophie in her usual pale browns and tans, Rae in her favoured primary colours and blacks.

Archie Campbell had managed to find them a small office in the local police station to use as a temporary base, so they called in to introduce themselves to the senior officer, an inspector. He was intrigued by their reason for being there, though Sophie only gave him a brief summary, focussed on the details of Wentworth's involvement in Grant Kirkbride's murder rather than his possible history of child abuse. That item of information was better kept under wraps for now. Once it was out in the open it would rocket around the local force's gossip channels and might leak out into the public sphere. Sophie laboured the point that their office was to remain locked at all times when empty. They would only be there for a few days so there was no need for anyone to enter, not even a cleaner.

They got down to the task of splitting the obvious lines of enquiry. Sophie was to follow up on the evidence relating to the abuse trial from a decade earlier, ploughing through the case file and the court records, looking for evidence of a missing perpetrator, someone who might have slipped away during the police raid, a man who had escaped the justice that ought to have been coming his way. If that's what had happened, she felt some responsibility. After all, she'd been there on the day of the raid.

Rae would continue Sophie's conversations with local people and would build up a picture of Wentworth's life in his short time as a curate in the parish. She'd also check through all relevant records, both civil and ecclesiastical, looking for anything that hinted something had been awry all those years ago. As is common in this type of investigation, she didn't have a clear idea of what she was looking for. But, hopefully, she'd spot something when it did appear. She started by reading the notes from Sophie's meetings the previous day, her chats with Marcus Dunn, Lillian Beckton and Dolly Knightly. Of course, Wentworth would have ensured all of his interactions while on official business in the parish were squeaky clean. If there had been any doubts in people's minds, they were likely to have occurred while he was 'off duty'. So, step one would be to trace where he lived. Rae also wondered if Marcus Dunn's wife might have had suspected more than her husband. Sometimes vicar's partners knew more about the realities of interpersonal peccadillos inside a close-knit parish than their spouses. Gossip would be everything, and someone might have let slip their suspicions, knowing that something said to the partner might find its way back to the spouse. She picked up her bag, collected her jacket and headed for the door. A brisk five-minute walk and she was standing outside the local vicarage, being asked inside by Judy Dunn.

Judy wasn't able to add anything to the picture of Gordon Wentworth painted the day before by her husband, but she was able to provide information of where he'd lodged for a few weeks on first arriving in the parish, and where he'd lived for the bulk of his time there, in a small upper-floor flat in a house owned by the church. She gave Rae both addresses.

Rae asked how Marcus was, passing on Sophie's concern about the vicar's health.

'He didn't sleep well,' Judy replied. 'The thing is, he acted in the way that was fairly common practice at the time when there was no proof of any wrongdoing. It had the unofficial approval of the upper echelons. He feels he's let people down. Badly. To be honest, he's inconsolable.'

'Would it help if my boss called in to see him again? She'd be happy to do so. It's me today because she's on a different part of the investigation.'

Judy thought for a while before responding. 'It might help. He said that she seemed an understanding sort.'

Rae asked her the key question. 'What did you think of Wentworth, Judy? You must have come into contact with him a lot during his time here.'

Judy regarded Rae warily. Of course, she'd see her prime duty as supporting her husband. She'd be unlikely to come forward now with any obvious suspicions because that would put Marcus in a bad light.

'He was always very efficient. Well organised. Careful and cautious. He didn't open up very much. That's all I can say, I'm afraid.'

Rae could tell Judy was holding back on something, but there was no point in pushing the issue, not yet anyway.

She left the vicarage and walked the five minutes to Dolly Knightley's home, in the middle of a row of single-storey, mews-type residences in a quiet cul-de-sac. Rae was in luck. Dolly was in. Her home was tiny but ideal for a single person living alone. Dolly told Rae that the row of small dwellings had been built by the church several decades earlier, deliberately planned for church stalwarts on low incomes who could never afford to buy their own homes nor manage commercial rents for larger properties.

'I've been thinking about that curate since the other detective mentioned him yesterday. I haven't remembered much though. He was one for keeping himself to himself. But he did help out with the local youth cricket team. That's what I heard.'

'Was that linked to the church?' Rae asked.

Dolly shook her head. 'No, it was just the local team. The ground's next to the park. That's all I remember.'

'What did you think of him? Did you get on?'

Dolly shrugged. 'He wasn't one who sticks in the mind. Didn't have much of a personality. And he was a right stingy one. I went round collecting for the local women's refuge once. He sounded really keen, but he only put ten pence in the collection tin. It sounded a lot more when it dropped in 'cos it was all single coins. He put his hand across so I couldn't see and would think it was a lot of cash. But it made me suspicious. He was the first person I called on, so I took the top off and looked inside. I ask you, ten bloody pence. What an insult! I think he might have been a bit anti-women.'

Rae thanked her and left after passing her a contact card.

Her next port of call was the official curate residence. She hoped to be able to speak to the resident of the upper-floor flat, rented out to someone local, but there was no answer at the door. Lillian Beckton was approaching the door of her ground-floor flat as Rae descended the stairs.

'Can I help you?' she asked.

'You must be Lillian,' Rae said. 'I'm DS Rae Gregson. I think you spoke to my boss yesterday. I'm up here trying to fill in some details about Gordon Wentworth when he was curate. I wondered if the person upstairs might remember him but there's no one in.'

Lillian looked thoughtful. 'That's our church organist, William Russell. But he's gone away for a couple of days. Back tomorrow. He's been here for yonks so he might remember something. Don't hold out any great hopes. He's getting a bit doddery. Still a good organist though. Listen, you look as though you could do with a cup of tea. I've just put the kettle on. Why don't you join me?'

Rae sighed with relief. Interviewing people in situations like this could be such thirsty work.

* * *

Back in the office Sophie was feeling equally thirsty, although her preference would be for a glass of local beer rather than a cup of tea. Shame. It was far too early in the day for alcohol.

She'd spent hours reading through the case notes and the trial transcripts. Archie had been right. There were definite hints that one of the perps had somehow escaped the net. Five men were on trial, but they didn't account for all of the detailed evidence that was supplied by the victims and witnesses. The problem for the police had been the reliability of some of the facts supplied by the abused teenagers, and understandably so. During their experiences at the house in question those young people were too often under the influence of drink or drugs. Their memories were vague. There might have been a sixth man, but no clear description of him was forthcoming. The teenagers' testimonies provided a start point, but so much of the trial's outcome depended upon forensic evidence, hard facts that couldn't be disputed. There was less doubt here: there were fingerprints found in a few spots around the house that belonged to neither the five defendants nor the abused youths. Person X. Unaccounted for.

The question for Sophie was this: was Person X, the suspected missing abuser, Gordon Wentworth, absenting himself from curate duties for occasional afternoons and evenings in order to drive across town and join his fellow abusers in drugging and raping teenagers? Boys and girls carefully selected because of their chaotic home lives? For Sophie there was one item of encouraging news in the background reports. A sixth

DNA profile had been taken from samples found on bedding in that house of evil. It had failed to match anyone on the police database, but it was there, ready and waiting, if they ever managed to make an arrest.

She phoned Archie Campbell and told him of her conclusions, but the conversation was cut short by the arrival of a text message from Peter Spence in Gloucester. A heavy, ash walking stick had been found downstream of the crime scene, caught up in a reed bed. It was undergoing forensic tests.

Was there a chance that this was the staff that had been used to strike Grant Kirkbride? Sophie had the feeling that the investigation was approaching the endgame. How clever was Wentworth really? Could he go on avoiding justice in the way he had for more than a decade? So much depended on whether his success in avoiding detection was down to careful planning or luck. She was beginning to change her judgement on this. Some of Wentworth's more recent actions at Millhead had been downright foolhardy. He was cautious, yes. But he'd also been stupid. It was time his luck ran out.

Sophie returned to the task in hand, working her way through the case records. One item suddenly leapt out of the page at her. One of the defendants was Gavin McCorquodale, nicknamed Corky. Hadn't she seen a reference to someone called Corky before? She phoned Rae.

'The nickname Corky. It rings a bell, Rae. Has it cropped up somewhere?'

There was silence for a short while as Rae checked her notebook.

'Yes. It's the nickname for one of the abusers here ten years ago. That's what I have in my notes.'

'I know that. But has it cropped up in a different context other than in the trial?'

'There was a piece of artwork on the wall of Wentworth's attic room, signed "Corky". It was abstract, if I remember right, but I didn't look at it much. Do you think it might be the same person?'

'Could be.'

Sophie closed the call and phoned Archie Campbell again to ask about McCorquodale. The news intrigued her. 'I think he's out of prison. Six months ago. He'll be on the sex offenders register, so it shouldn't be hard to find him.'

The news that McCorquodale was no longer inside the prison system shed a different light on things. Would Wentworth, if he was hiding in the area, seek out someone from his past? It would be a gamble for him. Surely he'd suspect that Corky, as he was known, was likely to be monitored in some way? Or would the lure of meeting up with an old friend in order to boast of his exploits be too strong? Somehow Sophie thought the latter might well be the case. Although he'd come across as careful and guarded in his face-to-face chats with members of the detective team, people like Wentworth often had extremely inflated opinions of themselves along with a sense of being invulnerable. It might be worth following up.

CHAPTER 41: JACK THE LAD

Jack Gillingham glanced through the front window before opening the door and emerging into the street. Of course, he wasn't really Jack Gillingham. That was a fictional name for a fictional person. But in the end, can any of us say who we really are? We each have a label that identifies us, a persona that we inhabit, a set of uniforms that we wear that helps to show the world the type of person we are or want to be, but it's all a creation, isn't it? Gordon Wentworth, Jack Gillingham, what does a name really mean? Not much, when you probe it deeply enough. It satisfies bureaucratic requirements for some kind of identity tag, that's all. He'd stepped out of his Gordon Wentworth persona, along with everything that went with it, and stepped into this handy new one. Blonde-haired, fresher-faced, and with several colourful tattoos on his arms. Along with a self-imposed commitment to totally immerse himself in his new persona. The name Gordon Wentworth was a thing of the past. He lived and breathed his new identity completely. He knew he had to. If someone were to call out 'Gordon' while he was out and about, he mustn't give the slightest glimmer of a reaction.

A neighbour called across the street. 'Hello, Jack. Off to work?'

So far, so good. Only a week here and people were being friendly to him already. They wouldn't be like that to a vicar. Interactions would be much more formal. Strained, even. He could get used to this.

He waved back. 'Yeah, pesky job. Need to pay the bills though.'

He laughed. He was serious about the need for an income. He had his nest egg, of course, carefully secreted away over many years, but it wouldn't keep him in a life of comfort for very long, not without some supplementary earnings. So he'd found a job at the local convenience store as a general assistant. He stacked shelves, served on the spare till when the shop was busy and even did a few deliveries. It meant that he was quickly getting to know people in the local community. More importantly, they were getting to know him and were starting to trust him.

He'd been lucky with the house. It belonged to a distant cousin of Corky's, the only family member who still talked to him after his spell in prison. The cousin was in Hong Kong for six months and had asked Corky to check his home occasionally. Corky, of course, was short of money, unable to find work. So when Jack contacted him and agreed to pay him almost the market rent, his dire cash-flow problem was partly solved. When Jack moved in, he told the neighbours that it was all above board, with the owner aware of the let. The reality was rather different though. Corky's cousin might throw a wobbly when he returned, but by then it would be too late. Jack would have found somewhere more permanent. Corky would have to handle the ensuing fireworks if the cousin ever found out. He was banking the rent Jack was giving him, after all, and doing sod all to earn it.

He had mixed feelings about Corky. The years in prison had changed him, made him wary and standoffish. He'd seemed cagey and reluctant to help on the single occasion they'd met face to face, just checking that Jack was who he said he was, passing across a set of keys, taking the first week's rent and then scarpering. He'd been rather more helpful on the phone, but even there he'd occasionally referred to Jack as Gordon, an absolute no-no. One slip of the tongue like that in public and Jack might have to do another runner. It was all a bit more disappointing than Jack had expected when he'd first contacted Corky. He'd hoped that their previous close friendship might be rekindled, but so far there were no signs of that happening. Maybe Corky couldn't cope with the name change. They'd have to meet again soon though. Corky wanted the rent in cash every week, presumably to avoid having to declare it in his benefits claim. The arrangement suited Jack. Bank accounts were too risky, leaving all kinds of data open to inspection by the fraud investigators. The only problem was, they had to meet up. A few minutes in the local park, just for the cash exchange. As long as they were careful, they should be safe.

Jack was already starting to make tentative plans for the inevitable six-month move, wondering whether to remain here in Wolverhampton or shift elsewhere for a completely clean break. He'd see how things turned out during the coming weeks. The problem was, if he started trying to rekindle some old contacts here, it might set ripples in motion, and who knows what unfriendly shores they might lap up onto? Cops had access to far better tracking systems than ten or twenty years ago.

He reached the store, ensured he had a blank, semi-vacant expression on his face and opened the door. One thing was true. This work was less stressful than being a vicar. Not the right kind of contacts though. Not for him.

CHAPTER 42: CORKY

Sophie looked at the list of names on the paper Rae had placed on the desk. Some were still in prison. Others had been released at various points during the last couple of years. Most had moved away on gaining their freedom. Only one or two had opted to stay in Wolverhampton. The middle entry in the list was Gavin McCorquodale.

'This is the one. Did you find anything else about him?'

Rae took out her phone and showed Sophie the photo that Tommy had sent her of the artwork from the vicarage attic. Dozens of intertwined limbs, seemingly detached from their bodies, radiating out from a central fuzzy cloud.

'And what was the message on the back?'

Rae examined the second image. 'To Gordon, from Corky.'

Sophie stroked the screen back to the first image. 'It's unsettling, don't you think? And those are young arms and legs. Pale. Slender. There's a hidden message in this. I wonder if it had some kind of meaning, if it was a gift.'

'So, do we go to see this Corky character?'

Sophie pondered for a short while. 'Not yet. He's been out of gaol for a couple of months. It's possible Wentworth has contacted him if he's come back to this area. If we suddenly turn up it will set the alarm bells ringing and we'll probably lose our man. We'll keep that approach up our sleeve and use it as a last resort. For now, let's just watch him from a distance. We need a dog.'

Rae's eyes widened in surprise. 'What?'

'Walking a dog, Rae. It gives us a good excuse to wander about, looking a bit vacant. I'll borrow the curate's spaniel, Queenie. Lillian was telling me it's a bit bouncy and she can't keep up with its constant desire for exercise. Favours all round. You can be Lillian's cousin if anyone asks. I'll be an old family friend.'

Rae looked disappointed. 'Not a princess, exiled from a faraway land? I've always wanted to be one of those. Tragic and sad.'

Sophie rolled her eyes. 'This is the modern police force, Rae. No room for romantic fantasists.'

Rae laughed. 'Shame. Dog walker it is, then.'

* * *

McCorquodale lived in a small end-of-terrace house just outside the city centre. It looked well-maintained, with clean paintwork and windows.

'How long has he lived here?' Rae asked as they strolled past, with Queenie sniffing the ground.

'It was his mother's house. She died while he was inside. He inherited. He's been here for six months, since he got out. Someone told me it was a bit rundown when he moved in, so he's obviously done some work on it. I don't think he's got much money though. He hasn't found a permanent job yet.'

'A good way of keeping in with the neighbours,' Rae suggested. 'They wouldn't know his background, would they? Best keep them onside.'

They allowed Queenie to take as much time as she wanted to investigate the pavement's doggy smells. They reached the far end of the street and were about to return to St Oswald's, when Rae turned and spotted a man emerging from the house. She nudged Sophie with an elbow, so they turned and slowly retraced their steps, trying to keep McCorquodale in sight. He walked as far as the local betting shop and stepped inside.

'Bang goes your theory about him having no money,' Rae said. 'He must have enough to place a bet. Strange priorities.'

'But the neat house is a reminder of our man Wentworth, when you think about it,' came the reply from Sophie. 'The vicarage seemed meticulously tidy, and he was always clean and well-dressed. But then, you wouldn't want to draw attention to yourself, would you? Not with his level of perverted behaviour. Hide in plain sight. Let's hang around to see what he does next.'

The man was out within five minutes and returned the way he'd come, passing the two women and their dog. He curled his lip at Queenie as he passed. He was clearly not a dog lover. Sophie and Rae followed at a safe distance and watched as their quarry entered his house. Rae sat on a wall that fronted a small play area, while Sophie took the dog back to its owner. She then returned in her car so that one or the other of them were watching the house from a nearby unobtrusive position. But there was no further move from McCorquodale that day. A local detective under Archie Campbell's command took over at night.

Sophie and Rae were disturbed before breakfast the next morning by a phone call from the local command centre. McCorquodale was on the move.

'At seven in the morning?' Rae groaned. 'Couldn't he have waited another half hour till after we've had breakfast?'

'Just grab some rolls and a couple of bottles of water,' Sophie replied. 'My guess is he's feeling suspicious. I'll check while you get the food.'

The detective duo were heading off in their car within ten minutes, making their way back to their quarry's locality. Apparently, McCorquodale had taken rather too many glances around as he emerged from his house, and it was this that had alerted the watching detective. The route he was following would take him towards the local park.

Sophie glanced at the digital clock on the fascia. 'Call Lillian. Tell her we want the dog ready and waiting. We'll be there in five minutes.'

CHAPTER 43: CAPTURE

Wolverhampton is well served for parks and open areas. Some are sports oriented, others more suited for wildlife-watching, with a natural feel to their layout. It was one of the latter that McCorquodale had entered. Sophie and Rae exchanged a few words with the plain-clothes officer from the local CID, then entered the park. There were several paths radiating away from the entrance. They followed a track heading almost due west that headed towards a large pond, partly hidden from view by trees and low bushes, as directed by the local detective who had followed their quarry's progress through binoculars. He remained in his car, parked near the entrance.

Sophie and Rae wandered rather than walked, allowing the dog to set the pace, but keeping the water in view. There were several bench seats positioned beside the path, all with views across the watercourse, some in more secluded positions than others. At this time in the morning all were empty except one. A solitary figure sat on the bench in the most isolated position. Having fixed the position, the two detectives moved away, but keeping the approaches to that particular corner in eyeshot.

'He looks as though he's waiting for someone or something,' Rae murmured. 'Maybe we're in luck.'

'It's about bloody time, then,' came the reply from her boss. 'I can't say we've had much luck so far. It's been sheer dogged hard work all the way.'

She stopped walking as a figure appeared in the distance, on the far side of the pond, moving towards the water and then around it. The man, tall and thin, stopped for a few minutes to watch some ducks but Sophie gained the impression that he was looking around him, gauging the lie of the land. He had blonde hair, almost white. Was it Wentworth? It was difficult to say. He was wearing a dark-coloured outdoor jacket with the collar turned up, along with trousers in a similar shade. Nothing about him stood out, apart from the shade of his hair.

'I'm going to head off with the dog, Rae. I can't afford to get close to him in case it is our man. We had a chat back in Millhead several weeks ago. He'd recognise me without a doubt. If he does meet up with McCorquodale in some way, follow him. Stay in contact and let us know where you are. I'll have the local squad staying back out of sight, but within easy reach. They'll have someone watching you. I'll stay with our friend Corky.' She paused. 'Don't lose him, Rae, in case it is Wentworth. Please.'

She tugged on Queenie's lead and headed away from the water, away from McCorquodale and away from the as-yet unidentified stranger. The problem was that Wentworth would probably recognise her, as she'd explained. But McCorquodale would probably recognise the dog, having recoiled from it the previous afternoon. Why did things always have to be so complicated?

* * *

Rae was initially puzzled by what happened next. The newcomer sat on a bench a good ten yards away from McCorquodale. Moreover, he didn't appear to look at the other man at any time. He stayed only a few minutes, then he rose and walked away, retracing his steps. What had he been doing? But Rae had clear instructions to follow the tall figure. She kept herself partly hidden behind a line of shrubs and found herself on a parallel path to the one he was using, heading further west towards a gated entrance. In fact, she was likely to arrive there first — no bad thing if she hoped to avoid suspicion. She spoke into her phone.

'He may have left something on the bench. I glanced back at one point and McCorquodale was moving towards the seat he'd just vacated.'

'Okay, Rae. Stay on your toes,' came the reply.

'It looks like rain,' she continued, talking in to her phone loudly as the tall stranger walked close by. She took a glance. 'Like we thought. Better be cautious, Mum. Take an umbrella. That green one I got for you. It's top quality.'

Rae followed the man out of the park, but turned immediately sharp left, away from the direction in which he was heading. She stepped behind a tree, slipped off her reversible jacket, turning it from dark blue to olive green, popped a red bobble-hat onto her head, and hurried back to the road junction. Good. He was still in sight, about forty yards ahead of her, on the opposite pavement. He took a glance back, but his gaze didn't rest on her. Instead, he seemed to take greater interest in two men who'd appeared out of a nearby shop. This could work in her favour. If they drew his attention, she might well remain unnoticed.

Her quarry walked quickly, heading closer to the city centre, but was clearly taking care over his route, occasionally glancing back, as if he was checking for people on his trail. He took a couple of diversionary routes and, once, called into a shop to buy a newspaper. This wasn't suspicious in itself, but the care he took to check his surroundings upon emerging onto the pavement, pretending to read the headlines but with his gaze clearly further afield, added some confirmation to Rae's initial judgement. He had something to hide. She was becoming more convinced that he was their target, Gordon

Wentworth, though she didn't aim to identify him definitively. All she had to do was stay with him, whoever he was, and find out where he lived.

She ducked behind a tall van, took the bobble-hat off and stuffed it into her pocket, then took a khaki baseball cap out of her bag and popped it on her head. The bright red hat had done its job. The man would have spotted it several times, mentally registering it as a clear identifier. Its replacement would perform a similar function. She would remove it after another few minutes, leaving her natural brunette colouring. By then his memory of her appearance in the park should have passed out of his mind, replaced by the more recent images. Hats were great identifiers to suspicious people, but that worked two ways.

In the event, she only needed another five minutes. Rae's quarry turned a corner into a street of Victorian-era terraced houses, slowed as he checked around himself once more, then let himself into a house halfway down the street. Rae kept going. She noted the number, passed by, turned into the next side street, then removed her hat. She pushed her hair behind her ears, removed her jacket and walked back to the previous road, crossing to the opposite pavement. She then walked slowly past, noting the target house in more detail. She went into a nearby grocery store, bought a magazine, came outside and made a phone call to her boss with the information. Things appeared to be going to plan.

* * *

Two hours later, things hadn't gone to plan. Not in the slightest.

Upon identification of the address, along with a judgement that the tall stranger was probably Wentworth, a carefully constructed plan had swung into action. A local surveillance team had taken over from Rae and were watching the small house. A check had been made on the ownership of the property and it hadn't taken too long for the details to emerge, along with the fact that the owner was currently abroad and was a cousin of Gavin McCorquodale. It seemed to Sophie and Rae that it was all fitting together neatly, like a child's jigsaw puzzle. Sophie and the local commander decided that a low-key raid was the most appropriate action. Forcing entry with a heavily armed snatch squad seemed unnecessary in the circumstances and might cause distress to the neighbours, several of whom were elderly or infirm. Sophie and Rae took backseat roles and watched as the house was surrounded by plain-clothes officers. A local DCI knocked on the door, but it wasn't answered, causing a heavier-handed approach to swing into action. A hand-held ram soon had the door open, and a team of black-clad cops swarmed in, spreading through the building, shouting as they went. They found the house completely devoid of occupants. Sophie shook her head in puzzlement and dismay. Rae felt as if she'd been kicked in the stomach. She felt sick.

'How?' she asked. 'He didn't spot me, I swear it. He must have got out by the gate from the backyard. But why? I don't understand.'

Sophie looked again at the diagram they'd drawn up while planning the raid. Three cops had been stationed in the narrow alley running alongside the fence at the rear of the house, timed to be in place a couple of minutes before the knock on the front door, one outside the back gate and one at each end of the path. She climbed the stairs in the building and looked out from one of the rear windows. They might have been spotted by someone sufficiently alert, passing by a window. But how would Wentworth have got away? No one had left by the front door, and those same three officers would have apprehended anyone leaving by the back gate. Shit. He'd done it again. Somehow Wentworth had repeated his trick of a decade ago and had found a way of eluding the squad. Unbelievable.

The two Wessex-based detectives trawled through the house again, helped by two local detectives on loan for a few hours. Still nothing. A third was still in the back alley, but she assured Sophie that no one had used the narrow path for the time she'd been there.

'He must still be here. Somewhere. Right under our noses,' Sophie said.

'But how did he know?' Rae was clearly still angry.

'It might be nothing more than sheer bloody bad luck,' the local commander added. 'He spotted something just by chance. It happens.'

They walked to the back door and looked out at the bare patio surface that covered most of the small, enclosed area. A shed stood in one corner, close to the gate. It was sitting on low timber blocks, raised a couple of inches from the surface of the paving slabs. That is, except for the side nearest the boundary fence, where a small flower bed ran up the length of the boundary. Here the gap under the shed's base was slightly deeper. Sophie felt a prickling sensation run up her spine. Was there enough space for someone to have wriggled into it? It was in shadow, difficult to spot from the middle of the yard. Could the search team have missed it?

She nudged Rae and, with a slight flick of a finger, indicated the possible hidey-hole. The local commander raised his walkie-talkie to his lips and spoke into it. 'On alert, everyone.' He pulled a taser from its holster. Rae did the same. They waited until a firearms officer joined them from the backup car.

Sophie pulled a torch from her bag, quietly knelt down and peered into the narrow gap. A small block of wood plugged the opening, but it wasn't fixed to anything. She ran her fingers around its edge and tugged hard, pulling it towards her. She shone her torch into the gap. Someone was there. Someone with blonde hair, squeezed somehow into the tight narrow space. There was a wriggling motion, but the gap left hardly any room for manoeuvre.

'If that's you, Gordon Wentworth, I suggest you extricate yourself. And don't try anything stupid. There are six of us out here and we're armed.'

The man slowly emerged, grimy, covered in cobwebs and with what appeared to be mouse droppings sticking to the folds of his clothes.

'Got you,' Sophie said. 'Ten years late, maybe. But you can't keep pushing your luck for ever.'

* * *

'So that's him?' Archie Campbell said. He had just arrived from headquarters and was standing next to Sophie watching the initial interview with Wentworth on a video screen.

'Yes, that's our man. The one who escaped us ten years ago. Gordon Wentworth, esteemed church minister, ex-army reserve and totally warped. I wondered what raised a few hackles in me when I first spoke to him a couple of weeks ago. It was his coldness. No real feelings, not ones of any depth. Everything in his brain is clinical and calculated. You know what he said to me when he came out of his hidey-hole? "You only got me by luck. It's not a real victory." I guess he saw it all as some kind of game. I think it was the same with one of our key witnesses back in Wiltshire, Miriam Boateng. He was planning something for her, we think, but then abandoned it when he realised how close we were getting.'

'And the two murder victims?'

'We think the son, Grant, was about to tell his mother about the assaults when he'd been younger. Wentworth overheard him at Bridget's party, hinting at what had happened, so he decided to kill the lad. But then she'd probably worked it out anyway. Wentworth saw no alternative but to get rid of both of them. To be honest, Archie, he was getting careless. He was dirtying his own backyard. That's never a good thing for a predator like him.'

'A church minister though. People are going to find it hard to believe.'

'No one wants it to be true, do they? But that's where they are, lurking in plain sight. Youth work, schools, church groups. Anywhere where they have contact with young people. We don't want it to be true. No one does. But that's where some of them are, just waiting for the right opportunity, for someone vulnerable enough to appear, a potential grooming victim. They got away with it for years. Thank God procedures have been tightened up now. But someone like Wentworth represents just the tip of the iceberg. There are people like him still out there.'

CHAPTER 44: WEDDING

The start to the day was wet, chilly and grey. Gwen wondered if such weather really mattered in the grand scheme of things. Surely what counted more was the emotional warmth of the friends and family members present at the ceremony? She and Barry seemed to be popular, both with their work colleagues and among their friends. Gwen, of course, was Welsh. She'd warned many of the local guests that her family members were loud, proud and happy to show it. Barry, coming as he did from Dorset farming stock, had kin who might appear to be a little more muted, though that difference would doubtless fade as the celebrations developed and the bar's stocks of local ciders and ales became depleted.

The couple had decided on a Dorset wedding, particularly when Barry, a long-time resident of Swanage, had taken Gwen for a visit to Durlston Castle, perched high on the clifftop, west of the town. Gwen took one look at the breathtaking views from both the function room and the outside terrace, and declared that she wouldn't look anywhere else. The fact that seals and dolphins were occasionally spotted just off the headland was the clincher. Were there other locations as beautiful as this? Possibly, but not many. And it was so easy to get to. All the couple needed was good weather, but it didn't seem to be playing its part, despite a positive forecast.

'I thought you said Swanage had its own special micro-climate,' Gwen complained to Barry on the phone after breakfast.

'It does. But just occasionally it works in reverse,' Barry replied. 'Anyway, it's early yet. It'll be fine by this afternoon.'

'I'll hold you to that,' she replied. 'You'd better be right.'

If truth be told, she had a slight headache, the result of one too many gins the night before, when the three Allen women, Sophie, Hannah and Jade, had talked her and Rae into a mini pub crawl in Wareham to help calm her nerves. Then the women from Gwen's family had joined them. The evening had got quite hazy at that point.

Barry had also been out the night before, in Swanage. He was staying with his best man, Jimmy Melsom, and they'd gone for a meal and a few drinks with Martin Allen, George Warrander and Rae's boyfriend, Craig. Gwen guessed that the behaviour of the men had probably been more restrained than the women, particularly when Sophie, Jade and Hannah performed a karaoke rendition of the Spice Girls' 'Wannabe'. Had it been entirely accidental that they'd included a pub with a karaoke night on their itinerary? Gwen wasn't entirely convinced despite loud protestations to the contrary. Then Sophie had got stuck into Gloria Gaynor's 'I Am What I Am' and Gwen decided, after the ninth flat note, that enough was enough. It was time to move on to the final pub, hopefully quieter and more restrained. She dreaded to think what some of the locals made of her husband's boss when she was in such an extrovert mood. A possible future chief constable, wearing a sequinned dress and performing karaoke in public? No chance! Maybe it was the singing that had left her with the headache, not the gin.

Gwen felt better after breakfast and even more so after coffee. It was time to climb inside her dress, helped by Jade, who'd volunteered to be the 'bridal dresser', whatever that was. She suspected that Jade had made the role up, just so she could get a close-up view of her lingerie and dress. Was there a clue there, somewhere?

* * *

Gwen and Barry gazed at the glorious view from the terrace. The sea was sparkling in the early-evening sunshine and sea-birds swooped low over the waves.

'It's perfect, Barry,' Gwen said. 'I should never have doubted you. It's turned out lovely after all. How did your evening go, last night?'

He shrugged and slid his arm around her waist. 'It was all very civilised. An Italian meal that Jimmy organised and then a couple of drinks in the pub. What about you?'

She paused. Would it help in any way if she shared the full gory details of the raucous night she'd experienced? What good would it do?

'Oh, fairly restrained too,' she said. 'I enjoyed it. Mind you, it'll be nice to get away just by ourselves, won't it?' She leaned across and gave him a quick kiss. 'I thought the ceremony was great. Jimmy did a really good job.'

'It was perfect. Though the boss looked a bit peaky when she first appeared,' he replied. 'Was she alright last night?'

'Oh, yes. Fine. Maybe she was just a bit tired.'

He peered back into the reception room. 'Oh. She's got the microphone.'

Gwen realised that the band were playing the opening chords to 'I Am What I Am'. She put a hand to her head.

Rae came out to join them. 'Looks like I've escaped just in time,' she laughed, then grimaced as the first bum note came echoing through the open doorway. 'You'd think she would be better after last night's practise in the pub,' she added.

Gwen couldn't help but giggle. 'Oh, she is. She'd already hit three flat notes by this point.'

Barry turned to his bride and frowned. 'I thought you said it was a quiet evening.'

'I was just trying to be diplomatic,' Gwen said. 'Apparently, all my family have been rehearsing "Land of my Fathers" especially for tonight. That'll be fine, but be warned. It'll go downhill after that. I heard through the grapevine that my brother seems to think he has a voice like Tom Jones. He's been practising a few songs.'

Barry looked mournful. 'I don't suppose we can leave now, can we?'

Gwen put a finger to his lips. 'No, Barry. Afraid not. Just grit your teeth and pretend you're enjoying it. You'll get your reward tonight, if I'm still in control of my senses. I'm Welsh too, remember. They want me to do a Shirley Bassey number.'

Rae raised her eyebrows. 'Which one?'

'"Fever". They want me to do the actions. Barry, you've got to be my prop.'

Rae tried hard not to laugh, but it was no use. The guffaw burst from her before she could stop it. 'Sorry, boss,' she said. 'But it's not only you. I've been drafted in as well.'

'Oh? What for?'

'Gwen's brother, in his Tom Jones stint. He's doing "You Can Leave Your Hat On". I'm doing the actions.'

Barry looked incredulous. 'Rae, you're joking.'

'Don't worry. I'll leave a few clothes on, not just the hat. I've been practising for days. You don't know how validating it is for a trans woman like me to be asked to do something like that. Craig will be standing by with a wrap for me. I'm over the moon about it.'

Barry slowly shook his head. 'You're all mad.'

'C'mon, Barry. You've known that for years.'

THE END

ACKNOWLEDGEMENTS

This is the eleventh Sophie Allen novel and it won't be the last. I want to take this opportunity to thank all the staff at Joffe Books for their help, particularly the editorial team for working on my original text so thoroughly. Special thanks to Kate Lyall Grant and Emma Grundy Haigh for their help and advice. They, and Matthew Grundy Haigh, have done a great job in editing my original text. Any errors are mine though. If you spot a typo, please email Joffe Books and they'll do their best to correct it.

Thanks are also due to my fellow Joffe authors; they're a great bunch and they use social media much more proficiently than me. I sometimes feel ashamed of my half-hearted attempts to use Facebook. I loathe the bloody thing! I'd like to reassure readers, though, that if they email me direct, at michael@michaelhambling.co.uk, I will always respond as quickly as I can. I do like email. Please visit my website at www.michaelhambling.co.uk. It had an overhaul earlier this year to bring it into the modern era. It carries relevant information and a selection of free-to-read short stories.

It was lovely to meet up with the Joffe staff and many of my fellow authors at our spring garden party. Helen Durrant, Janice Frost, Joy Ellis, Judi Daykin, Tania Crosse, Charlie Gallagher: thanks for being so supportive. The biggest thanks go to the boss, Jasper Joffe.

AUTHOR'S NOTES

Location

Cranborne Chase is one of the lesser-known Areas of Outstanding Natural Beauty (AONB) in the UK, spanning the Dorset–Wiltshire county boundary. The word 'chase' is derived from its role as an area reserved for hunting during mediaeval times. Royalty and the aristocracy hunted deer; half-starved and poorly nourished ordinary folk were hanged as poachers for doing the same thing. Deer still thrive on the chase, along with many other species of wildlife. It's mainly formed of chalk upland, cut by some fairly deep valleys. Salisbury, Shaftesbury and Blandford Forum, on the edges of the chase, are all worth a visit. The area is crossed by several long-distance footpaths and bridleways, and dotted with archaeologically important sites. The village of Millhead St Leonard, the main location in this novel, is fictional.

Subject Matter

I thought long and hard before starting to write this story. Child abuse is not something that should ever be treated lightly as a possible theme for a novel. I worked as a teacher for nearly forty years and became aware of some incidences of grooming and exploitation, although these were invariably nothing to do with school-based scenarios. In my view, schools always had more rigorous procedures in place than voluntary bodies, church-based groups and sports classes run by amateurs. The most distressing aspect of the scandals that have come to light in recent years is the way that young people were not believed when they reported incidents. They were too often treated as liars and fantasists. Too many evil manipulators were shunted sideways to get them out of the limelight, rather than ensuring that prosecutions were brought against them. They didn't just groom youngsters; in a different kind of way, they groomed senior figures within the church establishment to ensure that accusations against them were not believed.

The 2015 Oscar-winning film *Spotlight*, mentioned in this novel, is well worth watching. It tells the true story of the *Boston Globe*'s investigative unit probing child abuse by priests. There have also been several BBC documentaries about the exploitation of vulnerable British teenagers by predatory adults, both in religious and sporting situations.

Cheese and Beer

Apparently, I seem to have gained some influence as a source of information on cheese and beer in the areas I write about. So here goes:

Cranborne Blue is a very nice locally produced cheese. Definitely worth a try.

The Sixpenny Brewery lies within the Cranborne Chase AONB. It's named after the nearby village of Sixpenny Handley, and brews a selection of great local ales, available in some of the area's pubs. Try the Sixpenny Best Bitter.

If you visit Salisbury and are looking for a great historic pub in the city centre, try one (or more) from this list: the Haunch of Venison, the Pheasant, the Rai d'Or (evenings only), the Ox Row Inn, the Bell & Crown. Committed real-ale fans may also enjoy the Duke of York, the Village Inn, Deacons and the Wyndham Arms, although they don't have the picturesque draw of the city centre pubs already mentioned.

GLOSSARY

A & E: Accident and Emergency Unit in a hospital.
Flat: an alternative British name for an apartment.
Home Office: a ministerial department in the UK government, responsible for immigration, security, and law and order.
Pub crawl: A British tradition. Visiting a sequence of pubs, with a drink (usually a beer) in each.
Semi: Short for semi-detached house, one that is joined to another by a common wall that they share.
Terrace: a form of housing in which a row of attached dwellings share side walls. Called townhouses in the United States.

UK Police Ranks (in descending order of seniority)
Chief Constable (or Commissioner in London's Metropolitan Police Service)
Deputy CC (Deputy Commissioner in London)
Assistant CC (Assistant Commissioner in London)
Chief Superintendent
Superintendent
Chief Inspector
Inspector
Sergeant
Constable

Detectives hold the same ranks but with a prefix before the name (DC, DS, etc.) There is sometimes career movement back and forth between detectives and uniformed ranks.

THE JOFFE BOOKS STORY

We began in 2014 when Jasper agreed to publish his mum's much-rejected romance novel and it became a bestseller.

Since then we've grown into the largest independent publisher in the UK. We're extremely proud to publish some of the very best writers in the world, including Joy Ellis, Faith Martin, Caro Ramsay, Helen Forrester, Simon Brett and Robert Goddard. Everyone at Joffe Books loves reading and we never forget that it all begins with the magic of an author telling a story.

We are proud to publish talented first-time authors, as well as established writers whose books we love introducing to a new generation of readers.

We won Trade Publisher of the Year at the Independent Publishing Awards in 2023 and Best Publisher Award in 2024 at the People's Book Prize. We have been shortlisted for Independent Publisher of the Year at the British Book Awards for the last five years, and were shortlisted for the Diversity and Inclusivity Award at the 2022 Independent Publishing Awards. In 2023 we were shortlisted for Publisher of the Year at the RNA Industry Awards, and in 2024 we were shortlisted at the CWA Daggers for the Best Crime and Mystery Publisher.

We built this company with your help, and we love to hear from you, so please email us about absolutely anything bookish at feedback@joffebooks.com.

If you want to receive free books every Friday and hear about all our new releases, join our mailing list: www.joffebooks.com/free-books

And when you tell your friends about us, just remember: it's pronounced Joffe as in coffee or toffee!

Printed in Great Britain
by Amazon

56908420R00162